SHANNON'S
Hope

JOSI S. KILPACK

A NEWPORT LADIES BOOK CLUB NOVEL

SHANNON'S
Hope

Covenant Communications, Inc.

Cover image: *Newport Beach Binoculars Pier View* © Allen Donikowski

Cover design copyright © 2013 by Covenant Communications, Inc.

Published by Covenant Communications, Inc.
American Fork, Utah

Printed in the United States of America
First Printing: July 2013

19 18 17 16 15 14 13   10 9 8 7 6 5 4 3 2 1

ISBN 978-1-62108-469-3

Acknowledgments

I HAVE ENJOYED THIS SERIES so much and appreciate all the encouragement and support I've had from readers, family, and friends in making it possible. I'm beyond grateful for my coauthors on this project: Annette Lyon (*Paige*, Covenant 2012; *Ilana*, Covenant 2014), Heather B. Moore (*Athena*, Covenant 2012; *Ruby*, Covenant 2013), and Julie Wright (*Olivia*, Covenant 2012.) They are such important women in my life and have each made me better and stronger. Thank you, gals, for . . . everything. Big thanks to Deseret Book for supporting this project, which eventually led to them asking Covenant Communications to take over publication in order to retain continuity in the series. Because of that, I got to work with even more fabulous people. Specifically Jana Erickson, Deseret Book product manager; Lisa Mangum, Deseret Book editor (*After Hello*, Shadow Mountain 2012); Samantha Millburn, Covenant editing and typesetting; and Christina Marcano, Covenant cover design. I am grateful to be able to work with such talented people and appreciate each of you so much.

Thank you to Gregg Luke (*Deadly Undertakings*, Covenant 2012) for helping me with some of the pharmacist-specific elements of this book. With his own books to write, profession to work, a family to raise, and life to live, I am very grateful for the time he took to guide my words.

In my years of writing there are a few books I've written that have explored things that are a part of my personal experience. "Shannon" was one of those books for me. I am not Shannon, and I don't have a specific Keisha in my life, but I have been a participant in the "dance" of addiction and codependency and boundaries and letting go and forgiving (or trying to). The closeness of those issues made it a hard book to write, and at one point I determined I needed to abandon this story line and start something else; I felt that I was exposing too much raw flesh in the story and that I might hurt people I love. I explained it to my husband—who intimately knows the real-life people and circumstances that made this story difficult—and he encouraged me to stay with it. He felt that the value for me and other people involved in a similar "dance" was worth the discomfort. And so I wrote it. And I learned. And I'm still nervous. But the words are here, and I hope they are of value to others.

I believe in a God of healing and hope, and I believe our journeys do not end when we leave mortality and that some battles may continue indefinitely. There is a fine line between hope and hopelessness sometimes; between love and self-preservation; between kindness and enabling. I have much to learn in regard to these things but I am trying. If you are a dancer, on any side of the issue, of which there are many sides, I wish you peace and perspective as you figure out your own steps.

BOOKS IN THE NEWPORT LADIES BOOK CLUB SERIES

Set #1
Olivia—Julie Wright
Daisy—Josi S. Kilpack
Paige—Annette Lyon
Athena—Heather B. Moore

Set #2
Shannon's Hope—Josi S. Kilpack
Ilana's Wish—Annette Lyon
Ruby's Secret—Heather B. Moore

For ideas on hosting your own book club, suggestions for books and recipes, or information on how you can guest-write about your book club on our blog, please visit us at http://thenewportladiesbookclub.blogspot.com.

PRAISE FOR
THE NEWPORT LADIES BOOK
CLUB SERIES

OLIVIA

"I love to find a new series, and the Newport Ladies Book Club doesn't disappoint. I enjoyed . . . the personal connection I felt with the main character, and subsequently for her family members, book club buddies, and even her husband. It was extremely tender and so well written."

—Jenny Moore, *The Write Stuff* blog

"I really loved following Olivia through the process of self-awareness. She has become so wrapped up in making her home and family the ideal that she has forgotten her own soul is equally important in that whole "ideal" scenario. The book seemed to be made of very real-life-type stuff. It was easy to relate to and it was easy to find a bit of myself in there too."

—Aimee Brown, *Getting Your Read On* blog

DAISY

"I really enjoyed . . . the character growth in Daisy. It was so subtle and well crafted and really makes you take a look at your own inner child and what it means to grow up. The characters are so real and flawed; it added that sense of realism to the story in that it felt like we were peeking into these people's lives. Really well done."

—Julie Coulter Bellon, author of *All's Fair*

"I loved this book. I enjoyed getting to know the characters of the Newport Ladies Book Club through Daisy's eyes. I enjoyed the book club meetings, and it was as if reading them for the first time. I loved Daisy's character; she is a very strong, smart gal. I enjoyed her journey and the lessons she learns about herself, her family, and also the joys of close friendships. Most of all, how she needed to ask others for help."

—Mindy Holt, *Min Reads* blog

PAIGE

"This book is intriguing—the details and influences in Paige's life paint a deeper and more textured picture of her personality. Lyon has created characters that are both endearing and infuriating and woven them tightly with the characters previously introduced in the series. The book drips with emotional uncertainty and doubt, but it also engages readers in tender moments that pull at the heart strings."

—Melissa Demoux, *Deseret News*

"The premise—looking at the same four months in the book club from four different points of view—is increasingly intriguing to me. Author Annette Lyon, a much published writer and editor, treats her subject with her usual clarity and thoroughness. Lyon's writing itself is delightful. Her cleverness with language sometimes makes me laugh out loud. Paige's experiences at book club again make me pull the first two books from the shelf to remember how Olivia and Daisy learned from the discussions."

—Kaye Hanson, author & reviewer

ATHENA

"The Newport Ladies Book Club series is such an interesting, unique concept in publishing: a series of novels, each written by a different author and telling the story of one of the women in a book club. Heather B. Moore's writing is by turns funny, sad, and poignant. I had tears in my eyes reading about Athena's ailing father: 'What did my father dream about? Did he know my name when he slept?' And Grey: handsome and kind, handyman, cook, and owner of a bookstore—swoon!"

—Laura Madsen, *Laura's Books* blog

"Athena is a beautifully written and emotionally touching story that had me giggling and crying. This book is the only of the four in the Newport Ladies Book Club series that has a romantic ending, but that didn't take away from the reality of the story and the feeling. Heather B. Moore artfully uses true emotion to reach down inside her readers and leave them always wanting more. This book was a fantastic read for anyone who has ever been—or wanted to be—in love as well as for anyone who has experienced a hardship."

—Nashelle Jackson, *Just a Little Glimpse* blog

Chapter 1

THE PHONE RANG, AND MY brain and body reacted as only a brain and body can react to a phone call in the middle of the night: sheer panic.

I shot up in bed, scrambled across John's still-snoring form—causing him to grunt—and fumbled for the phone on his nightstand. "Hello?" I said, not yet fully awake but alert enough to wish I'd taken just one full breath so it wouldn't sound like I'd just been pulled out of REM sleep.

I could hear noise from the other end of the line—traffic, and a man's voice shouting in the background.

"Hello," I said again as I finished crawling over John, who was awake now, or at least not snoring.

"Can you come get me?"

My heart pitched, and I let out a breath as my grip tightened around the phone. "Keisha?" I asked, though we both knew I knew who it was; Keisha was my twenty-one-year-old stepdaughter, John's daughter from his first marriage. "Where have you been? Where are you?" She'd fought with her mother two weeks ago and had left the house with nothing but her purse and her phone, which she hadn't answered since then. I'd called her at least once a day.

"Please come get me. I don't have anywhere else to go."

I adjusted my position so I could sit on the side of the bed. John sat up behind me, listening. "Is it Keish?" he whispered.

I nodded and covered the mouthpiece of the phone. "She wants us to come get her."

John fell back on the pillows, worn-out by one more crisis following the years of crises involving his daughter. Drugs, rehab, drugs again. Living with her mom, living with us, living with friends, living with her mom again. But, despite the chaos, we had always known where Keisha was at any given time. Not knowing during these last weeks had been horrendous.

"Where are you?" I asked into the phone.

"Compton. By the airport," Keisha said, sniffling. "Can you come?"

"Of course I can come," I said. John's grunt from behind me communicated many things—disappointment in me, annoyance at this situation, and frustration with his daughter. I hoped, however, that within all those negative feelings was also relief that she had called, that we knew she was okay. I knew he'd been as worried about her as I was. I pulled open the nightstand drawer and found a pen and an envelope I could write on. "What's the exact address?"

She gave it to me and asked me to hurry.

"I will," I said. "I'll have my cell phone with me, so call if you need to, okay?"

John climbed out of bed and turned on the closet light.

"I don't know your cell number 'cause I lost my phone," Keisha said, still crying. "I found some guy who let me use his to call you guys."

The need for urgency was building in my chest. "Let me give you my cell number, then. Do you have something you can write it down with?"

"No, just come," she said, sounding frustrated. "Please hurry, there's some really creepy people down here."

"Okay," I said, standing up. "We're on our way."

I hung up the phone and relayed the information to John, who was buttoning up his jeans. "We should be able to get to Compton in about forty minutes this time of night, don't you think?" I grabbed the hem of my knee-length nightgown and fluidly pulled it over my head as I crossed the room to my dresser to get some clothes. Keisha was okay. She was coming home.

"I'll go," John said. "You stay here with Landon."

I stopped, holding up a pair of jeans and looking at him. Oh yeah, Landon, our twelve-year-old son. "I told her *I* would come," I said. "Maybe you should stay with Landon."

"And send you to Compton in the middle of the night by yourself?" He pulled a T-shirt over his head, sending his sleep-mussed hair even more out of control. His hairline was nearly halfway back on his head these days, and though he kept his remaining hair short, the half-inch strands stood up in fifteen directions.

He was right about me going alone, of course. It was bad enough that Keisha was there; to send me there too was ridiculous. But . . . "Go easy on her," I said.

He gave me a look that bordered on a glare and went back into the closet to get his shoes. It was an old argument between us—tired, worn-out, and threadbare. I was too soft on his daughter, and John was too hard. When she'd gone to rehab the last time, he'd become a big proponent for "tough love," and saying, "She's an adult." I wanted to believe that if he'd been the one to answer the phone he'd have agreed to get her like I had, but I didn't know. The poor choices Keisha had been making the last four years had sent us on an emotional roller coaster as we tried over and over again to help, only to have her fall further down the pit of addiction. Maybe for John anger didn't hurt as much as hoping did.

"We just want her to be safe," I said, reminding him of our shared alliance.

He nodded, though reluctantly, and kissed me quickly on his way to the door. "Try to sleep."

"I won't be able to sleep," I said, shaking my head at the idea. "Call me when you get there, okay? I want to know she's with you."

He nodded again and disappeared through the doorway, leaving me standing in the middle of our bedroom. I listened carefully for the sound of the garage door closing before putting my nightgown back on and puttering into the living room. It would be at least an hour and a half before they got back, but if I stayed in bed, I would just stare at the ceiling. I'd rather clean to pass the time; heaven knows with both John and me working more than full-time, and with John coaching whatever sport-of-the-season Landon was playing, there was always something in need of cleaning, but then I saw the yellow-and-purple book cover peeking out from beneath a pile of mail and newspapers on the kitchen table.

I'd bought *The Help* last week at Walmart after Aunt Ruby told me it was the title for next month's book group. We'd been meeting for four months now, and I had yet to finish any of the other book club books. I'd seen the movie for this one, though, and liked the idea of comparing the two formats. I glanced at the clock. It was 2:14. Was John to Anaheim yet?

I sat down in John's recliner and pulled back the stiff pages of the book. An internal hesitation almost stopped me; I'd developed a prejudice toward fiction many years ago. Why read fiction when there were so many fascinating truths out there waiting to be learned? I pushed away the thoughts and honed in on the first page, determined to make this work. I was thirty-eight years old and in most ways I was well-rounded, but I could use some more things to talk about and think about. Landon was almost thirteen and more independent than ever before. John was extremely involved in Landon's athletics, leaving me with time I didn't know how to fill. Hence, I'd accepted Aunt Ruby's invitation to join her book group and yet hadn't finished a book. This time would be different.

I looked at the clock again and hoped that this experience with Keisha would be different too. She'd lived with us half a dozen times since she'd turned seventeen and first starting hitting serious turbulence. Once she stayed with us for five full months; all the other times were just a few weeks here and there until she got back on her feet or repaired things with her mother. These last two weeks when she'd been gone were the longest weeks of our lives. We'd filed a missing persons report with the police, we'd contacted all of her friends we knew, and we'd called the local hospitals more than once. And now she'd called us. Thank goodness. I hoped that her calling us was a sign that she had finally hit the bottom of her trials and was ready to build her way up. I had always been able to see incredible potential in her, and I was determined to help her see it too.

But right now I needed to stop obsessing about her. I needed to get lost in something else and prepare for whatever tomorrow might bring. I smoothed my hand over the first page of *The Help,* took a breath, and started reading.

Chapter 2

WHEN JOHN AND KEISHA GOT home at 4:00 a.m., I hopped off the couch and fussed over my stepdaughter, who looked horrible. She was a tiny little thing, like her mother—just over five foot two, and a hundred pounds, if that. Without her makeup on, she looked about fourteen years old. She was usually fastidious about her appearance, but clearly she hadn't showered or brushed her hair in days. She smelled like a bar, and my stomach sank. I hoped she'd at least stayed away from anything stronger than alcohol. She was obviously exhausted and in no condition to talk, so I helped her to the shower, gave her a clean nightgown of mine, then tucked her into the guest room bed and told her we'd talk tomorrow.

"Thanks, Shannon," she whispered, closing her eyes and pulling the blanket up to her chin.

"You're welcome," I said. At the doorway I paused and looked back at her, my heart both heavy and light at the same time. I'd wanted more children of my own—well, sort of. I'd been pregnant before Landon. I had been a new wife of just a year at the time, establishing a relationship with my husband's six-year-old daughter, and I was both excited and nervous about becoming a mom.

At the twenty-week ultrasound appointment, however, the doctors couldn't find a heartbeat. Because of the gestation, it was a toss-up as to whether it was considered a miscarriage or a stillborn, but either way it was a difficult experience for John and me. I tried to be pragmatic about it; after all, my job as a pharmacist—a scientist—meant that I understood biological processes. I knew it was illogical to expect that every meeting of a sperm and an egg would result in a fetus and that every fetus would be viable.

But the reality *was* hard, and I mourned what could have been. I thought I'd handled it reasonably well . . . until I got pregnant with Landon a year later—then all my female emotion erupted.

I was constantly afraid my baby would die inside of me again. I couldn't sleep at night; I had nightmares that—even now—made me break out in a cold sweat when I thought about them. I wouldn't eat red meat for fear I would get E. coli. When the news reported a shipment of strawberries had been contaminated with salmonella, I gave up fresh fruit and vegetables altogether and only ate frozen foods.

On a psychological level, I knew it was completely unhealthy to be that obsessed, but at the time it simply felt like I was doing what was best for my unborn child. When Landon was born, I cried with relief and joy; I'd delivered a healthy baby boy: seven pounds, nine ounces, and twenty-three inches long. John and I both hoped that my panic would pass with Landon's safe arrival, but it didn't.

I insisted Landon sleep with me in the bed because I was terrified he would stop breathing, and I made John sleep in the guest room because I worried he might accidentally smother our baby due to how deeply he slept. After *ten months*, John sat me down and shared his concerns that I was unhinged, though he used nicer terminology.

At first, I went to counseling just to make John feel better, but once I began participating in the process, I was able to realign my thoughts and reactions, which I'd realized were based on unrealistic fears that were deeply rooted in that first pregnancy. By the time Landon turned two years old, I was off my meds and doing much better. I could let Landon sit alone in a grocery cart, and John had replaced him in our bed—though Landon's crib stayed in our room until he was nearly three.

After the drama and trauma of Landon's early years, John and I never talked about having another baby, both of us afraid to repeat my struggles. Instead of risking another pregnancy, we devoted ourselves to our son and to Keisha, who'd moved back to California with her mother. I didn't necessarily regret our decision not to have more children, but there were times that I missed the children we didn't have.

Looking at Keisha now and knowing she was safe was a powerful balm to my mother's heart. I pulled the door closed, then headed to our room, where John was under the covers but not asleep, his clothes discarded on the floor for the second time tonight.

We'd been out of bed for so long that the sheets had grown cold, and I shivered slightly as I slid in beside him. "Did she tell you anything? Did she say why she didn't call before now?" I whispered.

He was quiet for so long that I was trying to think of another lead-in when he spoke.

"I don't think I can do this again."

I took note of the discouraged tone of his voice more than I did the actual words and snuggled in closer so I could look into his face, which was heavily shadowed in the dark room. If not for the glowing numbers of the alarm clock informing me that I had to be to work in four hours, the room would be pitch-black. I reached out and traced the lines in his forehead. Life lines, I called them. He was eleven years older than I was— pushing fifty—and handsome in that rugged "man's man" kind of way.

"It's going to be okay," I whispered to him. "We did the right thing letting her come home. What else could we have done?"

He let out a tortured breath. "She's been so high since leaving Dani's, she doesn't remember days at a time. It's been a bad binge, Shan. She says she hasn't used in a few days, but I'm not sure we can believe her. I'm not sure it's safe for her to detox here."

"I'll take tomorrow off and keep an eye on her," I said. "If things look bad, I'll call Transitions." Transitions was the rehab clinic where Keisha had gone last fall. They had a detox program, though I didn't know where we'd get the money to pay for it. Keisha's last stay had pretty much wiped out our savings, and we'd only recently begun to build it back up.

John groaned, surely thinking the same things I was, so I hurried to offer some reassurance. "If she can keep her brain chemistries balanced, then she wouldn't need to use," I told him.

It was all based on science for me. Keisha had been diagnosed with depression when she was fifteen, and she had really struggled to feel good about herself and life in general since then. It had always been my belief that she'd started using drugs to numb the bad feelings, and then she'd gotten hooked. Because of the drug use, she didn't talk or act like a typical twenty-one-year-old young woman, but was more like the sixteen-year-old kid she'd been when she first started using. But I still had high hopes for her. If she could get well—*really* well—she wouldn't need to self-medicate. I had hoped Transitions had finally helped her find her balance this last time, but maybe the ninety-day program hadn't been a long enough stay.

I snuggled into John, and he rolled onto his back to accommodate me, wrapping his arms around my shoulders. "I think we can help her, John," I said, thinking of Keisha asleep down the hall. "I can find her a therapist and a good doctor, get her on her meds, supervise her behaviors, and she can create a new social group, find a job, and go to school." I'd said all of this six months ago when I'd wanted her to come stay with us, but both John and Dani, Keisha's mom, had chosen rehab. Now we had another chance, and who better to help lead Keisha to wellness than two of the people who loved her the most?

"I don't want her here with Landon," he whispered as though the words were hard to say. They were certainly hard to hear. "It kills me to say that, but he has to be our priority."

I agreed with him, and yet . . . "Where else can she go, John?" I said. "Dani's not a good fit—we both know that—but the only other resources Keisha has are those same druggy friends you just got her away from."

"When she's here, the whole atmosphere of our home changes. She becomes the focus, and I just don't know how many more times we can bail her out."

"She's had a hard road," I reminded him. It was difficult to say because I knew he felt guilty for the life his little girl had been exposed to after the divorce. Dani had dragged Keisha through a lot of her own dysfunctional problems: substance abuse issues, lousy boyfriends, and bouts of unemployment. Dani and Keisha had been out of state until Keisha was almost ten, far enough away that John didn't know the full extent of what was happening until years later when Keisha started telling us of the experiences she'd had when she was young. In hindsight, he wished he'd fought harder for custody. But he hadn't, and so Keisha had gone through a lot of garbage—too much. I wished his guilt would prompt him to want to go the extra mile now, but instead he seemed insecure about his ability to help her at all. He often kept her at a distance—emotionally as well as physically.

"She *can* get well, John, but she needs support, and we are the best people to give it."

"At what cost?" he asked, his voice still low. "Are we okay with having Landon exposed to her lifestyle?"

"She knows our standards, and she wouldn't have called unless she was ready to change." I knew that was the reason she hadn't stayed with us long-term in the past—because she couldn't use here. "She called us for *help*."

"Or, like you said before, maybe she called because she had nowhere else to go."

I couldn't help feeling disappointed in him for not opening himself up to what I was saying. "She's sick, John. She needs you; she needs *us*. We're her family, and we can give her a foundation to build on."

He said nothing, and after a few seconds had passed, he rolled onto his side, his back to me. I did the same, and we both lay there in the dark, defending our positions to ourselves. I closed my eyes and tried to sleep, but the heaviness of the discussion wouldn't allow it. I stewed and stressed and wondered what do to. How could I *make* this work? How could I convince John that having Keisha here was the right choice? The *only* choice. Could he really say no when she was so vulnerable?

Neither sleep nor answers came, but when the alarm went off, I was at least able to rise from bed more committed than I'd been when I'd lain down. When I looked into Keisha's future, I saw how it *could* play out. She could get well, go to college, get a good job, and look back on this time in her life with the knowledge that her dad and her stepmom loved her enough to give her another chance. She could be a success story—an inspiration to other people dealing with the same struggles she'd faced. I just had to convince John of that while assuring him that I wasn't putting our son at risk in the process.

Chapter 3

JOHN STAYED IN BED AFTER I got up; I was certain he hadn't slept any better than I had. He owned his own custom cabinetry business that had taken some hard knocks when the economy collapsed, which was why I worked sixty hours a week when I could. We usually did our morning routine together, but this morning was not like every other morning, and I wanted to let him sleep. I liked to go running before I woke Landon up, but with the night we'd had, that was out of the question.

I put on my bathrobe and peeked in on a sleeping Keisha before letting myself into Landon's room across the hall. It was a mess, and I had to pick my way through basketball gear, dirty clothes, and who knew what else to get to his bed. I knew I should take an afternoon and help him clean it, but honestly, I just didn't care that much. There were more important things than clean bedrooms.

"Hey, buddy," I said, grabbing his foot and giving it a shake. He grunted and shifted beneath the comforter.

"What do you want for breakfast?"

"Pancakes," he said from the head of the bed as he blinked his chocolate-brown eyes—the same color as John's and Keisha's eyes—at me. As a baby, he'd had the most beautiful, bright blond curls. I let them grow long until people kept mistaking him for a girl, despite his tractor T-shirts and camouflage pants. Now I wanted his hair short and he wanted it long, which I thought looked horrible. Funny how times changed.

"Okay, get in the shower and I'll make pancakes." I picked my way to the door, then turned back to give a second wake-up call before I left the room. "Landon."

"I know," he said, finally sitting up.

I flipped on his light to keep him from falling back into bed, then headed to the kitchen, where I took a minute to call into work. I felt horrible about missing work—I couldn't remember the last time I'd given the office such short notice about my schedule—but I had to keep an eye on Keisha today. The woman in the staffing office was professional about my call and said she'd find someone to fill in. Then I grabbed the pancake mix and turned on the griddle.

Over breakfast I told Landon about Keisha. He ate without looking up from his plate, making it impossible to read his reaction.

"So, what do you think?" I finally asked.

He glanced up and finished the bite he was chewing. "I don't know," he said with a shrug.

"Are you okay with this?"

"I guess."

I let out a breath and took a drink of milk before going back to my own pancakes. Keisha had doted on Landon when he was little, but in recent years, he'd become sensitive to the drama Keisha always brought with her. He also struggled with having to share the attention, but I thought that was good for him. My biggest fear about having only one child was that he'd be spoiled and expect to be in the spotlight all the time.

I considered what John had said about how Keisha's staying here would be bad for Landon. But they were both our children. They both needed us. Could we really be expected to choose one over the other?

John went to work at ten, and he called twice to see how Keisha was doing. She slept the whole day—literally. I woke her up every two hours and made her drink a glass of water, knowing dehydration would make the detox process worse, but then she'd lay back down and fall asleep again each time. I knew there were medications that could help with the detox process, but when I offered anything, she said she was okay.

At almost ten o'clock that night, just after putting Landon to bed, John and I woke her up enough for her to eat some red beans and rice I'd cooked for dinner. As soon as she finished, though, she went right back to bed, which I assured John was okay. I'd spent the day trolling the Internet and making sure I knew what to look for and what was considered normal for someone coming off a binge. If I knew what she'd been taking, I could have done more specific research, but she hadn't been awake enough for me to ask, and so I assumed she'd been doing what she'd done in the past—oxycodone, mostly, which she snorted for a quicker high than she'd get from taking it orally.

The information I found about oxycodone withdrawal said the worst symptoms could include panic attacks, depression, and nausea. While Keisha had experienced some of those in the past, she didn't seem to be experiencing them now. But it was the last item on the list—insomnia—that made me think that she had probably stopped using the really hard drugs. I glanced down the hall to the guest room where Keisha—clearly *not* suffering from insomnia—was sleeping off what must just be exhaustion and tension from the stress of the last two weeks.

I couldn't miss work two days in a row, so on Friday I worked my usual ten-hour shift, calling the house every two hours. I'd put the phone by Keisha's bed so she'd be sure to answer it. She answered each time I called, and she got up after I came home. She was back in bed by ten, but she looked better and said she felt better too. The next morning, she got up around nine o'clock, showered, and asked me to make stuffed french toast for breakfast. I couldn't make it fast enough, and the four of us had a nice Saturday morning brunch together.

Landon had a basketball game at noon so we loaded up and headed toward the rec center. I'd planned to go in and watch the game—John and I were big believers in parental presence—but Keisha and I stayed in the car and talked for over an hour instead. She told me about how great rehab had been, but that when she'd returned to her mother's house, it was just too hard. Dani had had episodes of drinking problems throughout her life, and I knew her current live-in boyfriend sometimes smoked pot in the garage. Keisha told me she'd tried to stay strong, but after a few weeks the tension of trying to establish a new life got the best of her. She started drinking here and there—though no one noticed—then she found an old stash of crushed narcotics in her room. It was all downhill from there.

"They said over and over in rehab that negative energy was the enemy of wellness. Do you know how *bad* the energy is in that apartment? Stifling. Mom's as big a mess as she's ever been. She's *so* done with parenthood."

"Didn't you have follow-up care after getting out of rehab?" I asked, knowing full well that she'd been set up with outpatient therapy.

She looked at her tiny hands in her lap. "It was all the way in Irvine, and I only made it to one appointment."

"And your antidepressants?"

"I was taking them for a while, but . . . they just didn't seem to help as much as the other stuff."

The two weeks she'd spent on her own were a blur, and I didn't push for details that I felt sure would hurt my heart to hear. She apologized profusely for having used again, and when I took her into my arms, assuring her she was loved and safe with us, she cried on my shoulder.

"I'm done for good now," she said when she pulled back, her eyes red and puffy. "I swear, Shannon, I'll never use again."

I wrapped myself up in that promise and believed it completely.

After Landon's game, John, Keisha, and I sat down and wrote up a contract. It was John's idea, and I wasn't completely comfortable with it—it seemed too formal for a family situation—but he was insistent that we spell out the expectations of this arrangement. Keisha agreed to get a job and enroll in some kind of school or certification program. She would communicate to us where she was going at all times. She'd make dinner Monday and Thursday nights. She'd go to therapy, take her meds, and attend Narcotics Anonymous twice a week. John would get her a cell phone on our account, but she would pay the bill as soon as she got a job. She would not drink—John had locked up our liquor cabinet years ago—and she would not use, and if she did, she would tell us immediately. If we found out she'd used and not told us, she was out.

"We can tolerate relapse if we know you're being honest with us," John said.

Keisha looked like a bobblehead doll as she nodded in agreement to every item on John's list. He kept looking at her as though he expected her to argue, but she didn't. I couldn't have been more proud of her. I knew it would be hard for her to make so many drastic changes—very hard—but I could feel her determination and knew she was serious about the change. I was also proud of my husband for finding a way to support a plan that, to me, was obvious. The contract wasn't my first choice, but it showed that he was reaching out for a compromise, and I appreciated that very much.

After that, the whole family went out for ice cream. Keisha talked to Landon at length, getting caught up on her stepbrother's life—which consisted mostly of video games and sports. He was hesitant to open up at first, but Keisha was both energetic and invested, and by the end of the meal there was a definite decrease in the tension between all of us. I reached under the table and gave John's knee a squeeze. When he looked at me, I smiled. He smiled back, though it didn't reach his eyes. He was trying, but he still wasn't sold on this idea.

Once we were alone in our room that night I gave him a big hug. "See, it's working out," I said, lifting my shoulders to my ears, excited about all the positive things we'd seen so far. "She seems excited about the plans we made, doesn't she?"

He put his arms around me and nodded. "She does seem excited."

"And she agreed to every point of the contract."

He nodded again, and I smiled even wider and went on my tiptoes to give him a quick kiss. "We're doing the right thing."

"I hope so," he said, then reached up and unwrapped my arms from around his neck before heading into the bathroom.

There would be no convincing him of anything with my words and, in truth, what could I convince him of? For all my optimism, I still didn't know what was going to happen. He didn't see the same potential I saw, and with only Keisha's past as a comparative study, it was hard to argue with John about his fearful expectations. Time would have to tell.

"She's going to prove you wrong," I said with a teasing tone to my voice. "Just you wait and see."

Chapter 4

BY THE FOLLOWING SATURDAY, NINE days into Keisha's stay, I was more confident than ever that we had made the right choice. Keisha seemed to have made it through some of the worst withdrawal symptoms and, for the last few days, had seemed back to her old self.

She'd picked up her things from her mom's house—though they weren't really speaking—and had started doing her hair and makeup again. She was looking for a job within walking distance of our house since John had refused to even discuss buying her a car, and she had decided to go to cosmetology school—something she'd talked about doing before. The school was just one bus ride away, and she said she was fine taking public transportation, though I said I'd drive her when I could. I thought Keisha would make a great cosmetologist; she had always had an eye for style and detail.

I'd asked around at work for a good therapist and found one just a few miles south of us who had an evening appointment open on Tuesdays. Keisha had only met with the woman one time, but she seemed to like her and had appointments set up for the next four weeks. John was loosening up, and Landon seemed to have accepted his sister being at home as though she'd always been there. Things were good, and I could not have been more pleased.

Aunt Ruby had called to remind me of the book group, and though I told her I'd be there, I was looking for an excuse to duck out until I mentioned it to Keisha and she asked if she could come with me. She hadn't seen Aunt Ruby in years and said she thought book group sounded "fun." And so, after a short three-hour shift in Irvine, I came home long enough to heat up a Hot Pocket before Keisha and I got back in the car and headed toward Newport.

"Did you read the book?" Keisha asked.

"I did," I said, unable to hide the pride in my voice. I'd read part of *The Poisonwood Bible* last fall, and started on *Silas Marner* after December's meeting, but I didn't finish them. *The Help*, though, I'd finished and was quite impressed with how well Hollywood had adapted the book for the movie. "Did you ever see the movie?" I asked Keisha.

"I think so," she said.

"I'm glad you're coming. I don't know the other women very well, so it'll be nice to have you with me."

The closer I got to Aunt Ruby's house in Newport, however, the more nervous I became. I dealt with people all the time at work, but those associations were short and centered on the service I was providing. Something about being behind a counter made everything easier for me when it came to conversation. Socially, I wasn't nearly as confident as I pretended to be, and I couldn't say that any of the women at book group would call me their friend. Well, other than Aunt Ruby, who was always attempting to include me in aspects of her life.

Aunt Ruby had kept me up-to-date about the lives of the other members of the group, and I was glad she'd developed friendships with these women, but I wondered how many of those friendships went below the surface—not just with the book group ladies, but with everyone Ruby had relationships with. I didn't like thinking negatively about Aunt Ruby; she was one of the kindest women I'd ever known, but there was a veneer about her, a desire for something she didn't have. Security? Safety? Belonging? I didn't know.

For all her reaching out, I wondered if many people reached in. I tried, but she didn't let me get very far, and I wasn't the most outgoing person to start with. I wondered if her caution had to do with Uncle Phillip—he'd have been a difficult partner to have in your life, I thought. As hard as his death was two years ago, I'd hoped it would be a new beginning as well and that this book group was part of that for Aunt Ruby—assuming she could let go of her fix-everything personality and let these women see the real her.

I had to analyze myself with the same measure though. Did I let people get past the surface? Did I let people see the real me?

I didn't like thinking about that, so I let my thoughts go from Aunt Ruby to Keisha, who was always easy to think and worry about. I hoped tonight would be fun for her. I knew she was struggling not having friends around here, and while none of these women were her age, it was a start.

There were a few cars at Aunt Ruby's when I pulled up, and I took a minute to redo my ponytail, smoothing my long brown hair and putting the ponytail higher on my head. I hadn't changed out of my Walgreens scrubs, but I wore them so often that they were as comfortable as pajamas. I deemed myself presentable, and we both got out of the car.

Aunt Ruby opened the door and gave us both a big hug, cooing over Keisha. I searched Ruby's face for judgment or censure—she knew Keisha's history—but didn't see anything except welcome, which helped me relax a great deal. Keisha seemed really touched by the fuss Aunt Ruby made over her.

Athena was talking to Tori at one end of the room, both of them thin and lovely, leaning toward one another and laughing about something. They were about the same age and, if I remembered right, both worked in journalism or something like that. They didn't look up at me, but that was okay; it saved me having to come up with a greeting. Olivia and Ilana, the Jewish woman, stopped their conversation to say hi to us. Keisha and I sat across from them, and Olivia introduced herself and Ilana to Keisha, who then introduced herself—all of them sparing me the task, which I appreciated since I was still so nervous.

It wasn't until everyone had said hello to each other that I noticed the sling Ilana wore on her left arm. I didn't want to put her on the spot by asking what had happened, but Keisha had no such hesitation.

"What happened to your arm?"

Ilana looked at the sling then shook her head, making a face. "I got hurt at work. Broken elbow."

"Ow," Keisha said, wrinkling her nose. "Does it hurt bad?"

"Not so long as I keep up on the pain pills," Ilana said. "They're talking about surgery, possibly. I go in again this week to get it checked out."

I wanted to ask what medication she was taking and when the accident had occurred. Was she sleeping at night? Did she know that stabilizing her wrist in addition to keeping it in the sling could limit the rotary movement which, in turn, would take some of the pressure off the tendons in the elbow? But I wasn't supposed to be a pharmacist with a passion for physiology right now; I was just a member of the group who'd finally read one of the novels all the way through.

"That totally sucks," Keisha said with a frown. Both Olivia and Ilana smiled, and I felt myself relax a little more. They liked Keisha, and she was comfortable here. That went a long way toward my comfort as well.

Olivia asked Keisha about where she worked and if she was going to school.

"I'm looking for a job right now, but I'm going to enroll in cosmetology school. I think I'd really like that."

Ruby returned with another member of the group—Paige, the young, single, Mormon mom. Didn't she have two kids? I'd never really talked to her much, but I remembered how she'd defended her church at the first meeting. I'd admired her confidence back then, even though I still thought Mormons were weird. I'd had a Mormon tech a few years ago who refused to work on Sunday or on Monday nights and who kept handing out postcards about her church to customers. I asked her to stop advertising, and she quit her job, just like that. The experience hadn't left the best impression on me, but Paige seemed nice, and Aunt Ruby thought the world of her.

"I guess we're all here," Aunt Ruby said, clapping her hands together and making her dangly silver earrings shake.

"Is Daisy still on bed rest?" Athena asked.

I remembered Daisy too; she was the pretty one with blonde hair and a big smile.

"She is," Aunt Ruby said, frowning slightly. "I offered to have us go to her place like we did last month, but she said she'd moved and her new place was too small." She looked at Paige. "I didn't want to pry by asking too many questions."

Paige picked up the cue Aunt Ruby was sending and tucked her hair behind her ear before speaking. "She got her own place a couple weeks ago, close to where her ex-husband and daughter live. She's still on partial bed rest, but the baby's doing well. She's able to work from home half-time right now."

"Did her life turn a 180 or what?" Tori said. I realized she wasn't wearing any makeup, but she was naturally gorgeous, with a casual attitude that made her even more striking. Her tightly curled hair was pulled into a sloppy bun that looked almost artistic. "But she's okay?"

"Yeah," Paige said with a smile that confirmed her words. "I think she's doing really well. She said to thank everyone for the phone calls and cards. She says she's felt every prayer."

Everyone commented that they were glad. I hadn't really gotten to know Daisy—well, I hadn't gotten to know *any* of the women, really—but Aunt Ruby had told me about her situation. Daisy had had a rough patch, but it sounded like it was all working out.

"Well," Aunt Ruby said, "Daisy chose the book, but since she isn't here, I guess I'll lead the discussion. What did everyone think?"

I mostly listened to what everyone said, nodding when I agreed with their assessment of the lingering prejudice and the lack of opportunity for black women during the time frame, and how they related to the characters. The part about the miscarriage had been hard for me to read. It had taken me back to the feelings of loss I'd had—still had—over my first pregnancy. But I wasn't about to share that experience, and none of the other women hit on that portion; instead, they had insights on all kinds of other details. It amazed me that these women could pull out such deep and philosophical things from the story. They did know *The Help* was fiction, right?

Tori's comments interested me the most, since she was the only black woman present. Her perspective was even more unique because she wasn't of African descent. Her family was from Barbados, where racial issues were different than they were in the United States. "For me personally," she said, "I haven't experienced racial prejudice in the US. Maybe because I'm in the entertainment industry, it just hasn't been an issue for me. I find it much harder to be a woman than to be black."

"You've experienced prejudice for being a woman?" Aunt Ruby asked.

"Oh yes," Tori said, raising her perfectly sculpted eyebrows dramatically. "There's still a lot of opportunity for me within my industry, but most of the top spots are filled with men, and most of the decisions on who *fills* the open positions are *made* by men. And a lot of women fall victim to unprofessional ways of furthering their career, if you know what I mean."

We all nodded; we knew exactly what she meant. I cast a look at Keisha to see if she was listening—she was. It made me a little uncomfortable even though she was twenty-one years old. She seemed so much younger than she really was, and I still wanted to protect her from the harsh realities of the world.

Athena shared some of her experience about being Greek. She'd had some painful experiences due to her ethnicity, especially when she was younger. Ilana and Paige had experienced religious prejudice. I was starting to feel left out for not having been discriminated against. Being a woman in a male-dominated profession had helped me in many ways—applying for scholarships and being in demand after school, for example. And my personal experience as a mother was priceless when others moms were nervous about the side effects of medications for their kids. Granted, I worked my tail off to stay at the head of my class and to do the best job I could every day, but I didn't feel that my race or my gender had ever stood in my way, and I didn't have a particular religious affiliation to set me apart either.

"Shannon, what did you think?" Aunt Ruby said, interrupting what had—thus far—been a nice meeting. It startled me to be singled out.

"Uh, I liked it." Leave it to me to come up with the cleverest response. I cleared my throat and tried again. "It's been a really long time since I've read a novel; I don't like much fiction." I immediately felt my face flush, since I knew these women *did* like fiction. "I really liked this one though."

I looked at the book I held in my lap. Across from me, Olivia had marked several pages with green Post-it Notes. Athena had already quoted something from the novel. All I'd done was read the book.

I barely noticed the silence that followed my lack of participation, but Paige hurried to fill it with more insight than I could muster. The discussion continued around me. I wondered if Keisha remembered that I'd been pregnant before Landon. Did she remember how neurotic I'd been during and after my pregnancy with him? I hadn't let her hold her brother for months after he was born, terrified she'd drop him or get him sick. Had that scarred her somehow, adding to the difficulties of her parents' divorce and her mother's chaotic lifestyle?

The discussion seemed to go on forever, and I distracted myself from my own anxiety by counting all the little white artificial flowers in the centerpiece on Aunt Ruby's glass coffee table—twenty-seven—the pleats in the curtain swag covering Aunt Ruby's big picture window—nine—and the number of tiles used in her fireplace hearth—sixteen. Numbers were unchanging and solid, much more so than ethereal concepts and personal insights.

Eventually the conversation died down, and Aunt Ruby brought out a chocolate pie that made everyone laugh. She assured us she had something else—red velvet cake bread pudding. Yum! I joined her in the kitchen and encouraged her to go back to the group, which she did. I knew she enjoyed entertaining, while busy hands always made me feel more at ease. Like at work, there was now a counter between me and the other women here. Once all the plates were filled, I took them out to the women—glad to see that Keisha was talking to Paige—then slunk back to the kitchen, where I ate my dessert alone.

While the desserts we had at the end of the meetings were always great, and I knew Aunt Ruby liked me to come, I didn't think this book group thing was going to work out. I just wasn't a fiction reader—let alone a fiction *discusser*—and even though I had a connection to this story, I wasn't comfortable sharing it, which made me question why I was even here if I wasn't going to participate where I could. Would Aunt Ruby understand if I called her tomorrow and explained why I needed to quit? I hated the idea of disappointing her, but I hated feeling like a fish out of water even more. With the number of hours I was working and the time I wanted to spend with my family, I just didn't feel like I had room for this. Landon was playing in Tustin tonight; John was there, of course, as assistant coach, but I hated missing it. Especially for something I didn't enjoy very much. Ruby seemed to be getting close enough to these women that I wouldn't be missed.

Maybe I could offer another interaction option to Aunt Ruby to ease her disappointment—did she like to garden? I wouldn't mind learning how to do that. My mom had had quite an herb garden when I was younger, and gardening was a hobby with a tangible result.

Eventually I had to return to the group, and I sat down next to Keisha in time to hear them discussing the date of next month's meeting—March Fifth. Once that was confirmed, it was down to choosing the book.

"Why don't you choose one, Shannon?" Aunt Ruby said.

"Oh, that's okay," I said with a polite smile. "I'm not nearly as well-read as you guys are."

"Oh, baloney," Aunt Ruby said with a wave of her hand. Her recent manicure—peach—caught the light just so and looked so elegant on her long fingers. I had to keep my nails short and unpolished because of my work.

Aunt Ruby continued. "You have a PhD; surely you're as well-read as anyone here. Just choose a book for us to read, something you'd like to share with us."

I didn't actually have a PhD. While I *was* a pharmacy doctor, the PharmD. wasn't equivalent to a traditional doctorate. It wasn't a point worth arguing though. As for a book for next month, I considered saying something glib like *The Amazing Mitochondria* or something, but that would be rude.

"Really," I said, looking around the group and hoping one of them would rescue me, "I don't know. I don't read much fiction."

"It doesn't have to be fiction," Athena said. "Do you read nonfiction?"

"Mostly only for work," I said, searching my mind for something. My copy of *The Help* was on the coffee table where I'd put it, and seeing it reminded me of something—a connection I'd made between that book and a book one of the techs had left in the break room last summer. I hadn't read the whole thing, but I *had* read portions of it and had meant to get a copy of my own so that I could finish it. "Well, there is one that might be interesting," I heard myself say. Wait? Wasn't I planning to stop coming?

"Oh, good," Aunt Ruby said, bringing her hands together in her lap—always such a lady. "What is it?"

"Well, *The Help* kind of reminded me of it since it also involves a black woman in the 1950s. It's called *The Immortal Life of Henrietta Lacks.*" I scanned the room, looking for someone to recognize it.

To my relief, Paige smiled. "I read a review about it," she said, nodding. "And I tried to check it out at the library once, but it had a few holds on it—that was almost a year ago though. I heard it was really well done."

Her confirmation gave me more confidence, even excited me a little bit. I did have something to say—imagine that! "It *was* really well done," I said, nodding quickly. "It's about a woman who had cervical cancer. The doctors biopsied the tumor and discovered that her cells reproduced continually, which opened the floodgates of medical research. Her cells are why we have a vaccine for polio, and why we've made such advances in cancer research. Fascinating history."

Everyone seemed surprised to have heard so many words come out of me all at once, myself included. But that book had been a story that was interesting to me. It was about science and ethics and factual representations of the behind-the-scenes things that affected people's lives without them even knowing it. It was truth, and truth was superior to stories . . . at least in my opinion.

"You're such a nerd, Shannon," Keisha said with a laugh.

I felt my face heat up, instantly embarrassed as Keisha's comment deflated my growing confidence. Why would Keisha do that to me? I was a nerd—an intellectual woman without the social graces of everyone else here.

"We love nerds," Tori quickly said. I tried to smile, but I could feel myself sinking deeper into the couch. Gosh, why did I even come?

"I think it sounds great," Athena said. I didn't look up at her because I was busy wiping at an imaginary spot on my pants.

"What was the title again? I want to order it from Amazon before I forget," she continued.

I was still trying to pull myself together, but luckily Paige provided the information. "*The Immortal Life of Henrietta Lacks.* The author had a weird name though. I can't remember what it was."

"Skloot," I said automatically, feeling saved by having the answer. "Rebecca Skloot—S-K-L-O-O-T." My mind remembered things like that without me even trying. It was one reason why pharmacology was a good fit; I was a master at remembering details and facts. But don't ask me to compliment someone's new shoes; I wouldn't notice in a million years.

"I'd have never remembered that," Paige said. She was probably smiling at me again. And I probably looked like a five-year-old folded up on the couch, so I forced myself to look up and smile back at everyone. As soon as I felt it was okay to do so, I got up and collected the plates, eager to disappear into the kitchen again. I didn't come back out until Aunt Ruby's kitchen was spotless and I heard her ushering people toward the door.

Chapter 5

"You ready?" I asked Keisha when I finally returned to the living room. She was slumped into the couch, texting on the phone John had picked up for her last week. Who was she texting?

Paige had already left while Ilana, Athena, and Olivia still talked at the far end of the living room.

"Sure," Keisha said. She typed another few words before getting off the couch.

"Nice meeting you guys," she said brightly, waving to the other women, who all echoed the same sentiment.

"I hope you'll come next month," Olivia said.

"Me too," Keisha said. "This was really fun."

Was it? I wondered. Was it *really* fun?

Once in the car, Keisha chatted about how nice Aunt Ruby's house was and how the other women were dressed. I smiled and nodded politely. Eventually she went back to her texting, and a somewhat comfortable silence descended. The thought of leading the discussion next month made my stomach tighten even though it was weeks away. Gardening was sounding better by the minute.

Twenty minutes after leaving Aunt Ruby's house in Newport, I pulled into the garage and shifted into park. John's truck was there, and I wondered how Landon had done at his basketball game. He'd improved so much on his shooting these last few months, and I hoped he'd impressed the coach enough that he would get more playing time than he had at the start of the season.

"Hey, could I borrow the car?" Keisha asked as I turned off the ignition. "My friend Jessica invited me to go to coffee, but she lives in Aliso Viejo."

"Who's Jessica?"

"Just a girl I met in rehab. She's really cool."

"Uh, I don't know," I said evasively.

"She's clean, Shannon," Keisha said, almost with an exasperated tone. "She's going to school to become a dental hygienist or something. So can I take the car?"

In the almost two weeks Keisha had been with us, she hadn't borrowed the car except for a few job interviews. And never at night, and never to hang out with friends. She'd never talked about this Jessica person before. But she *was* twenty-one.

"It's almost nine," I said, hedging. "Isn't it a little late for coffee?"

"It's never too late for coffee," Keisha said, smiling. She placed her clasped hands under her chin. "Plee-eease, Shannon. I just need to get out, ya know? Hang out with a friend. I can pay you back for the gas after I get a job."

"It's not about the gas," I said, smarting a little that I wasn't considered a "friend." "It's just . . ."

"Please?" she said again, her big brown eyes turning all puppy-dog on me even as she dropped her hands. "I just want to hang out for a little while. I swear, Jessica's a *good* friend."

I thought back to what I'd said to John when he worried about getting her an unlimited texting plan for her cell phone: "We need to trust her, even if we don't want to. She needs to be empowered by our faith in her."

"Sure," I said, forcing another smile as I decided to take my own advice. "Be home by eleven."

"That's, like, barely two hours," Keisha said, pouting.

"Okay," I said. "Midnight."

"Awesome!" She reached across the seat and hugged me. "Thank you, thank you!"

Keisha scrambled out of the passenger seat and ran around the back of the car. I handed her the keys once she reached the driver's side; she hugged me again and then jumped into the driver's seat. I reminded her once more to be careful, and she promised she would be. I stood in the garage until the taillights disappeared around the corner; then I took a breath and headed into the house.

John and Landon were watching a basketball game on TV, and I let them have their time while I slipped into the kitchen, feeling the burdens of the day fall away now that I was finally home. I didn't love working Saturdays, but I also hated turning down the chance to make some extra money. My willingness to work had saved us these last few years, but it wasn't easy. I missed having actual weekends and didn't like being at work when I knew John wasn't. Not that he liked that I was the breadwinner any more than I did, but sometimes my resentment crept up on me.

I took a breath and pushed away those thoughts, which were always stronger at the end of a long week. I had much to be grateful for. All the anxiety from the book group was finished, and the pending discussion about the book I'd suggested was a month away. My two favorite men were in the other room, and life was just good and calm and peaceful here. That's why I'd wanted Keisha to come stay with us. I wanted her to feel the warmth I felt in our home. I wanted her to know what it was like to be a part of a family so she could see a different, better future for herself.

I spent a few minutes cleaning up the kitchen before John came in for a soda.

"I didn't hear you come in," he said, leaning down to kiss me on his way to the fridge.

"I just got back," I said, adding soap to the dishwasher.

"I was going to clean up." He scanned the clean counters and sinks. Tonight was his night to do dinner and dishes.

"I really didn't mind."

He leaned in and kissed me on the back of the neck, giving me chills and making me smile. "Thank you."

"You're welcome," I looked over my shoulder and gave him a flirty smile. "How was Lan's game?"

"Great," he said. "He was two for three with his shots and made both free throws. He's come a long way."

"I'm so glad." I rummaged in the fridge for a yogurt cup. Keisha ate two a day, and I was having a hard time keeping up with the demand. "I wish I'd been there. That's the second game I've missed." I didn't say "since Keisha has come," but we both knew that's what I meant.

"Where's Keish?" John asked.

I paused for half a second, then kept any hesitation out of my voice when I spoke. "I let her borrow my car to meet up with a friend."

"A friend?" John pulled up on the tab of his soda until it made the *pop-hiss* sound. He sipped the soda from the rim. "What friend?"

"Her name is Jessica. I guess they were in rehab together."

Distrust pulled his eyebrows together. "She's never said anything about Jessica."

"I'm sure it's fine. Jessica's going to college; Keisha says she's a good influence." I turned my attention to pulling the foil top off the yogurt. "She'll be back by eleven." I said the lie before I even realized I was doing it. I knew why I'd lied though. John would be in bed before eleven, and I didn't want him to know I'd allowed his daughter to stay out so late without consulting him. My face got warm. It wasn't like me to be dishonest.

"Hmmm," he said before taking another drink. He looked at the clock on the stove. "I'll wait up for her and make sure everything's okay when she comes in."

"Don't do that," I said quickly, finding a spoon in the drawer. "You don't want her to think we're checking up on her."

"Why not?" he said as I took my first bite. We were both leaning against opposite counters. "She needs to be accountable, and it's good for her to know we're paying attention."

"She *is* accountable," I said, waving my spoon through the air. "And this is the first time she's asked for the car. We knew it would happen sooner or later. It's okay. She needs to build herself a new life here, and that means we have to let go enough for her to do that. She's with someone who's clean and goal oriented. Let's not make too big a deal out of this."

He was contemplative for a few more seconds, but then he gave me a playful smile. He reached across the space between us to grab my waist and pull me closer. I offered no resistance even though I almost dropped my spoon as I crossed the floor. "It's good you're here," he said, putting his soda down on the counter behind him and placing both hands at my waist, moving my hips as though we were dancing. It was kinda sexy. "I'm always thinking the worst, and you're always willing to give her the benefit of the doubt."

It felt good to have his compliments, or at least it would have felt good if I deserved them, but the lie I'd told sat heavy in my stomach. I did like seeing him softening toward this experience, though, and held on hard to that as justification for what I'd done. I reached up and tapped him on the nose with my spoon. "If we don't give her a chance to prove herself, she'll never feel successful or know how strong she can be."

John arched one eyebrow. "You don't think keeping her locked up in a tower will help her prove her strength?"

I laughed. "Probably not."

He leaned in and kissed me. I put my arms around his neck even though I was still holding my yogurt and spoon and kissed him back. "Thanks for loving my girl," he whispered against my lips before pulling me into a hug.

His girl? Wasn't she *our* girl?

John held me against him for a few seconds until Landon came in and made gagging sounds. John dipped me and kissed me hard on the mouth, causing Landon to leave the room completely and me to drop my yogurt. He stood me back up, kissed me once more, and helped me clean up the mess before returning to watch the end of the game, leaving me with a smile and a reminder of why I'd married this wonderful man. He had always brought out the best in me, and I liked to think I did the same for him. Especially with Keisha. I could tell him over and over again that he'd done the best he could at the time, but her drug issues had really done a number on his confidence.

"It's different this time," I said to the cupboards and dishes hanging out with me in the kitchen. That was why I'd lied about the curfew, because I needed things to be different and I could see how easy it would be for John to lose all hope. I could think of nothing worse than John giving up on Keisha when she was unsteady on her new legs. So I would hold her hand through this, and John's too, and one day we'd all raise our hands triumphantly over our heads and know we'd made it work. Keisha couldn't do this without us, and John couldn't support her without me. I would make this work. I had to.

Chapter 6

JOHN AND I WENT TO bed at ten thirty, but while he fell asleep quickly, I couldn't turn off my brain from both the growing guilt of being dishonest with him about the curfew and my anxiousness about Keisha being out. By lying to John I'd upped the stakes. It was no longer just Keisha's success on the line here; my dog was in the fight now too, and despite telling myself a hundred different times that she'd be home on time and everything would be fine, I looked at the clock at 11:22, and 11:53, and then again at 12:19, my confidence seriously compromised.

At 12:40 I slid out of bed and went into the kitchen to get my phone. Surely she'd texted me, right?

Wrong.

I texted her instead.

Shannon: Where are you?

I waited and waited for a response. Ten minutes later I called her phone, my stomach getting tighter by the minute as I tried not to imagine what was keeping her. She didn't answer. I contemplated waking John for exactly three seconds before determining that would only make things worse. We'd made progress tonight, and I didn't want to ruin that until I knew what had happened.

At two o'clock I was getting really worried. What if she'd been in an accident? Should I call the police? No, I'd have to wake up John before I did anything that drastic. I went into the laundry room and ironed for half an hour, then came out and opened the blinds in the living room so I could see the car as soon as it returned. I sat in the recliner, stood up and straightened the DVDs, sat back down again and tucked my feet underneath me. I texted and called her again.

I wished I had a copy of the *Henrietta Lacks* book already so I could distract myself with the story, but I'd left book group less than seven hours ago.

It was 3:00 a.m. At what point did I tell John that Keisha wasn't home? The very thought made me sick. Where was she? If she would just come home soon, it would be okay. I settled in to wait and must have fallen asleep because the garage door woke me, and I was on my feet and in the doorway at the top of the steps leading to the garage in mere seconds.

"I'm so, so sorry," Keisha said. She got out of the car before I had a chance to ask her what had happened. She hurried to the bottom of the steps and looked up at me apologetically, absolutely contrite. "We went to Jessica's to watch a movie, and I fell asleep."

I wanted so badly to believe her. "I texted and called you."

"I turned off the volume on my phone so I wouldn't interrupt the movie."

I looked closely at her. Were her pupils dilated? Was she twitchy and anxious? What would I do if she were? *Then* would I tell her father?

"I know you don't want to believe me," she said, her tone broken. "I'm so sorry, Shannon. I swear I'd never stay out this late on purpose—not after all you and Dad have done. I just lost track of time."

"I thought you fell asleep," I said, catching the contradiction.

"I did," she said quickly. "That's what I meant. I lost track of time because I was asleep." She took a step closer to the stairs. "Please don't kick me out," she said softly as tears rose in her eyes. "It won't happen again, I swear."

Ugh. What was I supposed to do? This was a violation of our contract. If John were the one waiting up for her, she'd have three days to find somewhere else to go. But I hadn't been comfortable about that part of the agreement from the start. She didn't even have a job yet. Kicking her out would be throwing her back to the wolves—her old friends who, I felt, held a lot of the blame for her problems. Telling John would be the same as kicking her out myself.

"You're putting me in a very difficult situation," I said, and I saw a momentary flash of something in her eyes. Was it victory? Oh, I hoped not. Surely it was regret or repentance. "This can't happen again."

"It won't," she said, sounding relieved. "I promise, Shannon, it won't ever happen again. Jessica felt really bad too. She didn't know I had such a strict curfew; she'd have woken me up if she knew. She thought I should just stay over, but I told her no way, I *had* to get home. You can call her if you don't believe me; she'll tell you all about it." She held out her phone, but I waved it away. I wasn't going to call a stranger at four in the morning.

I was too tired to fight and too scared to dig for the truth.

She frowned up at me. "I'm really sorry, Shannon," she said, coming up the stairs and giving me a hug I couldn't help but return.

"It's okay," I said, more for her benefit than because it was true. It *wasn't* okay. She smelled like mouthwash and perfume, which meant she was covering up something she didn't want me to smell. Something I didn't want to smell either. With her track record, I was a fool to let this incident go, but John wasn't going to give her any leeway, and I knew our home was the best place for her right now.

Also, I hadn't kept up my end of the deal in taking her to NA meetings. Our schedules hadn't lined up, and since she didn't have a car, she couldn't go to the meetings on her own. I needed to get her there; she needed to make new friends who were on a better course. Though I hated knowing she'd been drinking—surely that was all she'd done—I couldn't ignore the fact that she was an addict. Addiction was a disease, and she wasn't well yet. But she hadn't drunk or used since she'd been here; that was an accomplishment I wasn't willing to undo over one night of poor choices.

I pulled back but kept my hands on her shoulders. "This can't happen again, Keish, you understand that, right?"

"Totally," she said with a nod. "It won't, I promise."

I nodded and let her go. She gave me a quick hug again and then headed for her room. I shut the garage, locked the door, turned off the lights, and went back to bed, my whole body aching from both the worry and the lack of sleep.

"Huh, wha?" John said groggily, only half awake.

"Nothing," I whispered. "Go back to sleep."

He grunted but rolled back on his side and was soon softly snoring. I stared at the dark ceiling for a very long time before sleep overcame me.

Chapter 7

I'D NEVER KEPT SOMETHING LIKE this from John, and it ate at me all morning as we went about breakfast. I wanted John and Keisha to reconnect and find the relationship they'd once had, and I knew that John knowing about Keisha not coming home on time would prevent that. I didn't know what the *most-right* thing to do was, and my conscience was raw over it.

I woke her up at eleven o'clock—later than I usually let her sleep, but not so late that John was suspicious. We went to John's parents' house for an early dinner. John's dad had turned seventy-six last week, and this was our chance to celebrate with him. John's sisters and their families came too—his brother lived out of state—and we enjoyed a nice afternoon together. Though I could tell Keisha was hung over, no one else seemed to notice, and everyone was genuinely glad to see her. It had been awhile since she'd attended a family event, and, as the afternoon wore on, her mood seemed to improve.

After returning home, the four of us watched a Will Ferrell movie together and laughed our heads off. I went to refill the popcorn bowl, and when I came back, John was on the couch, Keisha snuggled against one side of him and Landon snuggled against the other. Seeing my husband wrapped up in his children was one of the most beautiful things I'd ever seen, and I chose in that moment to let the previous night go completely.

Rather than interrupt them, I went back to the study set just off the kitchen and caught up on some things on the computer: I posted on Facebook about how wonderful it was to have Keisha home, ordered *The Immortal Life of Henrietta Lacks* from Amazon.com, and checked some blogs I liked to keep up with—most of them written by medical professionals like me, but with a better sense of humor. With the pending health care reform knocking on our doors, all of us in the business were paying close attention to the changes taking place, hoping they would be good ones overall. So far, I was encouraged; we'd see if I continued to feel that way. The movie ended around nine, and Keisha surprised me by asking if the family could have a prayer together before we went to bed.

"It was something we did in treatment. Do you mind?"

We'd never been particularly religious, though John was raised Methodist and his parents still attended worship services most Sundays, but I wasn't opposed to prayer, especially if it was something Keisha had found comfort in. We knelt in a circle and held hands. I had Keisha on one side and Landon on the other, which put John and me directly across from one another.

Keisha bowed her head, and we all followed her example. "Dear God, thank you for this day. Forgive us our trespasses as we forgive others, and help us to have a wonderful week. Thank you for Dad and Landon and Shannon, for their love and acceptance. Help us be strong and do our best. Amen."

John repeated the amen, reminding me that it was a typical closing to repeat it. Landon and I said it at the same time a beat later. I was all choked up with emotion, and I hugged Keisha first, then Landon, trying to hide the tears in my eyes.

"Are you crying, Mom?" Landon asked when he pulled back from me. His surprise was warranted since I rarely got emotional.

I blinked quickly, embarrassed. "I think I just have something in my eye," I said as I stood up.

John laughed, a rich, throaty sound, and grabbed me around the waist before I could escape. Moments later I was draped across his lap, squirming as he tickled me. Keisha and Landon egged him on, and soon I could barely breathe, I was laughing so hard. I finally adjusted my position so I could knee John in the kidney, and with an "oomph" he let go, allowing me to roll to the floor.

"Okay, okay," I said, still laughing as I got to my feet. "Time for bed."

John grabbed my hand as I passed the couch on my way to make sure Landon was actually obeying my instructions. I looked at our hands and then into his face, where the tenderness and love I saw there nearly melted me completely. He squeezed my hand. "I love you, Shan," he said in a tone that said so much more than those four words. The moment filled me with emotion all over again, mostly gratitude at having such a good man in my life, but also a little more guilt. If he knew what had happened *last* night, would we have had *this* night? Would he have snuggled with his daughter and his son on the couch? Would he have tickled me while they cheered him on?

I knew the answer to those questions, but I still didn't see another way of handling the situation than to keep last night to myself. If Keisha continued to stumble, this day would haunt me forever. I could only add one more prayer to the one she'd already offered tonight that her commitment was sincere and that she really was beating this monster inside her. It could be done, I knew it, and she was stronger than she realized. I knew that too. She just had to realize it as well. I hoped and prayed she was moving in that direction.

I hadn't had as much time with Landon since Keisha had arrived, so I hung out with him after he got ready for bed, lying on the other twin bed in his room and asking him about school and the nearly-finished basketball season. There was a time when he and I would snuggle on his bed together, but a few years ago he'd deemed himself too big for such things. That was when I'd realized he was growing up; it had been harder for me than I'd expected it to be, but I was glad that we still had a special bond. I had to remember that it required me to be invested, however, if I wanted to keep things that way. He was twelve, after all, and prone to the same kind of independence that often spurred me to isolate myself from people.

"So, what girls do you like?"

"Mom," he said, disgusted. "That's gross."

"It won't be for long," I told him. "One day you'll go to school and think, 'Holy cow, who is that?'"

"You're totally going to make me throw up, ya know?"

I smiled at the ceiling and then turned onto my side to face him on the other bed. I propped my head up on my hand. "And how is it having Keisha here?"

"It's cool," he said, and the sincerity was a relief to hear.

"I've been kinda busy with her and missed a lot of your stuff."

He shrugged, but he looked at the ceiling and not at me.

"I'll do better, okay?"

"Could you also buy Pop-Tarts? 'Cause that would make me miss you a whole lot less."

I threw the pillow at him and then insisted on a good-night kiss on my way out of the room.

"I love you, little man," I said from the doorway, turning off his light.

"I love Pop-Tarts."

Chapter 8

I WAS RECRUITED TO WORK at Walgreens prior to my graduation and started working the night shift at the twenty-four–hour store in Long Beach as soon as I was fully licensed. After Landon was born, I cut back to part-time, usually working six to midnight, when John could be home. For a profession that required a doctorate degree, we didn't always get traditional white-collar hours. I didn't go back to work full-time until Landon was in first grade; I worked three twelve-hour shifts a week back then while John arranged his schedule so that one of us was home when Landon got home from school every day. For a two-parent, working family, we did a really great job of being there for our son.

John's father was a carpenter, and I had always teased John that he'd been born with a rasp in his hand like John Henry and his hammer. My John was talented and had built up his own custom cabinetry business before we'd married. His excellent reputation and unfailing work ethic were the only reasons his company survived the economic horror of the last few years, but he could sometimes go weeks between jobs, which was as difficult financially as it was emotionally.

My salary alone couldn't support the lifestyle we'd built in the years preceding the crash, and before we'd accepted that we needed to not live with the expectation of work right around the corner, we'd racked up enough credit card debt to put ourselves in a tough situation. We made some hard choices—selling our camp trailer, dropping the lease on John's workshop space and moving his equipment to his parents' garage, and trading in my Explorer for a used sedan, to name a few.

John started picking up small carpentry jobs here and there—installing crown molding into the few custom homes still being built, taking a few framing jobs to try to fill the gaps in his schedule—but it hadn't been enough.

After ten years at the Long Beach store, I put in for a management position in Fountain Valley. I got the job, the increased pay, and the year-end bonuses, which was great, but I missed the Long Beach store. Since John still wasn't working as much as we needed him to, I often picked up extra shifts, and I liked it when those extra shifts were at the Long Beach store.

Neither John nor I were happy with the overall situation. He felt like twenty years of building his company had been a waste of time, and I felt the same way about my eight years of schooling that now had me working at a mind-numbing pace. However, as we watched friends and neighbors lose their jobs completely and foreclose on homes they'd been paying on for a decade, we stopped complaining, even to each other, about how hard we were working to make ends meet.

We were able to refinance the house last year at a lower interest rate, which reduced our payment, and I'd pulled back on my 401(k) contributions so we could pay off the credit cards—which we'd done just before Christmas, later than we'd planned because we'd helped pay for Keisha's rehab. Now that John was working a little more, Landon came home to an empty house more often than any of us liked, but he hadn't had to skip a season of basketball or worry about where the money would come from for new shoes.

I was no longer picking up random shifts at any store that needed a licensed pharmacist in Orange County, though I still worked at the Long Beach store about once a week; I loved the staff, and they were often shorthanded. They would call me directly whenever they needed another pharmacist, and I said yes as often as I possibly could.

This week, I worked ten-hour shifts at Fountain Valley Tuesday through Friday but picked up six hours in Long Beach Monday morning so I'd be home in time to take Landon to his Monday afternoon practice. There were only a couple more weeks left in the basketball season, then he'd trade out the basketball for a lacrosse ball, which he'd eventually trade for a baseball in the summer.

The Long Beach store always seemed to keep up a steady stream of customers, which was fine by me since staying busy made the time go faster. I spent the morning talking to doctors and deciphering and filling prescriptions in between telling customers where to find toothpaste and flip-flops—the joys of working a retail pharmacy. It was fine. I was good with names and prescription details, and I could often remember what regular customers had been taking from the last time I consulted with them, which always surprised them since this wasn't my main store.

Today, Edna McDonald came in. She was ninety years old and lived a few blocks away. She came to Walgreens every day on her Jazzy chair with her Yorkie, Shoonka, in her lap. She always bought something—cookies, gum, Polident. Today she needed some prescriptions filled, two priors and one new script that made my stomach drop when I read the slip of paper.

You could learn a lot about a person from the medications they took. After filling the prescription, I told the tech I would ring up Edna myself. After her name was called, she motored up to the pick-up side of the counter, where I met her with a sympathetic smile. Up close, I could see how thin she was and how pale her skin was beneath the crème rouge she'd rubbed onto the apples of her cheeks.

"How are you, Edna?" I asked.

"Oh, I'm just lovely, dear," she said, smiling so that her over-rouged cheeks smoothed out and looked shiny under the fluorescent lighting. Her dentures were bright; I bet she soaked them every night. Though she was probably thirty years older than Aunt Ruby, she had the same sweetness about her. I'd assume it was a trait dependent on age except that Aunt Ruby had always been that way. I imagined Edna had too.

"You've taken these medications before," I said, showing her the two refills before I double-checked the labels and slid them into a bag, "but the dosage of the oxycodone is higher than your last prescription." I lowered my voice. "Be mindful of that in regards to going out on your chair. Oxycodone can throw off your perception and reflexes."

"Yes, dear, I will," she said, her voice reflecting the heaviness of our discussion. She knew I knew it was bad.

"This one is new," I said, pointing out the Cytoxan. I went on to explain when to take it and how much. Take with food, report any digestive reactions, drink lots of water, and urinate regularly.

She nodded and listened attentively. "Do you have someone to care for you, Edna?" I asked after I finished, leaning forward until she met my eyes with her somewhat watery blue ones. I could see the milky cloud of a cataract in her left eye. I was betting she wouldn't get it surgically fixed. Edna was dying.

"A home nurse will be coming to see me a few times a week," Edna said, petting Shoonka, who'd fallen asleep on her lap.

She meant a hospice nurse, someone trained to work with people who were not going to get better. Cytoxan would be more effective on someone younger, someone with a hope of recovery, but at ninety years old, Edna's chances weren't good, and she wasn't a good candidate for more aggressive treatments. I wondered what type of cancer it was. I imagined that giving her the prescription was mostly about making her doctor feel better about doing something, even if it wouldn't be enough.

"Do you have family you can call?" I asked. I knew how independent she was, but judging from the dosage of the pain medication she'd been prescribed, she'd have a difficult time caring for herself much longer.

"My daughter passed away five years ago," Edna said. "And my son lives out of state."

"You need to call him," I said. It made my throat a little tighter to think about her having buried her daughter.

She started blinking quickly, and I put aside the bag and the medication sheets so I could take her hand across the counter. Her skin was as soft and thin as parchment. "Edna," I said softly, giving her hand a squeeze, "you need to call your son."

Whatever strength had helped her put on a happy face that morning dissolved, and I held her hands while she cried and told me about her diagnosis, her fear of death, and her concerns about calling her son. She hadn't talked to him since Thanksgiving and didn't want to be a burden. I listened to her for a good ten minutes before she promised me she'd call him. She gave me her home number so I could check on her that afternoon and make sure she'd called.

Even knowing I had patients lined up for me, tapping their toes and impatient with my excuses, I walked next to Edna's chair as far as the parking lot. There was another pharmacist on duty, and three techs, but there still wasn't time for me to just leave like I had.

After Edna motored toward home, I hurried back inside and spent the next hour getting caught up. The store manager came over after the second customer complained about the long wait, and I did my best to explain. He muttered about bad online reviews as he headed back up front.

I apologized to the pharmacy staff, but they were sympathetic; Edna McDonald was part of our community, and a nice balance for the time-crunched professionals that made up the majority of our clientele. I took my break at noon, though I wasn't working long enough to warrant an actual lunch break. I was on my way out to my car with a banana and some string cheese I'd brought from home when a familiar face came through the front doors. We both looked at one another, trying to place each other in this out-of-context location.

"Shannon, right?"

"Yes," I said. "And you're Tori?" I said it as though I didn't know who she was, but I knew. I never forgot a face.

"Great to see you," she said, and her face broke into that gorgeous smile that lit up the room at book club. "I didn't know you worked at this Walgreens."

"I just fill in now and then," I explained. "Do you live around here?"

"Kinda," she said. "The house we're using for the show I'm working on is a few miles away." That's right, she was part of the production crew on some reality TV show. "But I was sent to find a special soap for sensitive skin. One of the girls on the set has developed a reaction to something in the hot tub. The on-site nurse told me what to get, but I've already made two stops and neither store had it." She waved a paper in her hand.

"Let me help you look," I said, reaching for the paper, which she gladly relinquished. Within a few minutes, she was in line for the cash register, gushing her thanks for my help.

"Not a problem," I said with a shrug. "It's what I do." We both stood there awkwardly for a few seconds. "Well, I'm on break so I better get to it." I held up the banana and she smiled again.

"Sorry I interrupted."

"Not a problem," I said again, waving away her apology. I really did like to help people. I started to turn away, but she put a hand on my arm and stopped me.

"I started that book you recommended," she said, her smile falling a little. "I feel so bad for Henrietta."

"I know," I said, reflecting on the story as well. "How far are you into it?"

"I just started reading about how that first doctor discovered that her cells weren't dying like the others. He's starting to sell them. Is the rest of the book as interesting?"

"It really is," I said. "There's so much left."

"Good. I'm really glad you chose it. I feel smarter already for having read just that first part."

I laughed, we said our good-byes, and I finally made it out to my car. It was overcast—February in Southern California—so I didn't need the air conditioner. Just solitude. As I opened the packet of cheese, I realized how comfortable I'd been talking to Tori whereas I'd been so uncomfortable every other time I'd seen her, which was only twice, I guess, but still. Why was today different? Was it because she was in my domain—my workplace—

and I was in my role as pharmacist? Or was it because she was one of those people who just made you feel comfortable?

I envied her and wondered what was so different between her and me. Obviously, we had different ethnicities, histories, and education, and I was at least ten years older than she was, but what was it about myself that made it hard for me to be comfortable in a group while she could be so at ease?

I thought about the next book group meeting, and the instant butterflies that took over my stomach reflected my anxiety, but for the first time since Aunt Ruby had talked me into attending the book group, I was actually excited to go. Tori liking the book so far gave me confidence, and like Ruby had said, I was an educated woman. I could lead a good discussion, and maybe if I opened up a little bit, I wouldn't feel like such an outcast. Keisha had done it, Tori had done it, why not me?

Chapter 9

KEISHA GOT A JOB! THE local Denny's just a few blocks away called her for an interview and offered her the job on the spot. She came home all smiles and confidence, and we celebrated by going to dinner—girls' choice—and an action movie—boys' choice. It happened to be the same evening as her NA meeting, but I was sure we'd make it to the next one. We'd already attended three since the night she came home late.

She and I had also talked about her antidepressants, which she'd been forgetting to take. I explained, again, the ramifications of not keeping her brain chemistries steady, and she promised, again, to be more consistent. That she hadn't been taking her meds helped explain her relapse—though we'd never talked about my knowing she'd been drinking or something that night—and she really seemed to understand when I explained that without the right medication, she would be driven to self-medicate, which would trigger her addiction all over again. She recommitted to the contract, and I think the fact that I was accepting and compassionate to her situation went a long way to renew her faith in my love for her. She said she would try hard not to work Tuesday evenings so she can continue with her therapy appointments. I felt validated in my decision to give her a second chance and was eager for more time to pass—more days sober and successful.

My copy of Henrietta's story came in the mail and though I didn't get to it right away, I started spending a little time every evening putting together my notes. I treated it like an assignment from school, highlighting key points, marking pages, and conducting additional research on both Henrietta Lacks and the author of the book, Rebecca Skloot.

By the Saturday before the next group meeting, I was completely and totally overprepared. I tucked the pages I'd printed from the computer into a folder and put the folder and the book on the table by the door so that I wouldn't forget anything, even though group wasn't for another week.

Keisha was at work so I went on a hunt for my husband and son. They'd promised to clean Landon's room today—it was starting to smell—and left me to my obsessive book group project. Now that I was finished, I was hoping they were close enough to being done that my offers to help wouldn't be needed.

"How's it goin'?" I said, leaning against the doorframe and looking over the nearly perfect room. I whistled under my breath in admiration. "Nice work."

Landon was organizing the books on the bookshelf mounted on the far wall and looked at me over his shoulder. "You probably don't even recognize this room."

"You're right," I said with a nod. "If not for having counted the doors in the hallway, I wouldn't know where I was."

John emerged from the closet with some articles of clothing thrown over his shoulder. He was putting a jacket onto a hanger. "Okay, bud," he said as he headed my way, "I think that does it. You need to transfer that last load of laundry in about fifteen minutes, okay?"

"Okay, Dad," Landon said without turning around. "And I promise to keep it clean from now on."

John rolled his eyes at the impossible promise, and I stifled a laugh. We knew better. I moved aside so John could exit, then followed him down the hall to the coat closet, where he hung up the jacket. "These are for Goodwill," he said, taking the clothing off his shoulder and handing everything to me. "Do we have a box for them?"

"Yep," I said, heading toward the laundry room. This time, he followed me. I showed him where the plastic tub was under the counter. I added to it as needed, then bagged everything up when it was full and dropped it off at the Salvation Army. I'd done a drop-off a few weeks ago, and these were the first new additions since then. The rumble of the washing machine beside the box was a welcome sound because it meant that Landon would have clean clothes on Monday. Always a good thing.

"When I was helping Lan with his room, we looked for the gift card from your folks—the one they sent for Christmas. We couldn't find it."

My parents had moved to Arizona last year. I missed them and we all missed their role in Landon's life. They'd only lived a few blocks away before the move, so we'd visited a lot. The phone calls, e-mails, and cards from

Arizona were wonderful, but they certainly weren't the same as chocolate chip cookies and golfing with Grandpa.

"I haven't seen it since, well, Christmas," I said. "It wasn't in his desk drawer? That's where I told him to put it."

John shook his head. "The card was there, and the envelope, but the gift card wasn't. Landon said he hadn't opened it since Christmas morning."

"Huh," I said, wondering why John was looking at me so intently. I picked up the basket of unmatched socks on the dryer and started rolling them while we talked. "That's weird. It was to Sports Authority, right?"

"Yeah," John said. "A hundred bucks."

"Did you check all his drawers and things?"

"We did," John said, leaning against the washer and folding his arms. "He also said Keisha was in his room last week, looking through his desk."

I gave him a reproachful look. "You think she took his gift card for a sporting goods store?" I could feel my defenses instantly kick in. Though I had seen great improvement in Keisha, John hadn't stepped up like I'd hoped he would, and this seemed like one more sign of the fact that he was still expecting her to fail.

"She could sell it."

I cocked my head to the side. "Really, John? You think she stole her little brother's Christmas present so she could sell it to someone who just happened to want new basketball shoes but preferred to use a gift card?"

"You sell them for a portion of the price. The buyer gets a deal, and the seller gets cash. When she was in rehab, she said she'd done it before—that her boyfriend had some system."

I hadn't remembered Keisha saying that, but now I understood why he was being so pointed. I paired two more sets of socks while thinking of what I wanted to say. "I think it's premature to put this on Keisha, and the gift card scam was more on the boyfriend's shoulders. I've been giving her some money as needed," I said, then looked up at him and added before he could ask how much, "not a lot, just some pocket money while she's been looking for a job, which she now has. Did she say why she was going through Landon's desk?"

He hesitated, then said, "She said she needed a pencil sharpener."

"Well, see, that's the first place I'd look for a pencil sharpener too. And Landon didn't see her with the card, right?"

John took a breath and looked to the side. "No."

I went back to the socks. "Did you tell Landon your suspicions?"

"No," John said again.

"Good."

Apparently neither of us had anything else to say, and after a few more seconds of silence, he left the room. I continued warring with all the thoughts in my head. I finished the socks—or at least finished the ones I could pair up—and headed for Landon's room. He was lying across his bed playing his Nintendo DS, which had been missing for two weeks. Each time he'd complained about not being able to find it, I'd told him to clean his room.

"You found it, huh?" I said, playfully smacking his foot.

"I guess it was in my room the whole time," he said, cracking a smile, though he didn't look up from his game.

"Imagine that."

I headed for his desk. "Hey, do you mind if I look for that gift card?"

"Sure," he said. "I want to buy an Airsoft gun. Treven has one. It's awesome, and Dad said he'd take me tonight."

"I'm sure Grandma and Grandpa will be thrilled to know their gift allowed you to buy weaponry."

He snorted.

I smiled and started going through the drawers. How many times in my years of motherhood had someone looked for something and not been able to find it, only to have me discover it within minutes? It was a mother thing. We knew our families so well that we made subconscious notes of where things could be. So I looked through every drawer, unfolding papers, moving things from one side to another, then emptying out the drawer completely.

Halfway through my search, I brought over the garbage can and began throwing out candy wrappers and stray Pokemon cards—who really collected those things anyway? I looked through the Christmas card and the envelope the gift card had been sent in three different times. Forty minutes later, I had to admit the gift card wasn't there. Then I looked around the desk, under the bed, and through the shelves in the closet. John announced dinner when I started eyeing the garbage can.

"Did you already take out the garbage?" I asked as Landon paused his game and jumped up from the bed for dinner.

"No," Landon said, hurrying from the room without a backward glance. I tried to remember when he'd have last emptied this garbage can. Seeing as how he hadn't cleaned his room in well over a month it had to have been awhile. If he'd accidentally thrown the card away after Christmas, though, it could be in a landfill by now.

At the bottom of the garbage can I found some red-and-green wrapping paper—scraps from the Christmas gift I'd help Landon wrap for John. A week before Christmas. Which meant the garbage hadn't gone out since then. Dang it. I'd been determined to prove the gift card was here, overlooked and waiting to be discovered. It would have proved both Keisha's innocence and John's obstinacy. But no card was found.

I joined the boys for dinner—sloppy joes—and pretended not to notice John's continued tension.

We talked about the upcoming week while we ate—Landon had basketball practice on Tuesday and Wednesday and then finals in Laguna Negro on Thursday. I worked all three days but said I should be able to make it to the game in time for the second half on Thursday. After dinner, I did the dishes while John went out to pick up a couple of Landon's friends for a Marvel Comic movie night. Then I sat at the computer and vegged out for a while.

After Landon and his friends were watching their movie, I dished myself some ice cream. When John came into the kitchen, I put down my spoon and immediately started getting him a bowl too.

"You didn't find it, did you?" he said.

For an instant, I didn't know what he was talking about, but then it all came rushing back, and I clenched my jaw in annoyance and embarrassment that he knew what I'd been doing in Landon's room. "I'm sure the gift card will turn up."

"I really hope it does," John said, but his tone sounded anything but hopeful.

I handed him the bowl of ice cream, and we both ate in silence for a little while before I said I was going to see what was on TV and he headed for the computer. When I knew he wasn't looking, I searched everything in the living room—behind furniture, all through the couch, in between books in the bookshelf. All I ended up with was dusty hands and hopes that if John's work kept picking up, we might be able to hire a housekeeper to come in a couple times a month. I really hated housework.

I returned to my now-melted ice cream and wondered where on earth that gift card could be. What if it had been accidentally thrown out and we never found it? Would John ever drop his suspicions toward Keisha?

Chapter 10

BETWEEN WORK AND BASKETBALL, THE week was brimming with activities. Keisha worked a lot—Denny's was short staffed, hence why they'd hired her so quickly—and, unfortunately, she had to cancel her therapy appointment for the week. I took comfort in the fact that she'd gone to four sessions already, and I reminded her to ask about getting Tuesday evenings off in the future. I also made sure she had appointments scheduled through the end of March.

Nothing more was said about the missing gift card, and the more time went by, the more I thought about how ridiculous the whole thing was anyway. I watched Keisha count out her tips every night. What did she need to steal from Landon for? And how did she sell a gift card anyway? I imagined Keisha standing outside Sports Authority and waving people over with a "Psst, want to buy a gift card?" Who would buy a gift card from a stranger anyway? How would they know it wasn't an empty card? The whole thing was silly.

Friday was a welcome reprieve and my first day off in five days straight—four ten-hour days and a twelve-hour shift. I was exhausted. John took the morning routine so that I could sleep in. Pure heaven. We'd gotten over our tension easily enough, like we usually did, and kept our focus on other things.

I got up at nine o'clock and thought about going running, but I got started on the laundry while John worked in the yard instead, and then I started reading up on Keisha's school information. I wanted to make sure I knew the different deadlines for tuition and what she'd need before her first day, which was just over three weeks away.

John came inside and made me an omelet for a late breakfast, and we talked about the new job he was starting—custom cabinets for a condo in Newport Beach that was being remodeled by a Realtor. If it went well, he hoped it would lead to other jobs. He was giving the guy a great price in hopes of future projects.

"So what's your plan today?" he asked while putting on his boots. He'd be working out of the shop at his dad's for a few hours this afternoon, building the cabinet boxes.

"To be as lazy as possible," I said, which was a joke. I really didn't know how to be lazy. I needed to pay some bills, get the flowerbeds ready for spring, and catch up on a hundred other things in need of doing.

"Are you going to be running any errands?"

"I was planning to get groceries. Oh, and I need a new sports bra." Assuming I'd get back to running anytime soon. It had been a few weeks, and I'd gotten out of the habit of my morning jog—the time just got away from me. Maybe a new bra would motivate me to return to my former hobby.

"That's perfect," John said without looking up from his boots. "We need new lacrosse pads for Landon, and practices start in a couple of weeks. Do you think you'd have time to take him after he gets home? You could get your sports bra while you're there."

Talking about lacrosse pads reminded me of sporting goods stores, which reminded me of the missing gift card and the argument from last weekend. I wondered if John was thinking the same thing, but I wasn't about to bring it up.

"I can totally do that," I said with a nod and a smile. I kissed him good-bye a few minutes later, then pulled open the kitchen drawer where we threw most of the mail. A few times a month, one of us would sort it, and today it was my turn. The drawer was overflowing, and I tried not to frown. What good was a day off if I had to fill it with another kind of work I didn't get paid to do?

Landon was home by three, and we headed toward the closest sporting goods store, which just happened to be Sports Authority. We found my bra—though Landon wouldn't come into the section with me—some lacrosse pads . . . and socks . . . and a jersey he just *had* to have before I put the kibosh on any more purchases.

We were in line when I saw the gift card display at the register. A horrible idea entered my mind, and I looked away in hopes the idea would disappear if I didn't give it my attention.

Landon asked, rather ironically, if he could go look at the airsoft guns he'd buy once he found the card. Apparently he'd taken me at my word that it would show up eventually.

I told him he could go look and then found myself staring at the gift cards again. There were a few different styles to choose from, but I knew which design Mom and Dad had sent because it had a collection of sports balls on it. It was right there. Landon would never know. No one would ever know.

I looked away again. *I* would know. I would know that I had manipulated the whole situation. I would be lying to my husband and creating false trust toward Keisha. But . . .

"Is this everything?"

I looked at the clerk and smiled. "Yes, that's everything," I said, reaching into my purse for my wallet. I slid my debit card through the machine and found myself staring at the gift cards again. It was such an easy solution. John wouldn't have to wonder if Keisha had taken the card, Landon would get his gun, and I would help create some extra harmony in our home. The pin number prompt came up on the credit card machine, but I hesitated. I looked around for Landon, but he wasn't close by.

"Is it too late to add a gift card to this?" I asked, turning back to the clerk, who was patiently waiting for me.

"Not at all. Which style do you want?"

Chapter 11

I WAITED UNTIL THE NEXT morning to plant the gift card. It was the day of book group, which Aunt Ruby had reminded me of twice this week. It was also my second day off in a row. I was making butterscotch brownies for the book club treat, which weren't really brownies at all since there was no chocolate in them. Regardless, you put one on a plate, top it with some ice cream and bottled hot fudge, and you had a somewhat-impressive dessert—at least by my standards, but it didn't take much to impress me where sugar was concerned. I wasn't a passionate cook.

John was at his dad's shop again; he planned to install the cabinet boxes on Monday and had some finish work to do before then. I waited until Landon was in the bathroom before taking the gift card out of my wallet and putting it between the cushions of the couch I'd searched a week earlier. To ensure it would be found, I put the remote between those same cushions, then hurried back into the kitchen and measured out the brown sugar. A few minutes later, Landon wandered into the kitchen, looking for food. I suggested a corn dog, burrito, or pot pie. He went with a peanut butter and jelly sandwich and asked again when I would be buying Pop-Tarts.

"Why don't you turn on the TV?" I said, waving toward the flat screen mounted on the wall in the living room. I couldn't really see the TV from here—half of it was blocked by a dividing wall—but still.

"There's never anything good on Saturdays," he said. "I think I'll play the Wii." The Wii was in the family room down the hall.

"Well, turn the TV on for me, then. I can at least listen. See if that medical examiner show is on."

"The gross one?"

"Yes," I said with a big grin. "The gross ones are my favorite."

"You're so weird," he said, but he obediently went into the living room.

I moved the mixing bowl as far to the left side of the counter as possible so I could watch him. It was ridiculous how nervous I was. I whisked the eggs into the batter between glances into the living room. His cell phone dinged and he stopped in the middle of the room to read the text. I shook my head, whisked too hard, and sloshed the egg-sugar mix onto my shirt.

While I cleaned my shirt, I continued sneaking glances. What kind of twelve-year-old took a full minute to return a text?

"Can I go to Kenny's?" Landon asked, coming back into the kitchen.

"Is your homework done?"

"Yes," he said with a proud nod. Since the start of the new term—and two C grades—we'd been working on him getting his homework done right after school. "And I can ride my bike. We're going to head over to the skate park. You don't even have to drive me."

"You can go," I said, pulling the hem of my shirt away from my waist and frowning at the big wet spot across my stomach. I looked up. "But will you please turn on the TV first?"

"Oh yeah," he said, hurrying back into the living room. I returned to my whisking and glancing and had counted to twenty-six before he said, "Where's the remote?"

"Uh, I don't know," I said—lied, really. Gosh, I was a horrible person, wasn't I? "Look for it." It would seem contrived if I told him right where it was.

The front door opened, causing my head to snap up. John had said he'd be at the shop until at least five, and Keisha was working until eight.

"Hello?" I called.

"Hi," Keisha said back.

A flush of heat smacked me in the chest. "I thought you worked until eight," I said, standing in the middle of the kitchen, trying to come up with a new game plan before realizing I didn't need a new game plan. Everything was fine just as it was. It didn't matter that Keisha was here. She didn't know anything about the card, so what was I worried about?

"They overscheduled the wait staff, which, like, never happens," she said, still not appearing from the direction of the front door. "But I volunteered to work the graveyard shift tonight if they'd let me come home. It's book group tonight, right? Hey, Land Rover. Whatcha doin'?"

"Looking for the remote. Mom wants to watch one of her gross shows."

"Oooh, I love those ones," Keisha said, making me smile.

I hadn't moved from where the surprise of her coming in had stopped me, so I refocused on the bowl. Would the brownies still work even though

I'd dumped half a cup of eggs and sugar all over myself? If I estimated there was three and a half cups of egg-sugar mixture, and I'd spilled one-seventh of that on myself, then I would need to decrease the ingredients I hadn't added yet by one-seventh as well to keep the ratios intact. What was one-seventh of a teaspoon of baking powder?

I converted the teaspoon into ccs—five—and then divided that by seven—.714—and rounded it up, though I should technically round it down, and converted it back to teaspoon equivalency. It came out to be just a touch less than three-fourths of a teaspoon. I wish I had my scale from work so I could use grams instead. Weight was always a more accurate measure than volume. In college I'd transcribed a cookie recipe entirely to grams and weighed everything—best cookies I'd ever made.

"Did you find the remote?" I called, feeling my tension rising.

"No," Keisha called back. "When did you last use it?"

This was ridiculous. "I don't know," I said. I didn't actually watch that much TV. "Did you check the cushions?" That should have been the first place they looked.

"Not yet," Landon called back. He said something else, and Keisha laughed.

I couldn't take it anymore and abandoned my baking in order to supervise. I got to the living room just in time to see Keisha hold up the remote triumphantly. "Ha, I found it!"

But not the card? Oh, for the love of—

"Hey," Landon said, stealing my full attention. I held my breath as he raised his eyes to mine and lifted his hand. "Look what I found in the couch—my gift card from Grandma!"

"What do you know," I said smugly, internally patting myself on the back. I was a genius. "Didn't I tell you it would show up?"

"Sweet! Can you take me to the store to get my gun?"

"What about Kenny? Aren't you going to—" I looked at Keisha and my train of thought derailed. She looked completely confused, her eyebrows pulled together as she stared at the card in Landon's hand. Why was she looking at him like that?

"Maybe Kenny can come with us," Landon said, digging his phone out of his pocket. "You can take us, right?"

"Um, sure," I said, turning toward the kitchen, but not before I saw the expression on Keisha's face as she looked at me. Pure guilt. My heart sank, and I held her eyes too long, realizing that she was likely seeing the same expression on my face.

Chapter 12

I HATED BEING LATE. THAT moment when everyone looks up at you and you have to make an apology was one of my least favorite things. And after this afternoon's nightmare with the gift card, I was feeling very insecure as Keisha and I hurried up to Aunt Ruby's door, knocked once, and let ourselves in. I'd kind of hoped Keisha wouldn't come. I felt like I needed a break to think about what had happened, but Ruby had called, again, to remind me of book group, and Keisha had answered the phone. By the end of the call, she'd promised we'd be there.

Aunt Ruby was in the foyer when we walked in. "Come in, come in," she said and hugged us both. At least she wasn't angry at our tardiness, though she was never really angry about anything.

I apologized for being late, and when she offered to take the dessert into the kitchen, I agreed and headed into the living room. I was halfway there before I realized Keisha hadn't followed me. I nearly turned around to go find her but made myself stay the course and sit down.

"Welcome, everyone," Aunt Ruby started once she sat down, her copy of *The Immortal Life of Henrietta Lacks* in her lap. That was the moment I realized I'd left my copy of the book *and* the folder of notes at home. Hours of work and preparation now sat on the table next to the front door.

I felt my cheeks heat up while Aunt Ruby gave a quick update about Daisy not being able to attend again before turning to me. I caught Tori's eye from across the room, and she smiled at me, which reminded me of the internal conversation I'd had with myself after running into her at work and how I envied her comfort with people. What made my work different than this setting?

Well, there were several things, of course, but in the split second of everyone looking at me I decided to try an experiment. I pushed everything out of my head except what I was doing right now—leading a book group discussion. I pretended that I had clocked in to this "work" and couldn't leave until I'd finished my shift. Worrying about anything outside of *this moment* was pointless because I needed to be focused and diligent.

As for having forgotten all my preparation, well, none of these women knew how prepared I'd planned to be, which meant they weren't going to be critiquing me against that expectation. I took a breath, centered myself, and took the lead as Keisha came into the room and sat down next to me. "I thought I'd start by asking if anyone had any questions about the medical events that took place," I said.

"I think I was lost half of the time," Tori said with a laugh. Olivia nodded her agreement as Tori continued. "My brain can compute production schedules but not so much how the different parts of cells work. It's amazing—and terrifying—to try to comprehend how anything that small could be so destructive."

"And *constructive*," Paige added. "Even though they were cancer cells, they spearheaded many important discoveries. I found the whole thing absolutely fascinating."

Athena commented on how many things had to come together just right for HeLa cells to have even been discovered and made available to the world. I nodded, glad to hear each of the women making such positive comments. I'd worried that its being a nonfiction book might be a challenge, but apparently it wasn't.

"It was interesting to read about the doubts that medical professionals had about the main doctor"—Tori looked down at her book—"Gey. He was revolutionizing medicine, and yet so many people discounted him."

"And this certainly isn't the only example of doctors who dealt with that type of thing," I said, excited to share my thoughts and glad I could remember the details from the notes I'd forgotten to bring. I talked about Harvey and Nott and the discoveries they'd made that the medical world had ignored for years. The women were genuinely interested, and I felt myself relax bit by bit.

"I also found it interesting that despite the eventual tragedy for Henrietta, she went to the right doctor at the right time," Tori said. "I don't know that any other hospital could have done what Johns Hopkins did back in the 1950s."

"I agree," I said. "Even with all the mistakes along the way and the breakdown of ethics, Henrietta left behind an incredible legacy that has changed the world."

"But an unwilling legacy," Tori said.

"I think this is one of the most important books of our century. Really, it's amazing how Henrietta's contribution has led to saving millions of lives and treating even more people. Her story should be required reading in every high school," Aunt Ruby cut in as though she were uncomfortable with Tori's comment, but I wished she'd let Tori continue. I was fully prepared to get into the medical ethics, the reason behind HIPA and the responsibility of patient advocacy.

"I would have loved to have read it in high school," Keisha said. I bit my tongue. Keisha dropped out of high school. My anger caught me off guard and just as instantly made me feel guilty. I didn't know how to act toward my stepdaughter right now. Was stealing Landon's gift card a cry for help? Was I listening? "Can I use your bathroom?" Keisha suddenly asked.

Ruby gave Keisha directions to the bathroom. Then Paige made a comment about God's plan and Ilana spoke up, pulling me back into the discussion. "The development of modern medicine was a rocky road, but it had so many breakthroughs along the way." She glanced down at her arm still in the sling. "I mean, with my arm, what they've been able to fix is remarkable when you think about it. Although now they explain things a little more before surgery. It made me sick to think of how they didn't inform the women about the side effects of those surgeries," Ilana's voice was sharp. "Henrietta had a real shock when she found out she'd been made infertile."

Tori broke in before I could agree. "But getting rid of her cancer was more important than having another baby."

"But they didn't get rid of her cancer," Ilana said pointedly. I felt like I was missing something behind her comments. Henrietta died before she could have had another child, which seemed to make her infertility a moot point.

Tori said how ridiculous it was for Henrietta to be mad that she couldn't have more children, but Ilana pinched her lips together. She'd always been very even-keeled at the other meetings, to the point of coming across as formal. In contrast, she seemed a little high-strung tonight.

"Women have to make hard choices sometimes," Aunt Ruby said, rubbing her hand over the cover of her book. "It broke my heart when Henrietta's daughter talked to the author in that first phone call." She flipped open the book and read from a page she'd marked. "Here, Deborah says, 'You know what I really want? I want to know, what did my mother smell like? For all my life I just don't know anything, not even the little common little things, like, what color did she like? Did she like to dance? Did she breast-feed me? Lord, I'd like to know that.'"

Suddenly I missed my mom. If she still lived close by, would I go to her and tell her what I'd done with the gift card? What advice would she give me about how to fix it? I could call her in Phoenix—I talked to her once a week or so—but it wouldn't be the same, and our conversations had become rather shallow now that we weren't involved in one another's lives so much. There was something about sitting with her at her kitchen table that was so much . . . safer.

I thought about the quote Aunt Ruby had read. How lucky was I to know my mother as I did? I had so many good memories. Deborah had none. I looked down the hallway to where Keisha had disappeared. How many good memories did Keisha have of her childhood? Things had been so chaotic when she was young. If her childhood had been different I was certain the choices she made now would be different too.

Keisha came back in and sat down next to me as the women discussed Henrietta's children. I was torn between compassion and frustration with my stepdaughter. Why couldn't we be honest with each other? Everything would be different if we could do that. Was it my fault we didn't have that kind of relationship? Were there things I could do to earn her trust that I didn't know how to do?

"No wonder Deborah didn't remember her," Ilana said in a quiet voice. I'd missed what had been said leading up to that, but I found myself focusing on Ilana. She'd calmed down since having seemed so offended earlier, but that made me wonder what she was taking for the pain for her arm. Some medications could cause mood swings. If those swings were too severe, she ought to explore other options, but how could I say that to her? I barely knew the woman and was likely trying to distract myself from thinking about Keisha by focusing on medical stuff.

"How tragic," Olivia said. "At least with my mother, I knew her . . . of course that means that I miss her even more. But I do have the memories and the heavenly reminders."

Athena sniffled, and I remembered that Athena's mother had died just a few months earlier. Did she remember how her mother smelled?

I made a note to call my mom; maybe I could talk her and Dad into coming out for a visit. Maybe she'd sit at my kitchen table and tell me what I could do to make things right. She might even have some advice on building a better relationship with Keisha.

Keisha plugged into the conversation. "Deborah sounded like a hillbilly."

"She wasn't well educated, and she lived in poverty her whole life," I reminded her, not wanting any judgment passed. "And yet, people were making millions off the tissues they biopsied from her mother while Henrietta's children couldn't get health insurance."

"Deborah passed away in 2009," Athena said, glancing up from her Blackberry with a sad smile. "She never even saw the book in print."

I knew that from the research I'd done, but hearing it made me sad all over again. Deborah never knew the legacy her mother had created.

"That's so sad," Aunt Ruby said, echoing my thoughts.

"At least she knew about it, and she probably read a draft," Tori said, smiling at Ruby in a compassionate way. "It would have been nice for her to see the book come out and to know about its success though."

"Are any of the other children still alive?" Ruby asked Athena.

Athena scrolled through her phone. "It looks like two sons are."

I knew that too.

"It sounds like her children didn't get much better health care than their mother did," Olivia added. "Maybe things haven't changed as much as we like to think they have."

This comment cast a hush over the room, and I glanced at Tori, expecting her to say something about the racial elements, but then I remembered the point she'd made about it last time. We all saw her as black, but she didn't seem to identify with the racial issues of either of the last two books we'd read. The moment passed when Olivia mentioned Henrietta's relationship with her husband, Day. "I wonder what would have happened if she'd lived. Would they have stayed together, do you think?"

"I bet they would have," Athena said, nodding and putting her phone down, done looking up facts for now, it seemed. "Times were different back then, and Henrietta knew Day was unfaithful all along. I think it was much more common in that generation for women to turn a blind eye to infidelity."

Aunt Ruby shifted in her seat and straightened up while looking at her hands holding the book.

Her tension in response to the comment startled me, but in the next instant I caught my breath—did she know about Uncle Phillip's affair? I'd always thought she was oblivious, that I carried a secret she was unaware of. Mom, Dad, John, and I had all agreed that it would tear her apart if she knew.

"But even though Day had been with plenty of other women, you could tell he loved Henrietta very much," I said quickly, feeling like I needed to build that bridge. I glanced at Aunt Ruby and willed her to relax.

"I agree," Paige said in a soft voice, causing me to turn my head in her direction. I had not expected to hear that from Paige—hadn't her husband been unfaithful? I wasn't the only one who'd turned my attention to her, and her cheeks turned pink under the sudden attention. She fingered the pages of her book—a library copy from the looks of it. "Remember how he took her to the hospital every day so she could be treated for pain? And when not having her children nearby upset her too much, he kept the kids right outside, under her window, so she could at least see them? I thought that was very sweet. Maybe he just didn't know another way to live."

"I wondered that too," I said. "How many of our choices are actually based on the choices our parents made? Not that it's their fault, or that Day wasn't accountable, but he didn't abandon Henrietta when she got sick and that says something. Their lives were a bit dysfunctional, but Henrietta seemed to be an overall happy person."

"Because she chose to be that way," Tori broke in, causing heads to turn in her direction. "Henrietta had really harsh trials to deal with. She lived in a time where she wasn't yet seen as an equal human with the white people around her—that was her reality every day of her life. And yet her sister Sadie said she was the life of the party, that she loved people and everyone wanted to be around her. I think she was a very strong, optimistic person. Maybe it's not so surprising that a woman like that would leave such a mark on the world—even if it took fifty years for the world to know it. Maybe the cells she left behind were the only way the world would notice this black woman from the South who was so easily discounted by the times."

"That's a great point, Tori," I said, appreciating her perspective very much as it so closely reflected some of my own thoughts. "Henrietta accepted her trials and made the best of them. She lived her life with such a great attitude and left that legacy for her children while at the same time creating opportunity for the world. She worked hard, and she loved her family. Even though they didn't know the impact she had on medicine, they knew the impact she had on them."

"She changed the world," Olivia said with a smile. "How many people can say that?"

"Mothers can," Paige answered. "Mothers have that kind of impact on the lives of their children. All of society starts with a child's mother."

Ilana stiffened up, much like Aunt Ruby had a few minutes ago. She looked at the floor, and I quickly worked out a formula in my head. The comments that had bothered her tonight had to do with children and motherhood. Ilana had been married for several years and was in her thirties. Was infertility an issue for her? Was that why things were hitting her so hard tonight? Again, I thought about trying to talk to her, but this was the wrong setting. I wished I'd gone over to see her after the surgery on her elbow. Ruby had asked, but I was so busy. Maybe if I had taken the chance to get to know Ilana better, I'd have more insight into her situation.

I almost didn't connect Paige's comment in relation to myself, but it sounded in my head again. *"All of society starts with a child's mother."* I glanced at Keisha. Her mother had been a mess, but Keisha had me too. Couldn't I make a positive impact? Couldn't I make up for what she didn't have?

"I'm really glad you chose this book, Shannon," Tori said, smiling at me. "I learned so much."

The other ladies murmured their thanks as well, and I nodded my head, accepting it humbly, but inwardly I was just relieved they'd liked it.

"I wonder what Hela will do in the future," Olivia said. "I mean, it's done so many great things already; I wonder where it will go from here."

We spent a few minutes speculating about cures for cancer, stem-cell research, and organ transplantation. Twenty years ago this kind of talk would have sounded like science fiction. How exciting was it to have such discoveries at our doorstep?

"So, Ruby, do you have any trips planned?"

We all looked at Athena. What an odd, out-of-the-blue question. Ruby and Phillip had once been world travelers, but since his death she'd become more of a homebody. But then the knowing look on Athena's face caught my attention. I turned to Ruby, whose cheeks were pink.

"Well, actually, yes, I do have a trip planned," Aunt Ruby said, smoothing her slacks. "I'll be going to Greece on a two-week tour with a group of people I met at the Senior Center."

"You are?" I said, sounding more surprised than I meant to. I was glad to hear she was planning a trip with friends but a little hurt she hadn't told me about it. "When are you going?"

"We leave March 10," she said, glancing over at me with a slightly repentant look as though she'd read my mind. I smiled back, not wanting to take away from her exciting news, but I couldn't believe she hadn't told me before now. It made me wonder if, like with Keisha, I hadn't created the right relationship with Aunt Ruby.

"How lovely!" Tori said. "I've heard that Greece is gorgeous."

"There's nothing like the Greek isles," Athena said. "Anytime my mother heard someone say Disneyland was the happiest place on earth, she would lean over and tell me that was only because they'd never been to Greece."

We all chuckled. "I'd certainly take Greece over Disneyland," I said. Another round of laughs boosted my confidence.

"Not me," Keisha said, shaking her head. "There aren't any princesses in Greece to sign my Mickey Mouse autograph book. Though there are a lot of hot guys if *Mamma Mia* is true to life."

More laughter.

"Yes, I went there many years ago with my husband," Aunt Ruby said, though I noticed her smile still held some reservation. I wondered if those earlier comments were still bothering her. I wondered how she would react if she knew that I knew about Uncle Phillip's affair, and I wondered again if *she* knew. "It will be a nice treat to visit it again, and I should still be able to find time to read our next book—whatever that is."

The women immediately started comparing different e-readers she could take with her on the trip. I didn't read enough to make one of those gadgets a worthwhile investment, so I took the opportunity to excuse myself to get the dessert. Once in the kitchen, I realized that, along with having forgotten all my notes, I'd forgotten the ice cream and hot fudge. So much for the blonde brownie sundaes I'd planned to make. I opened Aunt Ruby's freezer and smiled when I saw the French vanilla ice cream. It's like she knew I would forget! I didn't find any hot fudge, but ice cream was sufficient. I was laying out the plates when Olivia joined me.

"Want an extra set of hands?"

My first instinct was to say no, but why not? "That would be wonderful," I said. "Could you add a scoop of ice cream to each plate?"

"Absolutely."

We were a well-oiled machine, and we returned to the living room with desserts in hand just in time to hear Tori announce the title of next month's book. "*The War of Art* by Steven Pressfield." She paused to receive her dessert. "I read it a couple of years ago, but I'm due for another reading."

"It's that good?" Aunt Ruby said.

"It's that *important*," Tori emphasized. "It's about following your dreams and not letting anything stop you." She looked at me. "And it's another nonfiction book."

Ouch, had I branded myself as the fiction-hater? "Sounds interesting," I said, though in truth it sounded a little artsy-fartsy, which wasn't my style at all. Still, I was here to expand my horizons, right?

Olivia and I headed back into the kitchen for the last of the desserts.

"And it's on Kindle," Athena said as I sat down a minute later. She had her Blackberry out again and looked as though she were reading right off a website. *"The War of Art: Break Through the Blocks and Win Your Inner Creative Battles."*

Keisha had disappeared again. Wondering where she was made me think about the gift card fiasco and what, if anything, I should do about it. The intrusive thoughts "punched me out" of the work mindset I'd managed to maintain for tonight's book group, and I could feel my insecurities returning. I was hesitant to let the evening end, since I felt a little protected within this bubble of Aunt Ruby and her book group friends . . . well, my book group friends too, I guessed.

"So, Shannon," I looked up as Paige sat in Keisha's place next to me on the couch, "tell me about what you do. I considered becoming a pharmacy tech at one point and wondered how I would like it."

"It's not too late," I teased her, managing to hold on to my confident mood a little bit longer. I'd have to face the gift card situation sometime, but maybe not just yet. "Just promise me if you go to school, you'll apply to work for me before you go anywhere else. I'd love to have you on my team."

Chapter 13

I'D MANAGED TO PUSH AWAY most of the thoughts about the business with the gift card until Keisha and I got into the car after book group.

I wanted to come up with a theory involving Landon's gift card that wouldn't implicate either Keisha or me in what had happened, and since Henrietta's story was still fresh in my mind, I did a brief overview, looking for comparisons between that situation and this one. Who was at fault for the situation with Henrietta? Who turned a family's tragedy into a billion-dollar biological enterprise? Could there be one person in the line who could raise a hand and take the blame? Was it the doctor who ordered the biopsy? Was it the scientist who first noticed the immortal cells? Was it anyone at all?

Certainly the issue with Keisha and me wasn't on the same scale as Henrietta Lacks, but was I willing to ignore the morality and ethics in hopes that someone else would one day shoulder my accountability? I shook my head. I was making this too complicated, trying too hard to make a comparison between completely different things.

I took a breath and centered my thoughts. "We need to talk about this afternoon, Keish."

She shifted in her seat and looked ahead. "What about it?"

"The gift card."

I paused, waiting for her to explain herself. The light turned green before she answered.

"I'm sorry," she said, quiet and timid.

I had braced myself for defensiveness and justification, perhaps because that had been my reaction to John's first accusations against her. I wasn't prepared for humility, and it caught me off guard enough that I didn't have a quick answer, only more questions. It was essential that I not show my emotions.

"Why did you take it?"

"I needed money."

"You have a job."

"Yeah, as of two weeks ago."

"You took it before you started getting tips?" I said. For some reason, that made me feel better, though I couldn't be sure why. "I'd been giving you money. What did you need that I hadn't covered?"

She was quiet for a few seconds, then took a breath. "I owe people money, Shannon, and I had to make a payment."

"Why do you owe people money?"

She fiddled with her phone, turning it over and over in her hands, maybe willing a text message to come through so she could put her focus elsewhere.

I reached over and took the phone from her hands, placing it in my lap instead. "Why do you owe people money, Keisha?"

"I'm an addict, Shannon," she said, the humility in her tone edged with anger. "Drugs are expensive."

A burst of heat shot through me. "You're still using?"

"Not right now," she said. What did that mean? That she wasn't high right this minute, or that she hadn't been using for a period of time? "But I had to borrow money from friends last time, and they needed it paid back. I held them off as long as I could while I was looking for a job, but I had to give them something."

"When was the last time you used?" I couldn't believe I was staying so calm when inside I was freaking out. I was having a discussion about illegal drug use! I was talking about it as though we were discussing her messy bedroom. I had to be calm about it, though, because if I freaked out, she'd shut down. The calmness was a blessing, and I prayed that it would stay with me for as long as I needed it.

"Before I came."

"Those two weeks after you left your mother's?"

She was quiet for several seconds.

"Keisha, if you aren't honest with me, I will have to talk to your dad." It wasn't until after the words were said that I realized what I'd really said—if she was honest with me, I *wouldn't* be honest with John. I opened my mouth to restate the words in a way that didn't put her dad and me on opposite sides of the fence she was balancing on, but it was too late. She started talking—and talking fast—filling in details I didn't want to know about.

She'd started borrowing money from friends before Dani kicked her out; then, when she was on her own, she made promise after promise in order to get her fix. Why anyone thought she was good for the money she promised, I would never understand.

"And then I called you. If you and Dad hadn't let me stay with you, I don't know what I would have done." She'd turned in her seat so she was looking at me, tears running down her face. "I'd probably be dead, Shannon, I was using so much."

I wanted to stop this conversation, end it right here, but I couldn't. I'd already bartered away my husband's trust. I had to at least maximize what I got out of it. "Have you used since coming to our house?"

The pause caused my chest to tighten.

"Twice," she said.

My stomach turned to stone. She'd used in our home! "When?"

"Once, the day after I came. I had a small hit so as not to go into DT's. And then a couple of weeks later."

"With Jessica?" I asked, remembering that night exactly one month ago when she'd gone out and not come home until four in the morning.

"Yeah, but I only took a little of her oxy."

"A little is too much, Keisha," I said, torn between anger and just plain sorrow. "You can't do *any* drugs. That's what we agreed to. You brought drugs into my home? Around my son?" I had to shake my head to get rid of the thoughts of Landon walking in on her putting a needle in her arm—though I didn't think she'd done much IV drugs. Snorting or smoking was her method of choice.

"I'm so sorry," she said, crying even harder. "I'm so, so sorry. I haven't used since that night, I swear. I haven't touched anything but beer since then."

"You can't drink either, Keisha," I practically yelled. "You're an addict, and when you drink or use, your meds don't work. You can't touch anything that's going to throw off your chemistries. How many times do I need to explain that to you?"

She pulled her knees up to her chest and dropped her head, sobbing. I stopped yelling and took a breath, reminding myself yet again that she was not an adult, mentally or emotionally. She was still a child, unable to see very far into the future or to understand consequences the way she should at her age.

Calmness, please.

"How much money do you owe?"

She turned her head, still resting on her knees, and wiped at her eyes. "Sixteen hundred dollars."

I nearly choked. As soon as the shock passed, however, I recalled the street value of many of the narcotics I was charged with controlling as a pharmacist. Oxycodone sold anywhere from five dollars to twenty-five dollars a pill. For someone dependent on ten pills a day, that could be a $250-a-day habit. More than $1,700 a week.

"I've paid back almost $200 already, and they've agreed to let me pay them two hundred a week until I'm done."

"That's why you took Landon's gift card?"

She nodded. "I thought I could borrow the card, then replace it in a couple of weeks. I didn't think he would notice, and it would keep Tagg off my back."

"Tagg?" I repeated.

"The guy who spotted me the money," she said quickly, then lowered her voice. "Shannon, these are bad people I got mixed up with—really bad. If I don't pay them, I don't know what will happen to me." Her chin quivered, and makeup was running down her face.

I kept looking forward, weighing everything she was telling me. Was it true? Could I trust it? But why would she make this stuff up? It was so incriminating; she had nothing to gain from lying about any of it.

"I'm so sorry," she said again as I turned onto our street. I pulled to the curb a few houses away, not ready to alert John and Landon we were back.

"I have to tell your dad," I said.

"What!" she nearly screamed, causing me to jolt as I looked at her. "You said you wouldn't tell if I was honest. You told me you'd help me." Her whole face crumpled with anger, fear, and . . . betrayal. "You lied to me." She reached for the door handle—was she going to run? I grabbed her arm just as she pushed open the door. She tried to shake me off, so I grabbed her with my other hand too.

"Wait," I said, my mind racing. "Don't go. Let us figure this out."

She didn't close the door, but she did look at me. "Dad'll make me leave," she said, her chest constricting with sobs she was barely keeping at bay. "You know he will."

"Maybe not," I said, "He might—"

"Yes, he will," Keisha said, wiping at her eyes and tucking her chin to her chest. "He made me sign that contract so he'd have a way to get rid of me." She met my eyes with her tortured ones. "He didn't want me to come home in the first place, did he? I could tell by the way he acted when he picked me up. He could barely talk to me at all. I embarrass him."

I held her eyes, unable to think of anything to say. She was right— he *didn't* want her to come, and he *was* embarrassed by the choices she'd made. I understood why he felt that way, why this was so hard for him, and yet I didn't agree with the way he was handling it: leaving the work to me and keeping Keisha at arm's length.

I'd gone along with John's rules and his contract because I wanted to appease him long enough for Keisha to prove that I was right and that we could help her. On the surface it was working; even below the surface she was improving—she'd gone a whole month without using. That was a big accomplishment, but John wouldn't see it that way. He'd see the broken contract and the fact that she'd lied to us as proof that she was too high a risk. What would he think of the lies I had told? Of the ways I'd protected her already?

If he did kick her out, where would she go? Back to the mother who hadn't known Keisha had been using right out of rehab? Dani hadn't even bothered to call Keisha in the weeks she'd been with us. Or, would Keisha go back to the friends who had no problem loaning her thousands of dollars to keep her high?

I groaned and closed my eyes, letting go of Keisha's arm and leaning against the seat. I raised my hands to my face. "I don't know what to do," I said, feeling completely overwhelmed. I had to think, and I needed to be the strong one. I started counting by threes in my head, a cure-all for keeping back emotion. *Three, six, nine, twelve, fifteen, eighteen, twenty-one, twenty-four.*

Keisha put her hand on my arm this time and pulled the door shut with her other hand. "I'm so sorry, Shannon. Maybe I *should* just leave. I'm sure I can find somewhere else to go. You guys shouldn't have to deal with this."

I opened my eyes and looked at her. "Where would you go?"

She looked away. "I don't know," she said. "But . . . I make trouble everywhere I go. I'm so messed up. I don't deserve everything you guys have given me."

"We love you. We want good things for you."

Keisha removed her hand and looked out the window so that I could only see the back of her head. "Sometimes I think it would better if I just overdosed and got it over with."

"Don't say that," I said to her, unable to hold back the tears anymore. "Don't ever say that."

She turned back to me, more tears in her eyes, and looked at me with such pitiful sadness that I couldn't help but lean over and take her into my arms. We both cried all over again, and when I finally pulled back and tucked her hair behind her ear, I forced a smile. "We're going to get through this, okay?"

Keisha shook her head and looked into her lap. "I don't know how," she said. "Every day I want to use. I dream about it at night, and every time I get stressed out, I think that if I could just chill for a few hours, I'd be able to think straight again." She looked up at me. "Want to know the biggest reason I don't act on those cravings?"

"Why?" I asked.

"You. I know how disappointed you would be. I know you're already so disappointed."

I shook my head, more tears rising. "It's not disappointment. It's fear. Drugs and alcohol enslave you, Keisha; they have already robbed you of so many years—so much life. I don't want them to own another minute of your potential."

"See," she said, managing a watery smile. "You're the only person who sees any potential in me at all."

"That's not true," I said. "You're dad does."

Keisha shook her head. "He's waiting for me to mess up, I can feel it."

"Then prove him wrong," I said. "Go to NA, find friends you can trust, live your life in a way that you can be proud of. If you're proud of your choices, your dad will be *twice* as proud."

"I'm trying," she said, almost pleaded. "I'm trying so hard."

She *was* trying. She'd cut off her old friends, gotten a job, and enrolled in school. Those were big accomplishments—especially for a girl who'd only been out of rehab six months. I hugged her again, closing my eyes and taking a deep breath. "We're going to make this work," I said. "I promise."

Chapter 14

IT WAS ALMOST TEN O'CLOCK when we finally got home from our heart-to-heart. John and Landon were playing the Wii, which allowed Keisha to slip into her room and repair her makeup before either of them saw her. She got ready for work and then came out, her puffy eyes mostly disguised by freshly applied foundation. We shared a look as I handed her the keys to my car so she wouldn't have to walk in the dark—she'd walked to and from work many times without complaint. I knew trusting her with my car meant a great deal to her, and she hugged me before calling out a good-bye to John and Landon.

Not long after Keisha left, I headed to bed, thinking John and Landon would stay up longer; however, they ended the game immediately and John came into our room only a few minutes behind me.

"How was book group?" he asked as we went through our nightly routine.

"Good," I said, glad to be able to mean it and relieved to think about something other than his daughter. "It was really fun. We had a great discussion about the book."

"And how's Ruby doing?"

"Great," I said, sounding a little wistful. I was so jealous of her going on that cruise. The last few years had been all about working as hard as we could. John and I hadn't included vacations or indulgences. Right now I wanted nothing more than to step out of life for a couple of weeks and get lost in an adventure. "She's going to Greece." I explained what I knew about her trip while changing into my pajamas and washing my face.

"I'm so jealous," John said.

"Me too," I said, laughing at how similar our thoughts were. Laughter was good medicine for my troubled soul right now.

"We need to plan a trip," John said. "Maybe just a Baja cruise or something cheap like that. Landon would love it."

"He would." I sat on the edge of the bed and put lotion on my hands and feet. When John and I had taken a Caribbean cruise for our eight-year anniversary, Landon had stayed with my parents; they had still lived here at the time. We'd had such a great time and used to talk all the time about taking the kids with us on another one. But then the bottom fell out of the economy, and Keisha started having a tough time and, well, the cruise hadn't happened. But we were in better financial shape now than we had been the last time we talked about it. "Maybe we could do something after school gets out."

"I'll talk to Stan about it," John said, referring to a friend of his whose wife was a travel agent. "I'll see what he recommends."

"That would be awesome."

He disappeared into the bathroom, and I heard the buzz of his mechanical toothbrush. I pulled my hair up into a high bun and put my clothes and his socks in the hamper. John was so good about taking care of his own clothes, but for whatever reason his socks were always all over the place.

"Oh, hey," he said when he came out of the bathroom a minute later. "You didn't tell me Landon found that gift card."

I froze for half a second, then tried to look natural as I passed him on my way to the bathroom. "Yeah," I said simply, knowing I should say more but unable to as the guilt descended like a thunderstorm. I tried to summon the confidence I'd felt when Keisha had confided in me. I was the reason she was staying sober. *Me.* That was a big responsibility, and it was the only thing that made sense in regard to justifying why I was keeping things from my husband.

"I guess it must have fallen out of his pocket or something," John said. I could hear him turning down the covers while I stared at the reflection in the mirror. John's wife stared back at me—a woman he trusted, a woman he thought trusted him enough to be honest.

"I guess so," I said simply, breaking eye contact with the other woman in the mirror. Justifications aside, I felt horrible. I'd never kept anything from John before.

Suddenly he was right there, behind me. His arms reached around my stomach, and I closed my eyes when his lips kissed the back of my neck. "I'm really sorry for jumping to conclusions about Keish with all that," he said, horribly humble. My heart ached. "It was totally unfair of me."

If there were a script for this, I would say something like "It's okay" or "I understand." I could even say, "I need to tell you something." But

I couldn't say any of it. It *wasn't* okay, and I *did* understand why he'd jumped to that conclusion—the right conclusion, it turned out. I couldn't tell him the truth because I'd done what I'd done so that he'd trust his daughter and stop thinking the worst of her. What irony.

I opened my eyes to see him staring at me in the mirror. I forced myself to smile.

"Are you okay?" he asked, looking confused.

"I'm good," I said, though I wasn't good at all.

"Are you sure? You seem a little, I don't know, tight."

I tried to smile wider, but I felt worse than ever. "I'm fine. It's just been a long week, ya know?" I turned in his arms so that I could look up into his eyes. "I love you, John, so much."

"Whew," he said with a teasing grin. "That helps this whole marriage and family thing make a lot more sense." He reached over and flipped off the bathroom light, plunging us into darkness and giving me the relief of keeping any thoughts he might read in my eyes to myself.

Chapter 15

LANDON WAS DONE WITH BASKETBALL, which meant lacrosse was now on the top of our priority list. And since John was the coach, if he wasn't working, he was usually wherever Landon was. I loved watching Landon play, and a lot of my memories of him growing up were centered on his athletics. He would always look for me, even during practice, and give me a thumbs-up when he did well.

But instead of watching my boy play these days, I sat with Keisha in Narcotic Anonymous meetings and listened to addicts talk about the things they'd done in order to get their fix. Theft, assault, prostitution—it was unreal what addiction could drive people to. Keisha never shared her story or spoke up, but she was assigned a sponsor, a woman named Debbie who was in her thirties and had been sober for eight years. Keisha was supposed to call Debbie anytime she needed to talk—and especially if she found herself tempted to use. Debbie was missing most of her teeth—Meth-mouth—and had hair so thin I could see her scalp, but I tried to have confidence in her sobriety. She was Keisha's sponsor; she was part of the solution.

A young man named David came up and talked to Keisha after our third meeting that week. He was shy and nerdy, nothing like I'd expect from a recovered addict, but seemed to really like Keisha. She was sweet to him and gave him her number, which made him grin from ear to ear. I knew supporting Keisha didn't make everything I'd done okay, but as long as the results were moving her in a good direction, it helped me feel better.

Aunt Ruby left on her cruise, and I agreed to check on her house and water her plants while she was gone. I secured the alarm code for her house on the fridge with an Oreo-shaped magnet and hung the key on the rack by the door. I was glad to help but still jealous of her trip. Wouldn't now be a great time to take Keisha away?

Keisha worked a lot, often the night shift—which I didn't like—but I hoped that meant she was paying off her debts faster. She missed another therapy appointment, which I had to pay for because we didn't cancel soon enough. She usually came home before I got up for the day and then slept while we were at work and school. While the schedule meant she could use my car since I didn't need it at night, I missed seeing her, and my thoughts were never far away from her. Because I knew she couldn't afford it, I paid the first installment of her tuition. John and I had already agreed to pay half, so I figured I was just paying our half up front. I worried about Keisha being able work enough to keep up with her payments to Tagg once school started on the twentieth-eighth—just over a week away.

I asked her about her payments to Tagg on the way home from an NA meeting Saturday night. David had sat next to us this time. "I'm not sure what to do about all that," she said, her shoulders slumping. "Maybe I should wait on school."

"No," I said quickly, shaking my head. "You shouldn't wait. You need to develop a skill so you can get a better job. Besides, I already made the first payment for your tuition."

"I've got to pay off Tagg though."

"How much do you have left to pay back?"

She paused, then let out a breath. "Fifteen hundred."

I double-checked my math. "You haven't made a payment yet this week?"

"I did," she said, "But they changed it. Said they weren't charging me interest before because they thought I would be a repeat customer. Now that I'm not, I owe them more. I paid them three hundred dollars just a few days ago."

"They can't just change the payment you agreed on," I said, incensed.

"They're dealers. They can do whatever they want."

I clenched my teeth together. "How do you pay the money back? Do you meet them somewhere?"

"They come to my work, and I take a break."

"Which means they know when you're working. Do they call you and tell you they're coming?"

"We text."

I looked at the phone she was holding in her hands. I hated that she was still in contact with them. How did they get her new number? "Do they try to get you to use?"

Keisha said nothing, and I looked at her quickly.

"Do they?" I asked again.

"Of course they do," she said, exasperated, as though frustrated that I didn't know all of this stuff automatically.

We stopped talking about it, but I couldn't stop thinking about how this guy knew where she worked, knew where he could find her. What if he followed her home from work one day? It was all I could think about the next day, and it made me feel so vulnerable. What if this guy came to the house? What if Landon was home when he did?

A few nights later, Keisha came home and I could tell right away something was wrong. She walked past all three of us at the dinner table without a word. I exchanged a look with John and Landon, then pushed away from the table.

"What's wrong?" I said after following her to her bedroom and shutting the door so we wouldn't be overheard.

"I can't do school," she said, sounding angry. She sat down hard on the bed and pulled her work shirt out from where it was tucked into her pants. She wouldn't look at me, and she pulled her knees up to her chest instead, bracing her back against the headboard. It made her look like a little girl.

"We've talked about this," I said. "You have to go to school."

"I can't," she yelled, causing me to step back. "I can't, okay? I can't do it. I couldn't even finish high school. There's no way I can do something like this." She waved toward the door as though it were the program she'd enrolled in. I looked at her closer and felt my insides tightening up.

"Why are you acting like this?"

She wrapped her arms tightly around her knees and started rocking back and forth. I walked over to her, put my hands on her knees and stared her hard in the eye. Her pupils weren't dilated. "Are you high?" If she said yes, I didn't know what I'd do.

"No, I'm not high," she said, hitting my hands away and jumping to her feet. Tears filled her eyes. "This guy came to my work. He said Tagg sent him, that . . . that he could help me pay off the debt."

"What do you mean?" I asked, afraid of how much she was freaking out about this.

She met my eyes, and the tears fell faster. "I could work it off."

"I don't . . . " But then I did understand, and I froze as I thought of the things the other members of the NA group had said they'd done for drugs. I was speechless by the impact of the realization.

"Once school starts, I'm only going to be working fifteen hours a week. How will I get those guys paid off?" she said, her whole face crumpling. She grabbed two handfuls of hair in her fists before sitting back down on the bed and leaning her elbows on her knees. Then she started crying—no, sobbing.

I knelt on the floor in front of the bed and wrapped my arms around her shoulders. She clung to me like she never had before, crying into my shirt, saying over and over again that she was so sorry.

I didn't know what she was sorry for until I smelled the alcohol on her breath, hard to detect under the gum or mints she'd used to try to cover it up. It distracted me for a moment, but I was afraid that wasn't what she was apologizing for. "You didn't . . . do anything, did you?"

"He said he'd take two hundred dollars off my debt."

I almost threw up, and I grabbed her shoulders. "Please tell me you didn't do this," I said, absolutely sick to my stomach as tears filled my eyes. "Oh, Keisha, please."

"I didn't," she whimpered. I hugged her again and held on tighter than ever as she cried again. "But I freaked out," she said into my shoulder. "I got one of the cooks to take me to the liquor store. I just couldn't handle it—I *can't* handle it. I don't know what to do."

When her tears were spent and I'd regained my composure, I pulled back and brushed her hair from her tear-streaked face. "I want you to text Tagg," I said calmly, "and tell him you will pay him off tomorrow."

She pulled her eyebrows together, confused.

"*I'm* paying him, but he needs to understand that he has to leave you alone now. Your debt will be paid and that means he leaves for good, or I'll call the cops on him."

"You can't threaten him," Keisha said quickly. "You can't talk about cops. He'll freak and he'll come after me if he thinks I'm going to turn on him."

"Okay, then just tell him you're ready to pay off the debt and that he's not to come see you again—ever. We'll get you a new phone number."

Keisha's chin started to quiver, and she pulled me into a hug. "Thank you," she said, starting to cry again.

I closed my eyes and assured her that everything would be okay. I sat next to her while she texted him and read the messages. She told him she'd pay him off tomorrow. He asked her if she wanted a parting gift, and she glanced at me quickly before typing that she was done, for good. He agreed to meet her at Denny's the next morning at eleven.

I got her calmed down enough to join us for dinner but made her change her clothes first. I hoped John wouldn't pick up on the smell of alcohol.

She wasn't drunk, thank goodness, but John needed to see that she was okay or he'd start asking questions.

She came out and had a plate of spaghetti; John and Landon were finished by then. Landon was working on something for school, and John was cleaning the kitchen but mostly watching us. I finished my meal first but stayed at the table so Keisha wouldn't be alone. I talked about random things from work that no one cared about just to keep conversation going, then I suggested she and I find a NA meeting. She looked up at me with *do-we-have-to* eyes, which I returned with a look she couldn't misinterpret as anything other than *absolutely*. She agreed, then went to freshen up while I went to the computer and Googled the nearest meeting. We would have to drive into Irvine, but there was a group that started in ten minutes. We'd be late, but she needed to be there.

"What happened?" John asked, coming up behind me.

I took a breath and fought against the surge of anger that I was dealing with this all by myself. If he were more approachable, I could tell him all the things I'd been keeping to myself, and we could be a united front against the demon hunting his daughter, but he'd chosen an entirely different course, and so I was fighting this alone. Just like I'd paid the bills alone for months at a time over the last few years. It wasn't fair to be so angry, and yet it was too far into the battle to start renegotiating. "She had a tough day," I said, but I could hear the prickle in my voice and I knew he could too.

"Why?"

His ignorance about what was going on in his own daughter's life infuriated me. "Because she's an addict, John, *and* she's mentally ill, *and* she's trying to build a new life. Everything's working against her, and she needs a little more love and a little more patience." I stood up and glared at him. He looked completely confused.

"What did I do?" he asked.

"Expected the worst," I said, blowing past him to change out of my loungewear and into something presentable. "Again." I knew I was making no sense to him, and yet I was so angry I couldn't even explain myself. He followed me into the bedroom and stood with his arms crossed while I changed.

I continued to rant about being the one to take her to her meetings, talk to her about her day, and worry about what was going on with her. "All you ever seem to do is throw accusations around and think the worst possible scenarios about everything." I pulled on a T-shirt, realized it was dirty, and had to pull it off before finding another one. Clean this time. When had I last done laundry? Why wasn't John keeping up with it?

"I asked why she was upset," John said, his words measured. "I don't get why you're jumping all over me about it."

"Why didn't you ask *her*, John?" I said, stepping into my shoes and facing off with him, my hands on my hips. "Why didn't you talk to your daughter instead of asking me? Why am I the one in the middle all the time? Did you ever think that maybe she knows how you feel—that she knows you're disappointed and embarrassed and wish she wasn't here? Did you ever think about how that makes her feel?"

He pulled the bedroom door closed and crossed the room before I finished speaking. "What is going on with you?" he said in an angry whisper. "What if she heard you say that?"

"She doesn't need to hear me," I spat. "She told it to me."

He pulled back as if he'd been slapped. He opened his mouth but didn't speak.

I thought about what Keisha had told me tonight, about the option she'd been given to pay back the money she owed, and my anger renewed tenfold. Right here, right now, I blamed John for all of it. We could have paid off her debt months ago and she wouldn't even be in this situation right now. We could have bought her a car so she could have gotten a job sooner. We could have had her move in with us years ago when she was first struggling. We could have had her come stay after rehab and really created a second chance for her to succeed.

But John and his pride had stood in the way, and now his daughter was being approached by pimps. How disgusting was that? And yet I couldn't explain any of that to him, because he didn't know she owed any money and because, like Keisha, I didn't trust him enough to believe he would help her if he knew the truth.

I walked past him and exited the bedroom. Keisha was in the kitchen cleaning up from dinner. She glanced at me and I looked away, hoping she hadn't heard the argument. I'd tried to disagree with her when she'd said John didn't want her here, and I didn't want her to think that's what I believed even though I did.

"Ready?" I asked with a very false smile.

She nodded, and I led the way to the garage. It wasn't until we were halfway to the meeting that I remembered I hadn't said good-bye to Landon. How was I supposed to be everything to everyone in my life when Keisha needed so much of me?

Chapter 16

I WORKED THE NEXT DAY—Wednesday—and took my time coming home, stopping at a bookstore to buy *The War of Art* since I hadn't gotten around to ordering it, and then going to the mall for a new pair of work shoes. I didn't really need them, but I was still reeling from last night and the fact that I'd taken an early lunch in order to withdraw fifteen hundred dollars out of our savings account, which I'd then taken home to Keisha. She'd hugged me and left for work, texting me later to tell me it was done.

I'd just paid off a drug dealer. Whose life was this?

I called the cell phone company and got Keisha a new number, effective tomorrow, then texted it to her. I waited for a few minutes for a response, but when she didn't reply, I went back to my job as a medical professional and counted out legal drugs that would help people control their pain and misery, regulate their chemistries, and give them a greater quality of life.

I was shaking and nauseated most of the afternoon, and so confused about how I felt toward my husband and how to explain my reaction last night. It hadn't made sense and what I'd said wasn't entirely true, but it was as though I'd been holding in all this frustration and it had come out in a big, spewing rage. I didn't have these kinds of rages. It wasn't me. And yet it *was* me, and I stood behind what I said, which meant I couldn't apologize, and yet the idea of facing John tonight made my bones hurt.

I needed clarity. I needed to be centered, so I bought a CD of flute music at the mall and put high expectations on it as I listened to it on my way home. It was not the magic pill I'd hoped for, and yet I couldn't stay away from home much longer. It was almost eight o'clock.

I considered forcing a smile when I entered, but I was tired of all the falseness—most of which I had no choice but to continue playing along with. So when I pushed open the door I let myself look as tired and drained as I felt, steeling myself for either the silent treatment from my husband—which was what we'd done that morning—or another argument, which I did not feel capable of doing. Then again, maybe another argument was what I needed. I'd already let him have it last night. If it came up again, maybe I could just tell him everything—everything Keisha had told me, and everything I'd done to help her. He should have done better by her, if not when she was little, then now.

For the split second before I entered the house, I was overcome with relief at the idea of telling him the truth. I hated keeping secrets. There would be healing that would need to take place, for sure, but I wouldn't be burdened with this alone. That was where my anger came from last night—guilt and shame and frustration all scrunched together like a big wad of tinfoil. If I put it in front of him, I'd have a better chance of untangling it, right? But would he kick Keisha out? Was I willing to take that chance?

I entered the kitchen with these thoughts beating my brain, then stopped in my tracks. Instead of an angry husband and tense household, Landon, Keisha, and John were sitting around the kitchen table playing *Settlers of Catan*—our family's favorite board game. Keisha had just stolen the longest road from Landon and had her hand out for the card while he writhed in pain at having to give up the two points.

John met my eyes and smiled. I didn't know what to do with this scene, and then I saw the bouquet of flowers on the counter. A sudden lump in my throat caught me off guard. John and I had only had a few big fights in our marriage—fewer than most couples, I was sure. On the times when it was his fault, he would bring me flowers after taking the time to realize his mistake. When it was my fault, I bought him a new power tool.

I stared at the flowers and then looked at him as he stood up from the table. Keisha sent a quick glance our way but then went back to the game—it was Landon's turn. John came to me and put a hand on my shoulder, guiding me into the living room, away from our children. Then he faced me and managed a small smile. "I'm sorry," he whispered.

I couldn't talk, my resolve shaken up like a snow globe. I'd been almost ready to tell him, but now I had to rebreak the bone if I wanted to follow through on my decision to put it all on the table. Did I dare do that? Contrary to what people said about bones mending to be stronger than they were before, it wasn't usually true.

He reached up and touched my face. "I've thought about what you said, and you're right." He gave me a small smile with such tenderness in his eyes that I winced inside. His voice was soft, at least partly so as not to be overheard by the kids, I assumed. "I've let you take the lead, and in the process I haven't stood up for my daughter the way I should. She's done everything she can to prove herself, and I haven't allowed her to grow in my eyes." I understood how painful it was for him to admit that out loud. "That was wrong, and I'm sorry. She doesn't deserve that from me, and you deserve me to do my part. I'm sorry for not seeing it on my own."

I stared at him, taking in the scruff of his beard, the way his pale eyelashes were almost invisible. I loved this man—he was the beginning and end of all the great things I had in my life, and yet as I stared at him, I thought of the night Keisha hadn't come home until four in the morning. I thought of the gift card I'd purchased to cover her theft, and the money I'd withdrawn from our savings account this morning to pay off a dealer. Where anger had overcome me last night, now I was stunned with the burn of shame. I'd blasted him last night, and he'd forgiven me, just like that. I'd underestimated him. Had I underestimated him with those other things too?

I couldn't speak. All my words stuck in my throat as I tried to anticipate what he would say when I told him the truth. There was suddenly no doubt in my mind I would *have* to tell him eventually. Why had I ever thought I could hide it? Why had I wanted to? What kind of wife was I?

He took a step toward me and cupped my face in his hands, rubbing his thumbs beneath my eyes. With the tenderness of a man who had kissed me a million times during our lives together, he gently touched his lips to mine, held them there, then pulled back in order to wrap his arms around my shoulders. I couldn't help but wrap my arms around him as well, wishing I'd never have to let go, that we could exist in this state of doesn't-matter forever. I laid my head on his chest, closed my eyes, and wondered what on earth I was supposed to do now.

I opened my eyes to see Keisha standing in the doorway. She wasn't smiling as she looked at us; instead, she looked . . . sad. Why? And then Landon popped his head out from behind her and started making gagging noises. I felt the rumble of John's laughter in his chest before I heard it, then he pulled away and looked deep into my eyes again. "Are we okay?" he whispered. Landon writhed on his deathbed behind us, flopping on the floor in agony.

I still couldn't speak, so I just nodded. John's soft smile grew a little more, and he leaned in to kiss me once more while Landon said "I. Am. Dead!" before giving one last death spasm and going still, his tongue hanging out of his mouth. John turned to look at him, at which point Landon's eyes popped open, narrowed playfully. "It's your turn, lover boy."

John laughed again, and when I looked at Keisha again she smiled slightly. I knew she couldn't understand the weight of what I hadn't told John; maybe she thought I *had* told him, but I hoped she understood the sacrifice I was making for her.

Chapter 17

FRIDAY, TWO DAYS AFTER THE flowers, I was just getting into the shower when I noticed I'd missed a call from Aunt Ruby. I smiled, excited to hear about her trip, but I decided to call her back when I was on my way into work. It wasn't until I was in the shower that I realized she'd called really early in the morning—which was strange. I hoped nothing was wrong and hurried to get ready so I could find out.

Keisha was asleep when I left for work—she'd worked until six a.m.—and John had left for a job. I put in my earpiece for my phone and called my voice mail to listen to Aunt Ruby's message.

"Hi, Shannon. I'm back from Greece. It was a wonderful trip; I'll have to tell you all about it soon. I'm actually calling because I can't find my laptop. I left it at the house, but it's not where I put it. I thought maybe you borrowed it or something. Give me a call when you can. Thanks."

Borrowed her laptop? Why would I borrow her laptop? Besides, it was a PC and I was a Mac girl myself. Once you Mac-ed, you never went back. I erased her voice mail and called her number.

"Hi, Aunt Ruby," I said when she answered. "I just got your message. Are you sure your laptop isn't there somewhere?"

"I stored it in one of the kitchen cabinets when I left. I know I did because I had to put my mixer on the counter to make room, but I thought a mixer was safer in plain sight than a computer, you know? It's not there. The whole shelf is empty. You didn't borrow it?"

"No," I said with a smile. Storing a computer in a cupboard was silly—a laptop wasn't like a cup of sugar you borrowed on a whim. "And I never saw it during the times I came to check on things. I always locked the house up when I left, I swear."

"The security system recorded each time you disarmed it, and I know the alarm was reset correctly each time too, which is just so strange. How would anyone have gotten in without tripping the alarm? Do you think someone could have bypassed it?"

"I didn't get any notifications." Because of the security measures at the pharmacy, I knew a lot about security systems. They weren't impossible to disable, but most of them were set up with all kinds of internal safeguards to protect against tampering, and most attempts couldn't circumvent the system without leaving telltale evidence behind or an automatic call going to the dispatch center. At the pharmacy, the police were called if the code was punched incorrectly just two times, or outside of specific hours, and every employee had their own code so that we always knew who set or disarmed it. But of course, Aunt Ruby's house didn't have such a sophisticated system.

"Is anything else missing?" I still thought the laptop was in her house somewhere.

"Um, I haven't really checked, since I thought you'd just borrowed it. I'll go look right now. I don't leave valuables out, you know, especially when I'm going to be gone." I could hear her walking as she talked. "I locked up my jewelry box in the safe, along with some of my more expensive souvenirs I've collected over the years. Everything looks fine . . . oh, wait . . . someone's been in the master closet—that's where I keep the safe. My shoes are mixed up."

Maybe the laptop *had* been stolen. "Did they get into the safe?" I asked, sick to my stomach not only that something like this had happened to Ruby, but also that it had happened on my watch.

"No," Aunt Ruby said. I let out a breath. "But it looks like they tried to pry it open."

A missing laptop, mixed-up shoes, and a safe that had been tampered with, and yet there wasn't any evidence of a break-in at her house? I opened my mouth to ask if anyone else had the alarm code and then nearly choked on the words. *I* had the alarm code stuck to the fridge with an Oreo magnet. Heat crawled up my neck. *No*, I told myself. *Don't go there.*

"You said you looked at the history," I said a moment later, "and could see that I reset the alarm each time I came over. How many times does it show I came?"

Three, three, three.

"Four," Ruby said. She listed off the dates—the second and third stood out to me because they were the only two days right next to one another. There was no reason for me to go to Ruby's two days in a row. I'd only gone every three or four days—the last time had been Monday, the day before the meltdown with Keisha. I closed my eyes, refusing to picture Keisha in my mind looking at the fridge while sipping a soda a few days into Aunt Ruby's trip. I'd thought she was looking at the newsletter from Landon's school.

"I'm going to call the alarm company right now," Aunt Ruby said. "Maybe they'll have a more complete report for me by now."

Sympathy for Aunt Ruby made my chest ache, but I couldn't share my thoughts. That wouldn't be fair to anyone, least of all to Aunt Ruby if I were wrong—and I *had* to be wrong. "Do you want me to come over and stay with you? Do you feel safe there alone?"

"I'll be fine, dear. Thanks for asking. And thank you for watching the place."

It was like a knife in my chest to have her thank me when I knew what had happened. Wait—I didn't *know*. But I suspected it all the same. And that made me feel horrible too. Did I really think Keisha was a thief? She loved Ruby. She would never *rob* her—would she? And Keisha had been so sincerely upset earlier this week before I agreed to pay off Tagg. If she'd stolen Ruby's laptop, she wouldn't need money from me, right? I had to be wrong. Of *course* I was wrong.

"It seems I didn't do a very good job of looking after the house," I said, feeling terrible for everything—both what had happened and thinking Keisha might have been involved.

"Nonsense," Aunt Ruby said. "This is obviously the work of a professional. I suppose no security system is completely foolproof. I'd better go though. I've got more phone calls to make."

"I'm so sorry, Aunt Ruby. If you need anything, I can be there right away."

"I'll call if I think of anything, but I'm sure I'll get to the bottom of it."

We said our good-byes and ended the call. I was at a red light and picked up my phone from the middle console before scrolling to Keisha's number. My thumb hovered over the call button. I should just call her and ask her straight out. But what would I say? "Did you break into my aunt's house and steal her laptop after she's been so sweet to you?" Was there any way to ask it that didn't sound accusatory? I had no evidence it was Keisha, just circumstance and history. And was that fair? Gosh, I was as bad as John!

But was it fair to Aunt Ruby not to explore it?

I closed my eyes and took a deep breath. The light turned green, I replaced the phone in the console, and I moved forward with my fellow commuters.

Chapter 18

IT WAS A BUSY DAY at work, and then I had to hurry home to make dinner for most of the lacrosse team and their parents. It had been just a meeting where John would hand out schedules and call lists until I suggested making it a dinner. I'd been so distracted lately that it felt like an opportunity for me to make things up to him and Landon. And then I'd gotten the call from Ruby.

Nothing helped keep my mind busy like twenty-five extra people in my backyard, though, and John and Landon were both grateful about all my efforts. Keisha was at work during the whole thing, but I managed to fall asleep before she got off her shift thanks to a busy day and a busy evening and a busy mind. Though I fell asleep easily, I woke up, restless, around five o'clock in the morning, and finally got out of bed at six.

I was working in Long Beach from ten until three so I headed to Aunt Ruby's house early, desperately wanting to make things okay. Keisha had left fifty dollars from her tip money on the front seat of my car—it was how she paid me back without John asking questions. She was trying so hard to do the right thing, and I felt awful for thinking the worst of her in regard to Ruby's missing laptop.

Aunt Ruby was an early riser, and though I worried the jet lag might have her sleeping in, the drapes on the front window were open when I pulled up a little after eight o'clock. She'd always said the day didn't start until she could see the sky. She seemed happy to see me and immediately updated me on the theft—nothing else was missing, as far as she could tell. The security company was coming over later to make sure everything was okay with her system.

She poured me some juice and then listened to my version of events. I kind of glossed over the exact dates of when I came over and hoped she wouldn't ask pointed questions. I didn't know how to handle this, and being vague seemed to be the best choice. I worried she'd ask for specifics, but other than asking if I had noticed anything out of the ordinary during any of my visits—which I hadn't—she didn't ask me any questions I couldn't answer.

Once we finished, she insisted on making muffins, and even though I worried they wouldn't be ready before I had to leave, she started putting them together anyway. I sat down at the counter and updated her on our family and how Landon's basketball season had gone, glad to feel that even amid my worries and the theft of her laptop, we were okay with each other.

I finished telling her about the team party last night and then noticed a book on her counter. Uncle Phillip had been a buyer and seller for antiques—international, hard-to-find antiques—and Aunt Ruby's home was filled with beautiful pieces from all over the world and dating back hundreds of years in some instances. And yet, despite the aged furniture and décor, nothing ever looked used. Except this book. It had a ratty cover, and the pages were expanded as though it had been around too much moisture. It seemed completely out of place. I picked it up and read the title: *Zen and the Art of Motorcycle Maintenance*.

Motorcycle maintenance? I glanced at Ruby and imagined her in coveralls with grease smudges on her face while she took apart the transmission of a cherry-red Harley Softail. The idea made me smile.

"What's this book?"

She turned around too quickly, and a momentary expression of shock crossed her face as she looked at me holding the book. I pulled my eyebrows together. Aunt Ruby was rarely ruffled, but she was suddenly *very* ruffled . . . much like the pages of this book.

She explained that it was from the tour guide—Gabriel—and he'd snuck it into her bag, but she said it with a forced giggle that caught my attention even more.

"Have you ever heard of such a strange title?" she continued. Were her cheeks turning pink?

"Gabriel's the tour guide?"

"Well, he's part-owner with his sister, Maria, but he also works as a guide on a lot of the Greece tours."

Her cheeks were definitely pink, and I couldn't hold back my own curiosity any longer. "Aunt Ruby, I think you're blushing."

She stammered and turned back to the counter, focusing on the muffins.

"Do you have a picture of him on your phone?" I asked. I eyed her cell phone, which was within reach of me, though I'd never be so forward as to grab it on my own.

She didn't answer, and I looked at her, assuming her silence meant that she *did* have a photo of this mystery man who had her so uncharacteristically flustered. "Can I see the pictures?"

She paused but then reached for the phone and started scrolling while explaining that her friend had taken most of the pictures and she didn't have copies yet. She settled on a picture and then handed the phone to me, explaining where I could find Gabriel in the group.

"Oh, wow. He's good looking. And look at that smile."

She said nothing as I enlarged the photo to see his face better. He wasn't looking into the camera like everyone else in the photo. He was looking at Ruby, who stood on the opposite side of the group. I wondered what other photos might be on this phone that Ruby didn't want me to see. She was obviously uncomfortable with something, but I didn't want to make her any more uncomfortable. I couldn't resist teasing her a little, though, so I shared my observation about Gabriel's focus with her, and she flipped out, reaching for the phone and acting shocked. I pulled the phone away so she couldn't take it from me while she insisted he was looking into the camera.

"I don't think so . . . He's definitely smiling at you."

She came around the counter and looked over my shoulder at the enlarged image on her phone. Then she snatched it away and slipped the phone into the pocket of her housedress. She attempted to pacify me by talking about putting together a photo album of her trip that she'd bring to book group.

I looked at the book again—the one Gabriel had given to her—and picked it up while Ruby returned to her muffins. I flipped through the pages, then back to the inside front cover where handwriting in blue ink on the title page caught my eye. I lifted my eyebrows and read it out loud.

"'To Ruby. All my love, G.'"

Aunt Ruby whipped around so fast that I pulled back slightly. "What did you say?" she asked quickly.

I couldn't help but laugh out loud. "All his love," I said, wagging my eyebrows and showing her the book. "Tell me more about Gabriel."

Aunt Ruby's cheeks turned pink . . . again. "I don't know what you're talking about."

"There's an inscription." I held up the book, opened to the front page. "Didn't you see it?"

She didn't answer me but watched closely as I showed her the note. Her cheeks got even redder. "Like I said, he was very thoughtful—to everyone."

I wasn't buying it. This Gabriel guy was *important* to her somehow, which made me think of Uncle Phillip—the only man I knew of that she'd ever loved. She deserved better than Uncle Phillip—was Gabriel better? It made my heart ache a little to know the truth of what she hadn't had with her husband, and I decided to see where this conversation might lead us. Since her reaction at book group a few weeks ago, I'd wondered about how much she knew and had considered talking to her about it. Maybe now was a good time.

She opened a cupboard, removed some muffin liners from a basket and started putting them in the muffin tin she'd already set out.

"Have you ever thought about dating again, Aunt Ruby?"

She didn't say anything, but I waited her out in hopes of forcing her to answer me—due to good manners, if nothing else. It took her a bit of time to construct an answer she was happy with, and by then the muffins were in the oven. "I was married for thirty years, dear. I consider myself retired."

"Why is that?" I asked, resting my arms on the counter and giving her a strong look. "You've taken excellent care of yourself, you've got more energy than some women half your age, and you've got a lot of years left. Why not see if there's someone you could share those years with?"

She glanced at me, then wiped down the counters. My attention was making her nervous. "Thank you for your kind comments, but I guess I just had my fill of it."

I could almost hear her sorting through topics she could turn the conversation toward, and I felt now was as good a time as any to get to the heart of it. "Is this about Uncle Phillip's . . . ?" I was at the crossroads, and I couldn't say it. Couldn't spit it out. What if she *didn't* know? What if I inflicted a wound I could not heal? In the next instant I realized I had already started. I couldn't back out now.

She held my eyes for the count of three, and I saw within her the same battle I'd been waging—to speak or not to speak of hard things, painful things, things we wished weren't true. "Phillip's what?" she asked, the hint of a challenge in her voice. We both knew she could have ignored me, let me look at the pictures again, or told me something else about her cruise. But she didn't. Then again, she wasn't really *asking* either. It was an odd kind of stand off. "What are you talking about?"

"You know . . ." Again I couldn't say it out loud. Apparently, after two years of protecting her, I couldn't stop protecting her so quickly.

"Know what?" she said, then almost imperceptibly straightened and pulled her shoulders down. Her tone changed to light and casual—an attempt to pretend this conversation was light and casual too, perhaps? "What are you talking about, Shannon? This has nothing to do with my husband. A lot of widows remarry. It's just not for me."

I leaned back, folded my arms over my chest, and stared at her, trying to work out the equation of her words and her movements in my head because they didn't match the answer she was trying to convince me of. She scrubbed at something on the counter, but despite her pretended indifference there was fear and sorrow radiating from her. I bet she was regretting having invited me to stay for muffins.

"Ruby," I said softly, hoping she could hear the love in my voice, the understanding and compassion of it. She must know about the affair; why else would she be acting like this? I came around the counter; she pretended not to notice. I finally stopped next to her and took a breath before I spoke.

"Did you know Uncle Phillip had an affair?" I couldn't believe I actually said the words out loud, and I felt a little dizzy with the word "affair" echoing through the kitchen.

Aunt Ruby froze. I watched her stare at the stovetop she'd been wiping down, not moving at all—not even breathing. I reached out and touched her arm after a few seconds. She opened her mouth as though to say something, ward off my pronouncement, convince me I was wrong.

"No . . ." she said, but it was a broken attempt to deflect the conversation, not necessarily an answer to the question. I wasn't sure how I could tell, but I could. She knew. I was overcome with sadness for her. She swallowed, took a breath and looked up at me, giving up the pretense. "How did *you* know?"

I told her about my father catching Uncle Phillip out with another woman and watched Aunt Ruby crumble at the realization that her secret wasn't really a "secret" at all. I pulled her into a hug. She allowed it for several seconds; I could feel tears on my shoulder and glanced at the clock on the microwave, hoping the rest of the staff would forgive me if I was late to work—this wasn't the kind of conversation you cut off.

After some time, she pulled away and walked out of the room without a word. I followed her into the living room, where she sat down on the couch with enough room for me to sit beside her. She wanted to know details, so I told her about how my dad—her brother—had seen Phillip with a woman in San Diego and how I'd overheard my parents talking about it after Uncle Phillip died. I wanted to cushion each word so the impact wouldn't be too bruising, but there really were no words soft enough, and searching for them threatened my already-weakened resolve.

"When did your dad see my husband in San Diego?" she asked when I finished explaining how Uncle Phillip had begged Dad not to tear the family apart. It was a selfish request—a cruel thing to force between a brother and a sister—but my dad would never hurt Ruby. And so he kept Uncle Phillip's secret.

"It was about three years before he died," I said.

"Then that was Evelyn."

I felt my eyes go wide. "You know her *name?*"

She took a deep breath and looked up at me with a sad yet relieved expression on her face. "I knew all of their names, honey."

Chapter 19

I WAS GOING TO BE late for work—almost an hour late—and the muffins were inedible by the time we returned to the kitchen and realized they'd been severely overcooked. I drove down the 405 still stunned at what I'd learned. Not only did Aunt Ruby know about the affairs—plural—she knew about the women: their names, where they lived, what they did for a living. It kind of creeped me out that she'd also kept mementos of each woman her husband had cheated with. I couldn't imagine why she would want to do that, but maybe she just had to remember who her husband *really* was. He'd certainly put on a good show for the rest of us.

All the memories I had of her and Uncle Phillip raced through my mind as I tried to fit them into a new paradigm. I thought they were happy up until my dad stumbled across the affair. I thought they were in love to that point at least. Aunt Ruby, my domestic goddess of an aunt who'd doted on me, who always decorated for the holidays—my mom hated the clutter—who paid for the first year of my college education, and who gave me a high-end camera as a wedding gift so I could "treasure every memory" had been hiding a broken heart all those years.

Here we thought we were protecting her by not telling her what we knew, and perhaps in a way we were—knowing we knew was obviously painful for her—but she was much stronger than I had thought she was. She'd cared for a man she didn't love because it was the right thing for her to do, and despite my modern feministic ways, I couldn't disagree with her choice after hearing her defend it. She was raising her son at a different time. Who was I to say she'd made the wrong choice? My anger rose, however, when I thought of how Uncle Phillip was now standing in her way for something that could be beautiful.

"With all my love, G."

She hadn't had all of Uncle Phillip's love. What if she could have all of *Gabriel's*? What if Gabriel were the person she had expected Uncle Phillip to be? And yet seeing her pain laid out before me made it hard to imagine how she'd be able to overcome the betrayal of thirty years of marriage. I called Uncle Phillip some really ugly names during the last few minutes of my drive to work, then tried to think of how I could help Aunt Ruby see something more in Gabriel than she wanted to see—than she dared to trust. Then again, maybe this was something Aunt Ruby needed to do all on her own.

It was rotten how life played with us sometimes, giving us trials we couldn't just overcome and make better. Ruby was facing that. Keisha was too. So was I. Would any of us find the right resolution? I hoped so.

Chapter 20

I WAS HALFWAY THROUGH MY shift when a script came through for Edna McDonald. I hadn't seen her in several weeks, not since that day when she'd broken down and I'd told her to call her son. I had promised to check up on her, but I hadn't done it and felt terrible for not doing better by her. I filled the prescription, more oxycodone and something that would help her sleep, then came around to the front, looking for her Jazzy chair and her dog even though it was a frail hope. She wasn't there, so I walked back to the pick-up counter and announced her name. A man in his sixties stood up from the bench and approached the counter.

"You must be Edna's son," I said, taking in his blue eyes and slightly pointed nose, both features his mother had. I reflected on the fact that I had no idea how long ago Edna had been widowed.

He nodded his confirmation of the relationship, and I explained the medications while I was ringing up the prescription. "How is she doing?"

"Not well," he said softly. "She's in a lot of pain."

"But she can still swallow pills? You can run your card through that machine."

"Yes," he said, following my instructions for making the copay. "For now, but hospice told me to prepare for IV's within a few weeks. Mom's a fighter though." He smiled as he said it, but there was sorrow there. Real sorrow that bespoke of a relationship not as distant as Edna had seemed to think it was when she hadn't wanted to call him.

"I'm really glad you came," I said softly as I handed over the paper bag. "I was so worried about her being alone."

He looked up at me. "I wish I'd come sooner."

"But you're here now," I told him.

A woman standing behind him interrupted us to ask me where the Nyquil was. It broke the tenderness of the moment Edna's son and I were sharing. I ignored her. "Will you tell Edna that we miss her?"

He promised that he would and then stepped away from the counter, leaving me with the Nyquil woman, who looked annoyed that I had spent so much time with this man who was of no consequence to her. I held her eyes for a moment, then called over a tech to deal with her so I could get back behind the counter where I belonged. Knowing I would never see Edna again made my chest tighten off and on throughout the day. Knowing that her son had come to help her made me reflect on my own relationships, and my morning with Aunt Ruby kept playing over and over in my mind.

When I got home at four o'clock I set about making dinner. Landon and John had gone to John's parents' house to do some yard work, and Keisha had left a note saying she was working until eight o'clock. It had been a couple of days since I'd really seen her.

As I pulled open the fridge, the note with Ruby's alarm code caught my eye. I shut the door and stared at the numbers I'd left out in plain sight. I didn't need them now, so I pulled the paper off the fridge and crumpled it in my hand. Then I went to the hooks where we hung our keys and took Ruby's single key with the pewter butterfly keychain from one of them. I tightened my hand around it, then went to my room and put it in the bottom of my jewelry box. If I'd been more careful when she first gave me these things, I wouldn't be doubting anyone right now.

I cooked and pondered and cooked some more, and by the time the boys came home from John's parents' house, I had an entire meal ready to go. Chicken stir-fry, rice, egg rolls—from frozen—and a cucumber salad with sesame dressing. I made the boys shower, in part because they smelled like wet dogs—it had started raining—but also because I wanted Keisha to get home as well so we could eat together as a family.

It all came together when Keisha walked in not two minutes before John got out of the shower. Within a few minutes, the four of us were sitting around the table. Keisha hadn't done her hair, and she looked exhausted, which made sense since she was working so much, but it still had me worried. Was she sick? Was there something else? What would she say if I told her about the missing laptop? I could pretend I was just telling John and watch her reaction, but what if her reaction told me something I didn't really want to know? She started school on Monday, which was likely stressing her out as well.

We passed around the plates of food and made small talk for the first few minutes; then I took a breath to gather my courage and told them about the missing laptop. Keisha was sitting across from me, which made it easy for me to watch her reaction without being overt about it. She didn't react much at all. Was that suspect? Would she overreact or underreact if she were guilty?

Landon hung on my every word, entranced by the drama. "She could have been killed!" he said when I finished.

I smiled at him. "Good thing she was gone, huh?"

Landon nodded.

"They didn't take anything else?" John asked. "Just the laptop?"

"It seems that way," I said, taking a bite of my egg roll. "Though they tried to break into her safe—pry it open, I guess. I feel horrible." I didn't tell him about the extra disabling of the security code. Keisha didn't look up at me even once during the explanation.

"It's not your fault," John said.

"Can I go to Jessica's?" Keisha said suddenly.

"I don't know if that's a good idea," I said automatically, returning to my meal. Now that I knew she'd used with Jessica, Jessica was the enemy.

"Why not?"

I looked up from my plate, surprised at the question. She knew John had no idea what had happened the last time she went to Jessica's house and she was calling me on it right in front of him. I couldn't give a reason without revealing that I knew things that John did not—that I had kept the truth from him.

"Jessica's the girl from rehab?" John asked, oblivious to the standoff taking place. He sat between the two of us and dipped his egg roll in the sweet-and-sour sauce he'd spooned onto his plate. "The dental school girl?"

"Yeah," Keisha said, pushing her food around on the plate—she hadn't eaten much. "I told her I'd help her color her roots."

"That's nice of you," John said. "Are you excited for school on Monday?"

"Yeah," Keisha said, turning toward her dad and seeming to notice that she had his attention. "I hope I'm ready for it."

"You'll do great," John said, smiling at his daughter. "You've always had such a great eye for detail."

"Thanks. Can I borrow your truck to go to Jessica's?"

His truck—not my car. I looked back at my plate, embarrassed by the jealousy I felt. Why did it matter to me what car she took?

"Sure," John said, nodding toward the row of hooks holding our keys. "But make sure you're in by midnight, okay? I don't want to be up late worrying about my little girl."

Keisha smiled for the first time since she'd come in, and I had to get up from the table and walk into the kitchen even though I wasn't done with my dinner. *Now* she was his little girl? Where was he when his *little girl* was out until four in the morning? Where was he when his little girl was pawning her brother's gift card? Rage and jealousy and a few other ugly emotions were ripping at me even though I knew that I wanted John and Keisha to have this kind of relationship. It was what I was fighting for, right? What I was lying and hiding for.

"You okay, Mom?"

I snapped out of my thoughts and looked at Landon, who was standing next to me in the kitchen, holding his dinner plate. I'd stopped in the middle of the floor with my own plate in my hands. "Sure, I'm okay," I said with a smile, making my feet move toward the sink. He followed me with his plate, though his was empty. Except for his comments about the theft at Aunt Ruby's, he'd been quiet at dinner. "Are you okay?" I felt more out of touch with him than I ever had before.

"Yeah," he said, but it was noncommittal. I turned around and leaned against the counter. I could hear Keisha and John talking in the other room and had to suppress another ball of jealousy crawling up my throat. What was wrong with me?

"That wasn't a very convincing answer," I said, looking at him expectantly. "What's up?" As his mother I was supposed to ask questions like this, but I didn't really want to hear the answer. What if he were having problems at school or with friends? Was there any room left within me to deal with that? The thought of having to help him navigate his own troubles felt overwhelming, like being hit with ocean waves when I was already exhausted from treading water too long. But why was I so tired? Things were going the way I wanted them to, weren't they? Well, except for the stunt Keisha had just pulled about going to Jessica's.

"I was just wondering how long Keisha was going to stay," Landon said.

John laughed again, a big bellowing laugh, and Landon and I both looked toward the table. It was a few seconds before I turned back to my son and remembered the question he'd asked. "She'll stay here as long as she needs to," I said. There was finality in my words. Was he questioning me the way John had been? Did he not understand why it was so important that Keisha was here with us? Then I remembered my own exhaustion and my fears about her being the one who took Ruby's laptop, and I let out a breath. "Is it hard for you to have her here?" I asked, softer this time.

He shrugged. "It's okay, I guess, but . . ."

"But what?" I asked, really trying to tune in.

"But she acts really weird sometimes."

"Weird how?" I hadn't seen her act weird—well, except for tonight.

He paused, then shook his head and turned away. "Never mind."

I should have grabbed his shoulder, looked him in the eye, and pushed for the real answer, but I let him go. I didn't have the energy, and I wasn't sure I could handle whatever it was he was talking about. Surely it was just that Keisha left hair in the bathroom drain and wore tank tops around the house. Right?

Chapter 21

I took two Tylenol PMs in order to make sure I didn't wait up for Keisha and make myself crazy. When I woke up at eight the next morning, however, I peeked in on her before I did anything else. She was there, wrapped in the comforter, and it was a lead weight off my chest to know she'd come home. Well, it was *one* lead weight off my chest. There were three or four other ones still in place.

John and Landon went to his parents' house in Anaheim again. John's dad wasn't feeling well, and I knew that John helping out was his way of staying connected. I'd had several hours to replay last night in my mind and was becoming more and more bothered by it. Why had Keisha put me on the spot? Why would she want to hang out with Jessica at all? Why had she kissed up to John, and why had he responded to it like he had? I'd asked her to write her schedule on the calendar when she started working, and she'd done it for a while, but she hadn't kept up with it so I didn't know if she was working today or not. Noon came and went, one o'clock, two o'clock. Why was Keisha sleeping so late? Was she hung over again?

I couldn't stop thinking about Aunt Ruby's missing laptop. If Keisha had stolen it, it had to be because she needed money, but I'd paid Tagg off a few days before Ruby came home and discovered the theft. If Keisha had pawned the laptop, why hadn't *she* paid Tagg off with the money she'd have gotten from it? Did she owe more than she'd told me about? Had she needed the money for something else?

I was obsessing, so I called Aunt Ruby. I asked her how she was doing, and we talked about yesterday for a few minutes until she changed the subject, opening it up for me to ask for specific information regarding the break-in. I'd meant to ask about it yesterday, but the conversation had taken a very different turn. She had the times and dates of all the alarm disarmings, and I wrote them on the dates they'd occurred on the calendar as she reported them to me. I knew right away the date I hadn't gone—Friday the 18 at 6:54 p.m. Keisha had worked at eight o'clock that night, but I couldn't remember if she'd left for work early or not. "Did you find anything else missing?"

"No," Aunt Ruby said. "Just the laptop, but it had my banking information on it and there was money taken from my accounts. It's been very frustrating, especially since I'm trying to figure things out over a weekend. But the bank says they'll return the funds—it's part of the fine print, I guess. I just had to pay a hundred dollar protection fee."

"How much money did they take?"

"There was about twelve hundred dollars' worth of charges."

"Did they buy things, or just get cash?"

"Some of both," Ruby said. "They bought a car stereo from some place in Orange, and some gift cards from Target, of all places. But they also hit several ATMs for cash—taking out the max amount for two days until the bank did an automatic shutdown. I'd told them I was going to Greece, see, and so it had some alerts on the account—though they acted a little slowly, if you ask me."

"So the police are tracking the stereo, I assume," I said, feeling relieved to know that Keisha didn't have a car to put the stereo in, though the gift cards were damning.

"That's what they said," Aunt Ruby answered. "And they're looking at video footage at Target, I guess, but they haven't given me a lot of hope that they'll find the criminals. Because the amount was under two thousand dollars, they don't give cases like this much of a priority. Like I said, though, they're refunding the money. It should all be back in my account by tomorrow morning."

"I'm so sorry," I said, staring at the date on the calendar and feeling a headache starting from all the building stress. "You are the last person that deserves something like this to happen."

"Oh, I know this isn't your fault, and it's going to be all right. Athena stopped by last night to look at my pictures, and she helped me order a new computer and—like I said—the bank has been very accommodating. They have an entire department devoted to loss recovery. It would be a very difficult job if you ask me—all that negativity."

"I agree," I said, turning back to the kitchen and feeling the need for a change in subject. "So, have you talked to Gabriel? Does he live close by?"

It was the perfect topic-changing question, and from the way she hemmed and hawed, I guessed that she *had* talked to him but seemed to be struggling with her feelings. I asked a few more questions until finally making my good-byes.

Once I hung up, I returned to the calendar by the fridge. I reviewed the calendar on my phone as well as Landon's practice schedule, trying to remember the details of March 18, the day I *hadn't* disarmed the alarm. I'd worked Fountain Valley that day, and John hadn't been here when I got home from work, which would have been around six o'clock. Landon was at a friend's house—it was on the calendar in orange pen. Keisha had been home when I got home, though, but had left soon after. I'd let her take my car because she worked and I wasn't going anywhere. I raised a hand to my forehead and took a deep breath. I didn't want to do this anymore.

I needed to take a Tylenol for my headache and then switch the laundry, but though I went through the motions, I kept thinking about Keisha and Ruby and all the things I hadn't told John that I wished I had so we could talk about everything. The information was bursting inside of me.

When I'd finally run out of things to clean—well, not really, but I was sick of cleaning—I sat down with the book Tori had chosen for book group, *The War of Art*. I tried to give it a fair shake, but it annoyed me. It talked about "resistance," which was some ethereal concept centered on the idea that we are out to sabotage ourselves away from success. It was kind of artsy—which I'd worried about when Tori first told us about it—and, honestly, I didn't really get it. I wasn't resisting anything in my own life. I wasn't distracting myself from my potential. I was simply working hard on several fronts to fulfill my obligations. I didn't like thinking that there was more to me than what was here right now. I didn't like the idea that I wasn't doing something I was meant to do.

I heard Keisha's bedroom door open and looked at the clock: 2:45 p.m. I put down the book, got up from my chair, and met her in the living room. "Are you okay?" I asked. I'd wanted to sound direct, but it came out tentative, careful.

"Sure," she said, rubbing her forehead.

"How was Jessica's?"

"Fine." She walked past me toward the kitchen. I turned and followed, determined to talk but hesitant to bring anything up too. I didn't like confrontation and therefore spent so much time avoiding it that I wasn't really sure how to confront someone correctly when it had to be done.

"Do you work today?"

"No, it's my day off."

"You haven't been writing your schedule on the calendar."

"Oh, sorry."

She pulled the cereal from the cupboard and the milk from the fridge. We'd run out of things to talk about much too soon, leaving me with only one option: face it head-on.

I took a breath. "I don't appreciate what you did last night."

She looked at me, cereal in one hand and milk in the other. "What did I do?"

"You knew why I didn't want you to go to Jessica's."

She moved to the counter, put down her things, and turned to the cupboard to get a bowl. She busied herself with breakfast in the middle of the afternoon, and I waited her out. "Sorry," she finally said as she poured the milk. It was a flippant apology, the kind someone said when they didn't mean it but felt obligated to say it anyway. It was the kind of apology I would expect from a teenager, not a grown woman who owed me better than this for all the help I'd given her.

So, did I push harder for information or just let it go? Ugh, where was my owner's manual on how to handle this? Should I ask her if she used last night? Did I want to know the answer?

"Are you okay?" I finally asked again, giving her the chance to tell me something and hoping that my compassion would be more effective than my questioning. If she chose to tell me, then I would feel as though I'd created a trusting relationship that made her feel comfortable enough to tell me the truth.

"I'm good," she said. She took the milk back to the fridge without meeting my eye.

I stood there for a few seconds, scrounging my brain for something I could say to her. For all my worries about her and Ruby's laptop, I couldn't pin it on her. It seemed too unfair, but I needed to say something. Preferably something that would motivate her in good ways. I finally settled on "I love you, Keisha. I want good things for you. If you need to talk, I'm here, okay?"

She smiled, but there was something fake about it. Did she not believe me? "I love you too, Shannon. I'm going to watch *Jersey Shore,* okay? I TiVoed it." She walked past me with her cereal and out of the kitchen.

I stared at the cabinets. I liked to feel strong and in control of a situation, but right now I feared I was completely delusional.

Something was changing—or had changed—and it worried me. Yet I hadn't pushed for information—didn't want to. Didn't know how. The dryer dinged, and I was relieved for something else to do. Something I knew, something I could control, something that didn't terrify me.

As I went about the rest of the afternoon, I told myself over and over again to be positive, to stay focused, not to give in to my fears. School started soon, and it would change everything. It had to. I would not focus on these negatives; I would look ahead, instead of backward, and be the support system she needed. I needed her to make this work more than ever. She could not fail. For both our sakes.

Chapter 22

KEISHA STARTED SCHOOL ON MONDAY. I was so excited I could hardly stand it. This was her ultimate chance to prove all the naysayers wrong, to move forward with her life and show the world what she could do. She was really nervous in the morning, to the point of getting snappy with me, but I didn't take it personally. This was the first time since her sophomore year of high school that she was entering a school of any kind. I dropped her off on my way to work—she could take the bus home afterward—and texted her at lunch, asking how it was going.

Keisha: This is going to be so hard.

My stomach sank, but I responded with optimism and encouragement.

Shannon: You can do it. I know you can! Tomorrow will be better.

Tuesday wasn't better, though, but I had high hopes for Wednesday until she came home with a list of things she needed to buy—$1,500 of equipment, makeup, and accessories! She hadn't finished her financial aid application but had to have all her supplies by Monday.

"Maybe this is a sign that I'm not ready for this," Keisha said, flopping onto the couch and throwing the papers into the air. They fluttered down to the ground almost poetically. She threw an arm over her eyes. "It's just so much . . . stuff."

I picked up the papers and sat down in the chair, smoothing them out on my lap and reading the list of supplies included in the kit: a mannequin head, pin curl clips, blow drier, ceramic straightener, brushes, combs, foils, curlers, picks, etc., etc., etc. My eyes focused on the price at the bottom of the page again. Nine hundred and fifty dollars for the complete hair startup kit. And another $600 for the required makeup kit. Holy cow. I took a deep breath, though, and schooled my expression. "It's stuff you'll use once you're fully licensed though," I pointed out. "And it says right here that it's all top-of-line, so it will last."

Keisha took her arm off her face. "I don't have fifteen hundred dollars," she whined.

"Well, how much do you have?" I'd paid off Tagg and made the first payment for her school. She had to have saved up something in the meantime.

"I only have, like, two hundred, and now I can only work evening shifts. And the course work is *so* hard, Shannon."

Two hundred dollars? I wanted to ask why she only had that much, but it was her confidence and commitment I was the most worried about. "It's always hard to start new things, but I really think this will be a good thing. You need something to focus on, something that will build a future."

She groaned and threw her arm over her face again. I looked back at the list. "Okay, what if I buy this stuff for now, and when your financial aid comes through, you can pay me back."

She didn't answer right away and kept her arm over her eyes. Finally she sighed loudly. "I guess."

It wasn't quite the grateful answer I had hoped for, but I had to remind myself of how overwhelming my first few weeks of college were. I remembered looking over my course syllabi and thinking there was no way I could keep up. She needed a cheerleader right now, and I needed her to make this work. How else could I keep justifying all I had done? "You're going to do great, Keisha," I said, reaching over to shake her leg. "We'll get the kit and you'll get into a new groove, and eighteen months from now you'll get a job in an awesome salon and fill your pockets with cash every day."

She still didn't respond. When her phone buzzed in her pocket, however, she sat right up and pulled it out, reading the text before looking up at me. "You really think so?" she said while typing a response into her phone. I didn't know how people could carry on a verbal conversation at the same time they were texting with someone else.

"I know so," I said, still using my cheerleader voice. "I'll go order the kit right now."

"Okay," she said, putting her phone in her pocket. "I've got to go to work."

"I didn't realize you worked today," I said as I stood along with her. She still hadn't written her schedule on the calendar.

"Until midnight," she said.

"That late? You have class again in the morning."

She headed down the hall to her room. "The joys of a twenty-four–hour restaurant and being completely broke."

Less than five minutes later she was back, dressed in her uniform with her hair pulled back and wearing more makeup than usual. "Can I take your car?"

I'd hoped to meet John and Landon at Landon's practice tonight, but I'd expected Keisha to be going with me since her schedule wasn't on the calendar. "Maybe I could drop you off," I offered.

She made a face. "Then you have to pick me up at midnight. Or, well, maybe I can get a ride home from someone." She pulled her phone out of her pocket. I hated her being a burden on her coworkers, and she was already taking the bus from school, which I knew was really hard for her. I wouldn't like taking the bus either.

"It's fine," I amended, heading into the kitchen. "Let me get the keys."

After she left, I ordered her kit, having to charge it to my credit card because funds were low in our account thanks to the money I'd given her to pay off Tagg and the tuition I'd paid. I was going to have to talk to John about this one and didn't look forward to it.

When he came home, I explained about the kit.

"I wish you'd have talked to me before you paid for everything," John said, opening cupboards in search of something to eat. I hadn't made dinner, and Landon was at a friend's house. "Maybe she should have waited on school if she isn't prepared to pay for at least part of it. Why doesn't she have any money? She's been working for almost a month, hasn't she?"

I didn't know where all her money was going either, but it wasn't like waitresses made a ton, and she'd been out of work for a long time. I explained to him, much as I'd explained to Keisha, about how important it was for her to be working toward her future. He agreed.

"What can we do to get the financial aid stuff done?" John asked.

"I'm not sure, but I'll talk to her about it." Having one more thing added to my to-do list reminded me of how much other stuff was on it. I'd have suggested John help with that part if not for fear he'd look too closely at things.

"That would be good," John said, sitting down and taking off his shoes. He looked up at me and held my eyes. "Before you put more money into her school or anything, let's talk about it, okay? It wasn't that long ago that we didn't have the cushion we have right now. I don't want to blow through it."

"Of course," I said, but mentally I was adding up all the money I'd spent on Keisha since she got here. We'd done some shopping—she hadn't had much of a wardrobe when she got here, at least not an appropriate one—and she'd needed makeup and things. There was the money to Tagg, tuition, the school kits, and then the twenties I handed her here and there to cover little expenses and for gas money. All told, it added up to more than $5,000, which was a shocking number. John would freak if he knew I'd put that much toward helping her get on her feet, and yet every expense was justifiable, and most of it she would be paying back. Still, I needed to rein it in. I'd ensured she got started and now she was in school, so it was the perfect time for me to pull back and let her spread her wings. And hope that John never found out the dollar figure on this investment.

Chapter 23

KEISHA RECEIVED HER KIT AT school the next morning, and things seemed to be going well for the next week, though I was surprised at how much she was working. She'd been offered some shifts at another Denny's a few miles away—graves mostly—and though I worried she was taking on too much all at once, school and so many hours, I only had to remind myself of how much money she owed me to hand over my keys in the evenings and wish her well.

I found myself anxious when she wasn't home, though, or on the days I didn't see her in between school and work. I'd text her during the day, and if I didn't hear back from her, I'd call. She would usually text me back after that, and then I could calm down and go forward.

Book group was on April 9, and though I'd told Aunt Ruby I'd try to make it, I was secretly pleased when the Long Beach store needed someone to work four to ten o'clock that night. Aunt Ruby was disappointed, but I hadn't read the book and was still uncomfortable about my thoughts concerning Keisha and Ruby's laptop—though I had convinced myself it was ridiculous—but mostly, I was just worn out.

By the time I finished that Saturday night shift, I'd have clocked in sixty-two hours that week. Keisha had finished her second week of school, but I was still worried about her. She was working almost every day and sleeping whenever she was home. I couldn't wait up for her at night, since I was working so much too, but I'd gotten into the habit of checking on her if I woke up in the middle of the night. Sometimes she was there, but sometimes she wasn't—though she was always there by the time John and I got up the next morning.

I'd asked her about her schedule but could tell she was frustrated by my questions. She'd only paid me back $150 since school started, even though she was working more than ever.

I told myself she was saving it up to pay off a bigger chunk all at once, but in my heart of hearts I wasn't sure I believed that. She hadn't shown great ability to handle stress in the past, but as long as she was going to school—I dropped her off most mornings—and working hard, it was difficult to justify making too big a deal about my concerns. The fact was that this was real life; you had to work hard all the time to make ends meet. It was a tough lesson to learn, but everyone had to figure it out sooner or later. At least she had a stable home and a family to support her through it. That was a gift, even if she didn't recognize it.

I glanced at the pharmacy clock Saturday night and then turned my attention back to the three prescriptions I'd just filled. I was totally working out of order, but I was the only one on staff until the night pharmacist arrived in fifteen minutes, so no one would care that I was working in batches instead of one at a time. Honestly, I was running on fumes, and it was all I could do to finish out the day. Thank goodness it wasn't busy tonight. The twenty-four–hour clinic down the street kept us busy around-the-clock on most weekends, but they must be pretty quiet tonight.

I paused to make a note to the day-shift pharmacist to order more promethazine DM cough syrup before closing tomorrow; we were at half our usual stock. They'd want to make sure there was an order put in by the end of the shift tomorrow since it was cough and flu season.

I turned back to the computer but glanced up when I saw someone out of the corner of my eye. But it wasn't just a random customer, and I felt myself smile at unexpectedly seeing a friend instead.

"Tori," I said from back behind the second counter where the meds were counted and filled. She must have just come from book group, which meant she'd talked to Ruby. Gosh, did Ruby suspect Keisha and say something about it? "What are you doing here?"

She smiled, but there was a hesitation to it, a reticence to be up front with why she was here, which made me even more cautious. Still, I kept my smile in place and made sure none of my thoughts showed on my face.

"I was planning on giving you grief for no-showing tonight at book club. When I got there, I hoped you were late too so I wouldn't have to be the only miscreant in the group." The playful tone in her voice surprised me. Maybe this visit was purely social.

I teased her about being late while I finished updating the final patient record, trying to center myself so I could be more focused on our conversation. I made a final keystroke, closed the program, and came around to the front counter while asking how book group had been. I felt bad for not reading the book—she'd chosen it this month—but I could be polite about the first twenty pages if I had to.

"We had donuts for dessert," she said, shaking a paper bag at me. I was as relieved not to have to talk about the book as I was excited to eat something completely horrible for me. Maybe it would give me an excuse to run in the morning. I needed a run in the worst way.

"Any chance there's a cruller in there?" A cruller would be worth five miles, easy. I heard the front door open and looked up in time to smile at Michelle, the night pharmacist. She stopped to chat with one of the clerks, and I turned my attention back to Tori and her bag of donuts.

"Are you kidding? Any self-respecting purchaser of baked goods would get plenty of crullers. Can you eat back there, or will you get in trouble?"

"I'm actually about to turn things over to another pharmacist. Give me a few minutes to get things squared away, and I'll meet you out here."

"Sure thing," Tori said, smiling at Michelle as she came to the counter.

I signed out of the computer, hung the refills I'd finished on the rack out front, and gave Michelle the shift report. With a little luck the night would stay quiet and she'd be able to complete the inventory and update the files before the day shift came in.

Tori was sitting at the blood pressure machine when I came out from behind the counter. I had to smile. People couldn't resist a free medical test.

"Having fun?" I asked when she didn't notice I'd arrived.

She pulled her arm out of the cuff. "Sorry. Just . . . you know." She waved at the machine and shrugged.

I waved it off with a smile. "It's the most popular seat in the store. So, what's up?"

"Uh . . ." She looked around then down at the bag in her hand. If she were just bringing me a donut, she could leave now, which meant there must be something else. I wasn't nearly as reluctant to hear it now as I had been before—probably because there were baked goods involved.

"Thank you," I said, accepting the bag. I could sense she was a bit anxious about being here; maybe if we had a task to complete, we would both be more comfortable. "I need to pick up a few things. Want to tag along with me?"

"That would be great," Tori said, sounding relieved.

I reached in the bag while we headed to the front of the store for a cart—I was suddenly starving. The confection melted in my mouth, and I swear it filled me with sunshine. I was in desperate need of some sunshine.

"So . . . how was book group?" I asked when I finished chewing. I couldn't *not* bring up the book group I wasn't at—it was the reason Tori and I even knew one another.

"It was fine," Tori said, looking a little nervous. "Ruby doesn't know I'm here. But she's the reason I came."

I could feel my chest tightening in anticipation. "Oh yeah?" I tugged a grocery cart out of where it was nested with the others. I prepared how best to handle this if what Tori said was about Keisha.

"Well, kind of. And Ilana."

"Ilana?" I said, leaning forward to take a bottle of nail polish remover off the shelf and hoping the movement covered my surprise and relief.

Tori took a breath before she explained. "Ilana was acting strange tonight. I probably wouldn't have thought much of it, except that when she went to the bathroom, she didn't use the main one—she went upstairs, I could see her from where I was sitting. She was gone for a while and when she came back, she seemed different. Calm."

I'd stopped shopping at this point and was leaning on my cart, visualizing the scene Tori was setting for me. She continued, "After a bit, I excused myself as well and went upstairs; I guess Ruby's room is up there."

I nodded, even though I knew Ruby didn't sleep in the master bedroom because she didn't like to climb the stairs all the time. But Tori didn't need to know that.

"The light in the master bathroom was on," Tori continued, "and when I looked around to try to figure out why Ilana would have come up there, I found this on the floor. I thought maybe you could identify it for me." She opened her hand so I could see the small white pill with 512 stamped on one side.

"Mallincrodt oxycodone," I said automatically. I'd used the specific generic name most Medicare users—Ruby included—would get in place of the brand name. "Percocet," I amended.

Tori stared at the pill in her hand and took a breath before looking up at me. "It's possible that Ruby just left the cabinet open and dropped this pill, right? It's possible that it wasn't Ilana who dropped it at all."

"Possible . . ." I said, taking the pill from Tori and turning it over in my hand. "But Ruby never takes anything that isn't absolutely necessary." And she didn't use that bathroom. *And* the last time she'd filled a script for Percocet was about a year ago, after having some dental work done.

"Maybe Ilana has her own prescription," Tori said, sounding desperate for an explanation. "Is that what you're thinking?"

"But why use Aunt Ruby's private bathroom for that? And a private bathroom on a different floor than the guest bath," I said, switching into devil's advocate for a minute.

Tori let out a breath. "Right. She just seems too classy for this sort of thing. Ilana isn't the type."

"Everybody is the type. I've seen some really fabulous doctors and other pharmacists destroy their lives and families because they thought they weren't the type." I said the words automatically; I talked about *prescription* drug addiction and abuse all the time, and yet, in the wake of what had been happening with Keisha lately, the words hit home in a different way.

"What should we do?"

Such a question. "The first step is trying to make sure we're right about this. If we're not, it could be devastating to confront her about it."

"Okay," Tori said, nodding. "Good point. How can we find out?"

I shrugged. "Spend time with her, ask her how things are going since her surgery."

Tori was thoughtful for a few moments. "I need to get a birthday gift for my mom. Maybe I could invite Ilana to go shopping with me."

"That's a good idea," I said. "Do you mind letting me know how it goes? Maybe I could invite her to lunch or something." When was the last time I had "lunch" with anyone? I barely knew Ilana, hadn't ever even had a one-on-one conversation with her. But I could see how plausible Tori's concerns were. If Ilana was already struggling with family planning, got injured, lost her job, and found that pain meds made all the pain, sadness, stress, and worry go away for a little while . . . who *wouldn't* want the pain to disappear? But stealing meds was a sign that things were out of control.

"Do you think we should talk to Ruby?" Tori asked, then smiled slightly. "And by 'we' I mean you."

I smiled back but felt frozen by the thought. There was so much between Aunt Ruby and me right now, even if Ruby didn't know all of it. But I couldn't say no to Tori, not without admitting what was going on. "Sure," I said.

Tori reached over and gave me a quick hug that I feared I returned rather awkwardly. Gosh, I missed having friends.

Tori pulled back. "Thank you so much. I knew you would be the right person to talk to. I'll let you know how things go. Can I get your cell number?"

We traded cell phone numbers, and she hugged me again before she left. When was the last time I'd had a girlfriend?

I drove home feeling depressed and a little overwhelmed by Ilana's situation. I hoped Tori was wrong about the pills, that Ruby had had a toothache and had dropped the pill herself, but I knew that wasn't likely. Maybe I *could* talk to Aunt Ruby. Maybe if I opened up some other discussions, I could feel more comfortable with her again.

At a stoplight I texted Keisha and asked her how she was doing—she was working late tonight but was getting a ride home. I wasn't sure which Denny's she was at or I might have stopped by to say hi. She texted back almost immediately; I must have caught her while she was on break. I read it at the next intersection.

Keisha: I'm great! Love you.

I smiled to myself as I put the phone away and noted how much better I felt with such a positive answer. She hadn't said she was okay or good— she was *great*! I wished Ilana the best and hoped Tori would be able to help, if help was needed, but I didn't have room to put myself into that situation. Family would always be more important than friends. I was doing what I could to hold mine together, and I couldn't afford to lose my focus now.

Chapter 24

JOHN WAS STILL UP WHEN I got home, which surprised me since it was after eleven and he rarely stayed up that late.

"Hey," I said, hanging up my purse and keys as I entered the kitchen. As I moved toward him, I could see that the expression on his face was tight, checked. I slowed down.

He got right to the point. "I talked to Stan about that cruise, and his wife found some good deals for us, so I went online to transfer some money into our checking account in order to put down a deposit."

I held my breath, but inside I started to panic.

"Did you pay Keisha's tuition?"

It was ridiculous to be relieved, but I was. He wasn't asking about my payoff to Tagg.

"And withdraw $1,600 in cash a few days before that?"

Oh no.

"What's going on?"

"Uh," I said, pausing to clear my throat, which meant I could go to the cupboard and get a glass so I could get a drink—all in order to stall a little longer. I felt John watching me every step of the way as I filled the glass and drank half of it. He didn't say a word, just looked at me. Watching me. Waiting.

Finally, nearly a minute after he'd asked me the question, I put the glass in the sink and looked up at him. "She just didn't have the money for the tuition, John, but she had to start school, she had to start working on her future. She's going to pay me back."

"And the cash?"

"Uh," I searched my mind for an answer, knowing there was no way I could tell him the truth about that money—not when things were so confrontational. Wait, the school kit was fifteen hundred dollars. Close enough. "The school kit," I said quickly, instantly relieved to have an excuse.

"The school kit," he repeated, but he cocked his head to the side and continued to stare at me. There was something wrong with that look.

I nodded but held my breath.

"I checked out the credit card balance while I was online. The school kit was charged to our credit card after she started school—you told me about it right after you ordered it. The cash was taken out weeks before school even started."

A heat wave washed over me, and I stared into the sink as my ears started ringing. This couldn't be happening, and yet I'd known it was inevitable. I didn't lie often enough to do it well.

"The cash was taken out in the middle of the day," John said, the anger finally emerging in his voice. "You would have been at work, and you *never* take cash out."

I lifted my eyes to meet his. Where was this going?

"Did Keisha steal your debit card?"

"What?"

"And you're covering for her? What the heck is going on, Shannon? Why would you do that?"

I was completely trapped and stuttered over my words. "I . . . I . . . "

"She's gone, Shannon," John said, standing up from the barstool. "I'm not going to put up with this."

"Gone? What do you mean gone?" Had he kicked her out already? Without even telling me?

"I mean that we made that contract for a reason, and she broke it and you covered for her. I'm going to wait up for her tonight and then she's got three days, just like we agreed."

I ran around the counter, relieved he hadn't kicked her out already but overwhelmed by what he was saying. "We can't do that, John, not now. She's in school; she's working hard."

"She's a thief!" John shouted and pointed his finger in my face. "And you're protecting her."

"She's not a thief," I said, though I instantly remembered Aunt Ruby's laptop. I pushed the thought away. "*I* took that money out of the account."

John lowered his finger but his eyes narrowed. "Why?" He didn't believe me.

I looked at the floor and wished it would swallow me—and Keisha too. "I paid off a dealer," I said, so quiet it was barely a whisper.

I think he heard me, but he said "What?" anyway.

"She owed a dealer some money, and he was harassing her and . . . propositioning her. So I paid it."

He was quiet. Oh, so quiet. I continued to stare at the floor. After several miserable seconds, I looked up and tried to read the expression on his face—anger, definitely, but he also looked sad, and that was surprisingly harder to see.

"Why didn't you tell me any of this?" he asked, his voice at a normal level.

I wished I had a reasonable answer to that question.

My attempt to explain was paltry in the wake of his shock at what I had done, and I could see that he was overwhelmed by it. And yet, I hadn't told him everything. Explaining the money part was horrible, and I knew it hurt him so much—how could I also tell him about the night Keisha didn't come home, and the time she'd left work to go drinking? I should have told him, I knew I should have, but things were so intense. It killed me to see him so hurt.

It was nearly midnight before he scrubbed his hand over his face and said he was going to bed. He didn't ask if I was joining him, and I didn't follow him down the hall because I was afraid he'd want to talk some more, and I didn't know how to handle that. When the door to the bedroom shut behind him, I put my elbows onto the kitchen counter and dropped my head into my hands. I had never felt so small, and yet I still hadn't told him everything. I felt terrible and asked myself why I was doing any of this. Why was I working so hard to protect Keisha?

I expected Keisha home by twelve thirty, but she didn't come. I texted her, but she didn't text back. I waited up until I was sick to my stomach, I was so tired. The night had completely worn me out; I had nothing left. Where was she? Why wasn't she returning my text messages? How would I deal with her tomorrow?

At two thirty I couldn't keep my eyes open and so I went to bed, undressing quietly as though I thought John was asleep. I slid carefully between the sheets with my back toward my husband.

"Is she home?" he asked in the dark.

I took a breath. "Not yet. She probably had to work later."

He didn't answer me. He didn't have to. I knew what he thought and clenched my eyes closed, praying he was wrong. He hadn't said anything about the contract after I'd explained what happened with the money—there wasn't anything in the contract against Keisha borrowing money—but he was keeping score all the same.

Please come home, I begged the walls and the heavens and anything else that might listen and help Keisha get home. *Please, please, please come home.*

Chapter 25

AT THREE THIRTY I HEARD something and got up to see what it was. I peeked in the hallway in time to see Keisha's bedroom door shut. I let out a breath I feared I'd been holding for hours. She was home. She was safe. Everything else could be dealt with in the morning.

She slept all morning, but I kept checking in on her to make sure she was there, and though John didn't say anything, I knew he was watching too. Finally, around noon he asked me what time she came in. It was so tempting to lie to him, but I didn't. "About three thirty."

I braced myself for his response, but he just nodded and went out to the garage.

Landon was working on a school project at the kitchen table and had watched the exchange but didn't say anything until John left. "Keisha came home at three o'clock in the morning?" he asked.

"Yeah," I said, opening the fridge to find something for lunch. This was my first day off this week, and I found myself wishing I was working. I hated this tension.

"If I did that, you'd kill me," Landon said.

"You're twelve years old," I reminded him, pulling out the fixings for some turkey sandwiches.

"Even if I were thirty, you'd kill me."

I clenched my jaw, annoyed with his comment.

I thought John was cleaning the garage—I could understand the need to burn off his stress—until he came inside with a list he put on the table in front of me. I scanned it in confusion and looked up at him.

"Have you seen any of these things?" he asked.

I looked back at the list.

Impact driver drill—Makita
Hand sander—Dewalt
Golf clubs with drivers

When I didn't say anything—I feared I knew where this was going—he asked again if I'd seen them.

"Mom hates golf," Landon said, glancing over the list before looking up at his dad.

"I don't think Mom took them," John said, taking back the list. "I think Keisha did."

"John!" I couldn't believe he would say that in front of Landon.

"Keisha golfs?" Landon said, looking confused.

John looked at me while he answered our son. "I think Keisha sold them to get money for drugs."

I pushed out from the table and stood quickly while glaring at John. "Stop it."

"It's the truth."

"It's not the truth. Where is this even coming from?" I stopped, suddenly mindful of our audience. "Can we talk about this in the bedroom, please?"

"Sure," he said, oozing confidence. I smiled weakly at Landon and then followed John down the hall, closing the door behind me.

"Those things are missing," he defended, keeping his voice low.

"So maybe they're at your dad's house," I said, staring him down. "You take stuff back and forth all the time."

"And maybe Keisha stole them and pawned them."

"My gosh, are you listening to yourself? This is why I didn't tell you, John, because you overreact and look for the worst."

He shook the list at me. "Why would I take my clubs to my dad's?"

"Why would Keisha steal them?" I countered. "She has a job."

"And yet has only paid you back a couple hundred dollars of the money she owes you. Where's the money going, Shannon? She's using again—can't you see that? That's why she's been acting different, why she's gone so much. I bet she isn't going to work all these nights she's gone."

I blinked. I had wondered myself where her money was going, but I wasn't going to accuse Keisha of using again. Not after how hard I had worked to create a successful environment for her. "You're taking this too far," I said. "You're looking for reasons to accuse her of this, and you have no proof at all."

He shook his head; I had to look away from the disappointment on his face. "I'm taking Landon to my folks, but when I get back later tonight, the three of us—you, me, and Keisha—are going to sit down and talk."

My mind was spinning. "Can we wait until you're not so upset?"

He glared. "Why do you think I'm going to my parents?"

Chapter 26

KEISHA DIDN'T GET UP UNTIL after four, and when she came out of her room, I looked at her differently, noting that her eyes looked bigger on her face due to the fact that her face was so thin, like the rest of her. I could tell she didn't feel well, and as much as I scrambled for another excuse, John's accusations were too fresh in my mind for me to ignore. Was she really using again? It broke my heart to consider it. What more could we do to help her?

I decided to preempt John's meeting by confronting her myself. She didn't take it well.

"Of course he thinks I'm using," she said, pinching off a corner of the piece of toast she'd made for her breakfast-lunch-dinner. "He always assumes the worst." She looked up at me. "And you hadn't told him about paying for my school?"

The accusation was not subtle—it was my fault he was surprised by the expenses, thus triggering his fears.

"And I didn't know you hadn't talked to him about paying Tagg off. I thought he knew."

A second stab, and I didn't know how to defend myself against either one. I'd never told her I was keeping those things from my husband; of course she'd assume he was in the loop. And if I had told him those things, none of this would have happened. "I'm sorry," I said, but hearing myself apologizing to her after everything I'd done for her was a bit of a shock, one that didn't sit well with me. "I've done everything I've done to help you, Keisha."

"By getting me in trouble with my dad?"

I stared at her for a few seconds. She went back to her toast.

"Keisha," I said. She didn't look at me. "Keisha," I said again.

She finally looked up, but her expression was annoyed.

"You *are* using again, aren't you?"

"You know what, I don't have to put up with this," she said, pushing her toast away and standing up. "I can go somewhere else, ya know. If you guys want to go ahead and think the worst of me, I can leave."

"I'm not asking you to leave—I'm asking if you're using."

"So you can make me leave," Keisha said, heading toward her bedroom. "I knew you guys didn't want me here. I knew it."

"Keisha," I said sharply, following her to her room. She tried to shut the door, but I put out my hand and stopped it, leaving a space where the two of us faced off with one another. "I am not trying to kick you out, but I need to know if you're using. If you are, we need to deal with it. I just need you to be honest with me."

She stared at me for a few seconds, then let go of the door and raised a hand to her eyes. "I'm trying so hard," she said in a soft, shaky voice. "I really am, Shannon, but it's never good enough, is it? What's wrong with me?"

I pushed the door the rest of the way open and pulled her into a hug as she crumbled, crying into my shoulder. "He's going to kick me out; you know he will."

"Maybe not," I said, smoothing her hair and trying to calm her down. "But we have to be honest." I did not miss the hypocrisy of my words. "We'll sit down with him tonight, and we'll tell him everything, okay? All the stuff we should have told him sooner."

"He'll make me leave," she said again into my shoulder.

"It's my house too," I reminded her. "And he wants you to be well as much as I do. We just need to reassess things, that's all. We'll figure this out."

As the time for John's return got closer, Keisha's anxiety grew stronger. She said she was supposed to work tonight, but I demanded she call in—this was more important. She didn't want to, we argued about it, she said she'd be fired, but I held my ground, knowing that this discussion with John would be a defining moment for all of us. He needed to see that we'd both made it a priority. In the end, she took her phone into her room and closed the door while I threw together a roasted tomato soup for dinner and set out some frozen rolls to thaw.

John and Landon returned at seven o'clock. Landon must have already been given instructions, because he went straight to his room with barely a smile in my direction. I heard the door snap closed and turned to face John.

"I made dinner."

"I want to get this over with."

I bit back my argument, well aware of the part my actions played in this situation, and went down the hall to Keisha's room. I lifted my hand to knock and took a deep breath, centering myself and trying to remain calm. I knocked and waited for her to open the door, but several seconds passed. I knocked again and listened closely for movement. I heard nothing and was beginning to feel annoyed, thinking she'd fallen asleep, when the worst-case scenario entered my mind. She'd threatened suicide before. I turned the knob, but the door was locked. I ran for my room and grabbed a bobby pin that would help me trip the thumb lock.

"What's going on?" John asked, entering the hallway.

I ran past him on my way back to her room.

"She's not opening the door," I said, jamming the curved end of the bobby pin into the door while jiggling the handle. "It's locked." Right then, however, the knob turned in my hand and I threw the door open. John entered with me, both of us scanning the disaster area of her room, the bed, the closet, looking for her. It took several seconds for my heart to slow down and my brain to admit she wasn't there.

"She's gone," John said, standing by one of the two windows that faced the back of the house. The window was closed, but the blind had been pulled all the way up, and as I approached, I could see the screen lying against the outside of the house. I stared at it and then closed my eyes, pressing one hand over my stomach and bringing the other one up to cover my eyes. I felt dizzy. Sick. I felt John's hand on my arm, but I pulled away and left the room.

"I need a few minutes," I said, going into our bedroom and shutting the door behind me. I sat on the bed and took deep breaths while trying to understand what had just happened. She'd left because she felt sure she'd be kicked out once John knew the truth. Where would she go? Would she come back?

Please come home, I said in my mind over and over again. I'd said this prayer before. *Please, please, please come home.*

Chapter 27

JOHN DIDN'T CORNER ME, WHICH was a good thing since I felt very, very frail. I called and texted Keisha half a dozen times, begging her to just make contact. She didn't. At midnight, I had to take a sleeping pill to fall asleep, a silent John beside me. I knew he didn't know what to do and I didn't know what to ask him to do, so we simply circled one another, not wanting to make anything worse and certain that the other was in no position to make things better.

I had to go to work the next morning, but I texted Keisha as soon as I pulled up to the Fountain Valley store. I waited for a response all day, the familiar fear building in my chest by the minute. Was she with Jessica again?

I thought about calling her school, but what would I say? "Hi, I'm checking up on my twenty-one-year-old daughter—is she in class?" I didn't want to embarrass her or damage her reputation with her instructors. I told myself that maybe she just needed a day to get a hold of herself. She'd come back; I was sure of it. Hadn't I promised her we'd make something work?

I got home from work a little after six. Keisha wasn't home, and it didn't look as though she'd been home all day. I didn't know what to do, so I did nothing.

John had a late job in Aliso Viejo, so Landon and I ran some errands and then he worked on a school project—a PowerPoint about the circulatory system. We both knew I would be no help on a techy project like that. Once he was occupied, I went to Keisha's room, standing in the doorway for several minutes before walking into her space.

Her room was a mess. Clothes I'd recently bought for her were piled everywhere, with very few hanging on hangers in the closet. The paperwork from school was stacked haphazardly on one end of the dresser; an assortment of makeup was scattered on the other end. There were dishes here and there, despite our rule about not having food in the bedrooms, and all types of miscellaneous papers were strewn about.

I started with her clothes, picking them up and determining if they were clean or dirty. I hung the clean ones up and threw the dirty ones in the hamper, as though I believed a clean room would bring her home. I didn't know why I was doing this—maybe to keep myself busy, maybe so that when Keisha came home she'd feel guilty for the extra things I did for her. Maybe I was doing it because it was the only thing I *could* do.

When I finished with the clothing, I straightened the dresser top, and then I started picking up the garbage—a to-do list here, a receipt there. I glanced at each piece before throwing it away to make sure it wasn't anything important. I didn't throw out her pay stubs or her receipts for school supplies. And then I picked up a piece of paper that made my heart stop as key elements jumped out at me.

JJ's Pawnshop
One laptop computer. $300 pawn. Sell immediately.
$400 to reclaim within 30 days if item doesn't sell.

I sat down slowly on the edge of her unmade bed and stared at the receipt. There was no point in playing dumb with myself anymore. I'd been pushing away the suspicion since the first time I'd talked to Aunt Ruby about the missing computer. By the time I remembered to blink, my eyes were burning.

Keisha had pawned Aunt Ruby's laptop.

It was more than that though. Keisha had taken the code and the key from where I'd put them—trusting they were safe in my home—and had broken into Aunt Ruby's house, searched until she found something quick to sell, tried to break into the safe, and then used Aunt Ruby's financial information to steal more than a thousand dollars from Aunt Ruby's accounts. Keisha had used me. She'd robbed Aunt Ruby. I looked at the date on the receipt—it was a couple of days *after* I'd given her the cash to pay off Tagg.

My hands started to shake, and I dropped the receipt and the trash can I'd been carrying with me around the room, spilling everything I'd worked so hard to clean up all over the floor. I put my hands over my face as though I could hide from this. This wasn't happening. It *couldn't* be happening because I didn't know what to do about it. I'd risked my marriage and my own sense of integrity to do what I felt I had to do to help her. And yet it had all been a game, a smokescreen.

I don't know how long I sat there, but I finally stood up, turned off the light, and closed the door behind me. I put Landon to bed and took another sleeping pill in hopes I'd be asleep before John got home—I couldn't talk to him right now. It was all too much to process. My stomach knotted every time I thought about Aunt Ruby. How would I tell her what Keisha had done? She'd be devastated.

I woke up late and had to hurry through my morning routine. John was rushing too and said he'd drop off Landon on his way to the shop. I wondered if John was avoiding me the same way I was avoiding him. What would I say when I had to talk to him? I was so embarrassed.

The empty house beckoned me to stay in it, curl up under the covers, and spend the day sorting through my thoughts. My thoughts were not good company, however, so I went to work and let it absorb me.

I texted Keisha half a dozen times throughout the day, and when I called to check on Landon after he got home from school, he confirmed she wasn't there. Instead of going straight home after work, I went to the Denny's where she worked.

I pushed through the glass doors, and a young woman asked me if I wanted a table for one.

"I'm actually looking for an employee. Is Keisha Griffiths working tonight, by chance?"

"Keisha?" the girl said with an unusual amount of surprise in her voice. "No, she doesn't work here anymore."

They'd fired her already? "Do you know if she left a forwarding address or phone number for her last paycheck or anything? I'm her stepmom, and I'm having a hard time finding her."

"Uh, let me get the manager."

She returned with a very tall, lanky Hispanic man who put out his hand and introduced himself as Juan. He invited me back to his office, which I didn't find very comforting. In his office, which was tiny, he invited me to sit in one of the chairs that matched those out in the dining room and asked what I needed. I repeated that was trying to find Keisha.

"I'm her stepmom, and I haven't seen her for a couple of days. The hostess said she'd already been fired. Was she scheduled to work today?"

"Keisha was fired weeks ago."

"Weeks?"

He nodded.

"Why?"

He paused, and I repeated in my mind the labor laws I knew backward and forward. "Please, I just need to know where to start looking." She'd said she was filling in at another Denny's and that she was working a *crazy* amount of hours in hopes of paying me back. I'd never doubted her enough to check her facts.

"She left in the middle of her shift a few weeks ago and came back with alcohol on her breath," Juan said after a few moments. "It was her third offense. I had no choice."

I remembered the night—Keisha had said Tagg had sent someone to proposition her about repaying the money she owed him. "Third?"

"I had no choice," Juan repeated, his tone surprisingly gentle.

I started to cry and wiped at my eyes, then smiled gratefully as he handed me a napkin. "I'm sorry," I said, feeling humiliated as I stood. "But thank you for letting me know."

"You're welcome. I hope she can get some help."

I thought that's what I'd been doing—helping her. What had I *really* been doing?

I was in the driver's seat with the engine on and the seat belt stretched across my chest before I allowed myself to admit what all these things meant. Keisha had been lying to me for a long time. She'd thrown her fit about not being able to pay off Tagg knowing full well she didn't have a job to pay me back. Had she even owed him money at all? Then she'd pretended to work for weeks after that. She'd completely played me, and yet the anger I knew I should feel didn't come. I needed to talk to her. I needed to understand her intent.

There was only one answer, of course: her addiction was spiraling to the point where it was controlling her, rather than her having any control over it. Where would it take her before it spit her out, used up and desolate? Where was she right now? Was she okay?

If John had been home when I walked in, I couldn't have hidden my feelings from him a second longer, but he and Landon were at a game. They hadn't even bothered to ask if I was going to go because I hadn't gone to one of Landon's games in nearly a month. I had the house to myself and was so exhausted that I reheated the tomato soup from the other night, ate it without tasting it, and then went to bed. I heard John come in just after nine but pretended to be asleep, putting off for just one more night what I knew I couldn't run away from for much longer.

Come home, I begged in my mind again, thinking of Keisha. *Just come home and give me one more chance.*

But a chance for what? I didn't even know anymore.

Chapter 28

THE RAWNESS FROM THE NIGHT before had scabbed over by morning, and I managed to send John off for work with just a minimal conversation about him having talked to Dani—she hadn't heard from Keisha—and my finding out Keisha had been fired. We had a lot to talk about now that I'd run out of reasons not to tell him everything, but he had a big day and I didn't want him distracted from his work. When we talked, we needed to really *talk*, and that wasn't going to happen amid a rushed morning of getting lunches packed and shoes found and tools loaded into his truck.

When I called Keisha's phone on my lunch break, it went straight to voice mail, which I took to mean that the battery was dead. I called the cell phone company to see about tracking the phone, but the GPS app we'd put on her phone when we bought it had been disabled. I called her school and learned she'd attended the first four days, then never came back. The receptionist thought Keisha had sold the $1,500 supply kit I'd ordered to another student. I requested a refund of Keisha's tuition, minus the twenty percent nonrefundable portion. They said the check had to be in Keisha's name, but it would be waiting for her to pick up Monday morning.

I texted her again, asking her to please just let me know she was okay. No response.

Aunt Ruby called and left a message about the next book for book group. It was *Zen and the Art of Motorcycle Maintenance*, the book Gabriel had given her. I wondered what was happening between her and this man. I'd only talked to her that one time since the morning at her house when we talked about Uncle Phillip. Did she think she'd run me off by confiding about Uncle Phillip's philandering? I felt horrible and hollow when I thought of her and the good she'd done for me all my life. How could I tell her that Keisha had robbed her? And yet, that feeling was tempered with the thought of how desperate Keisha must have been to steal from Aunt Ruby in the first place. My poor girl was so broken. Did she even know what she was doing when she'd done these things to us? Did she have the ability to comprehend the choices she made?

I got through my shift, but just barely. I was exhausted. In the parking lot I started the car and took a breath. I needed to tell John everything before he found out for himself, but the idea made me cold. He would be so angry with me. And yet I still blamed him for parts of this mess. If he was more approachable . . .

I parked in the garage and took longer than usual to gather my things. Before walking inside the house, I said a prayer in my head and just asked that we could get through this.

"Hey," I called out, after letting myself in from the garage. I put my purse on the counter and hung up my keys on the rack where Aunt Ruby's key no longer hung. I heard John come into the kitchen and turned to him with a careful smile that quickly fell when I saw the look on his face. "What's wrong?" I asked, a hundred scenarios rushing through my head, all of them centered on his daughter. "Keisha?" Had he heard from her? Had she called him and not me? Was she okay?

His eyes narrowed ever so slightly at the mention of her name, and it made me pull back. Not Keisha. In fact, the sound of her name made him angry. No, the sound of her name made him *angrier*. He raised his hand, holding a piece of paper I recognized as the pawn shop receipt I'd found two nights ago and dropped on Keisha's bedroom floor. My eyes moved from his hand to his eyes, hard, cold, and very angry.

"I was going to tell you," I said.

"What is going on, Shannon? And don't you dare leave anything out."

Chapter 29

I TOOK A BREATH AND explained the basics of what had been happening behind his back these last several weeks: Keisha not coming home on time, her admission that she'd used, my covering for her and then finding the receipt in her room. He listened in silence. I finished with a teary apology, and then we just stood there for several seconds, John leaning against the doorway, and me standing in the middle of the kitchen. The island served as a barrier between us, as though we needed a physical reminder of the distance that seemed to have grown between us with every word I'd said. As the seconds ticked by following my explanation, I tensed. Would he yell? Would he hold his arms out for me?

Oh, please hold your arms out. Please forgive me for all of this.

"When did you realize she stole Ruby's laptop?"

"Two nights ago," I said.

"And when did you find the drugs?"

I looked up at him. "I didn't find any drugs." He cocked his head slightly. He didn't believe me. "Did *you* find drugs?"

"Yes, Shannon, I did. I found a baggie of pills in her room—the room right next to our son's room. You're surprised?"

I looked at the floor and wrapped my arms across my waist. "I didn't know, John."

"You didn't?"

I met his eyes. "Of course I didn't. I wouldn't let her use drugs in our house. I had no idea she had any here."

"But you were fine lying for her about other things and covering her tracks. Do you even understand what you did? You made that contract null and void. You hid things from me—your husband and her father. Why would you think that could possibly be a good thing? You enabled her."

It was like being shot through the chest to hear his accusations. Did I bear responsibility for what she'd done? Why was there something satisfying about that idea? If I shared the blame, then maybe it wasn't all her weakness. If I shared the blame, than maybe fixing *my* mistakes could help her. Was that possible?

"You need to tell Ruby."

My breath caught in my throat, and I closed my eyes. "I can't do that," I said after a few miserable seconds. I looked up at John, then to the single receipt in his hand. "I'll go to the pawn shop and buy it back."

John tightened his fist on the paper and shook his head. "No, you won't. You'll take this to Ruby, who will give it to the police and press charges."

"No!" I said, louder than I meant to. I glanced toward Landon's door and lowered my voice. "Where's Landon?"

"Oh, so *now* you're going to think about your son?"

"John," I said, a sob in my voice.

"Landon's at Jeffrey's house. You need to tell Ruby."

"No, John. Not like that. Let me talk to Keisha first and then—"

"Are you listening to yourself?" John said, shaking his head and holding up the receipt again. "She broke into Ruby's house and stole from her. Don't you see what that means? It means she's a criminal, Shannon, and that she's willing to use the people who care about her the most to get whatever fix it is she needs. She's used you, she's used me, and she's used Ruby. Can you not see how horrible this is?"

"It is horrible," I said, "and I do understand. But you're talking about possibly sending her to jail. She's your *daughter*."

"I'm talking about accountability, which is probably the only thing left that will save her."

I shook my head, overwhelmed by the very idea. Had he no compassion for the battle she was fighting?

"And I'm changing the locks in the morning."

"John," I said, a sob shaking my words. This was why I had kept things from him. He was proving me right for doing what I'd done.

"She's not welcome here anymore," John continued, straightening in the doorway. "I won't have her here again."

Anger shot through me like a bullet. "She's not Dani, John. You can't just walk away from her."

Fire lit up his whole face at the sound of his ex-wife's name—his first wife, the woman he'd vowed to share a lifetime with, who had completely broken his heart. He'd always blamed Dani's addictions for the breakdown of their marriage, always harbored anger for her lack of control, which had ruined everything they had tried to build together. But I'd never thrown that in his face before, and he was not ready to hear it.

He walked toward me but stopped a foot away, waiting until I looked up at him. "She's not Dani," he said, low and angry. "But because of Dani I have been down this road before, Shannon, and I will not do it again. I don't know why you can't see the big picture here, and I obviously can't make you see the truth, but I can decide who comes into my house, and she is not welcome here. I'm going to pick up Landon."

He held my eyes for another moment, then stormed into the garage, leaving me, shaking, in the middle of the kitchen, repeating his ultimatum in my head and wondering how he could be so cruel.

Chapter 30

THE NEXT MORNING, I WOKE up to the alarm in a daze, replaying the night over and over again, wishing I could believe it was a dream. The tension radiating from John when he got up and headed into the bathroom to take a shower was intense and convinced me that it had all been real. I tried to keep my distance by getting breakfast for Landon—cereal. I hadn't made him pancakes in over a month.

I worked at eight, and I thought John and I would maintain our dancing around one another until Landon ran out the front door for school. I turned to find John standing in the kitchen, putting his phone into his pocket. "I'm meeting a locksmith here at two o'clock. When do you get off? Six?"

"John, please don't do this."

"You need to talk to Ruby."

My stomach sank. He stared at me, holding my eyes for several seconds. "I texted Keisha and told her not to come back. I'll be cancelling her phone in a couple of days. She can call if she wants to talk about this, but she's not living here again."

Tears filled my eyes, and all the times Keisha had said how much she appreciated being here—how comfortable she'd been—flooded my brain. I thought about the conversation she and John had had just a few weeks ago, when she told him about how excited she was about school. Yet she'd already stolen the laptop by then; she'd been fired by then too.

I looked at the floor and heard him come closer to me. I thought maybe he was going to raise my chin and tell me he loved me and that we would get through this. I should apologize for bringing Dani into our fight last night—that was cruel of me. But he just stood there, then moved past me and out the front door without saying a word. I stayed where I was, a tornado of thoughts and feelings spinning around in my head. I texted Keisha again, stared at my phone for a full minute in hopes of a response, then took a breath and faced the day.

I feared the hours would drag by, but they moved at record speed, which was actually worse. I checked my phone every half hour, waiting for Keisha to contact me. I almost wished she'd been in an accident because that at least would be a valid excuse for her not coming home. On my lunch break I called hospitals. I got a text from John around four o'clock.

John: Locks changed. New key under front mat. We're off to practice.

I let myself into an empty house a couple of hours later with a shiny new key and immediately checked the caller ID to see if Keisha had called the house. She hadn't. I wondered what John had told Landon, and I wondered if Keisha would ever sleep in her room again. Would John *ever* let her return? Would John and I ever get back to who we'd been before I begged him to pick Keisha up in Compton?

When they got home, he asked if I'd talked to Ruby yet.

I clenched my jaw shut, which he took as an answer.

Landon was looking between the two of us, his expression cautious and confused. I continued to face off with John for a few more seconds, then turned away from both of them and headed to our room. I sat on the edge of the bed and gripped the edge of the mattress, rocking slightly back and forth while trying, and failing, to make sense of all of this. After a while, I changed into my pajamas and crawled into bed, wanting more than anything to just sleep and forget. I didn't understand what was happening, and I didn't know what to do about it. And I was so scared for Keisha.

I pretended to be asleep when John came in, but he called my bluff. "You're really going to keep defending her?" he said. I stared at the wall while he got undressed. "This is sick, Shannon."

"Your daughter's sick," I said without looking at him. "And she's so desperate for help that she'll use drugs to make her feel okay. She needs help."

"What help have we not offered?" John asked, his voice rising. "What more could we possibly do?"

I still wouldn't turn to face him. "You could have spent more time with her. You could have gone to a single NA meeting with her. You could have made her feel important."

"So this is my fault? You'll put the responsibility for what *she's* done on me, but not on her? How can that possibly make sense to you?"

"You're not even listening to me," I said, finally sitting up and looking at him and letting my anger filter through. "She's sick, John. She can't think clearly. It's like . . . it's like a diabetic not having insulin, or a cancer patient not being able to get chemo. She can't get better until her head is right and she—"

"She won't *get* her head right," John shouted, throwing out his arms. "You got her a therapist, you took her to meetings, you talked to her and coddled her and got her enrolled in school. She had every chance to get her head right, and she chose not to do it. She chose to put us and *our son* at risk instead. She *chose* not to get help, Shannon!"

"She doesn't know how to help herself!" I shot back, my fingers clenching the bedspread. "Maybe it will take another try, maybe it will take six more tries, but she is *not* well, John. You judge her as though she is purposely trying to hurt us, and she isn't."

He clenched his hands at his sides and groaned so low and loud it was almost a scream. His face was red and his jaw tight. "I can't talk about this anymore," he said, suddenly pulling open a drawer and grabbing some pajama pants and a T-shirt. "I'll sleep on the couch."

"Fine by me," I said, lying back down and pulling the covers up to my chin. He didn't say anything but slammed the door on his way out. I heard muted voices in the hall and knew he was talking to Landon, who had to have heard the argument. I clenched my eyes shut and pulled the pillow up around my ears. I hadn't had more than a passing conversation with Landon in who knew how long, and yet it felt like he and John were on one side, and Keisha and I were on the other. Except that I was fighting by myself.

I wanted to scream and yell and cry and beg and grovel. But to whom? And for what?

Chapter 31

IT TOOK ALL MY ENERGY to put on a happy face when Landon got up Friday morning. John had to leave early, and I had the day off. Landon asked me what was wrong as though he didn't know what was going on in his own home. Still, I appreciated him not jumping right into the topic of his sister. "I'm not feeling well," I said, which wasn't necessarily a lie. I got a box of cereal out of the cupboard.

"What feels sick?" he asked. It was the question I always asked him when he was sick, an attempt to identify whether he was dealing with something bacterial, which could be treated, or viral, which had to be waited out. I feared my problems were the viral kind—I had no control.

"Everything feels sick," I said, sitting across from him and sipping my morning tea. He looked concerned, and I reached over to ruffle his hair. He needed a haircut. "But I'll be okay. I just need to rest."

"So you can't come to my game tonight?"

It took me a moment to remember that today was April 15—his first lacrosse game of the season. I was totally out of the loop on his schedule. I smiled even though I didn't really want to go. "I'm hoping that if I rest all day I'll be able to make it." I'd missed every practice of the season so far in order to attend NA meetings with Keisha, or because the meetings had been the night before and I had other things to catch up on. Sure, there were plenty of parents who didn't attend practice, but until now I hadn't been one of them. Until Keisha had moved in, Landon and his activities were at the top of my list. Where were they now?

After getting Landon off to school, I tried to go for a run for the first time in several weeks, but my legs felt like logs, and I turned around after a mile and walked back. I wondered how ugly things were going to get between John and me. What could I have done differently? What *couldn't* I have done differently was a better question. I texted Keisha twice. No response.

I did get some sleep in the afternoon, but my head and heart were still heavy when I woke up just before Landon came home. I had an idea in my head that we'd make cookies, or watch a movie together, but he had already planned to go to Kenny's house to practice before the game.

John didn't come home until an hour before it was time to leave. He took a shower, got dressed, ate some of the enchiladas I'd made, and thanked me as though I were the waitress at a Mexican restaurant. He didn't make eye contact with me. We didn't talk. But we all loaded up in the car together and headed for the game.

As soon as we got there, John was on the field, calling out practice runs, checking equipment. I set up a camp chair and watched. Last year, I'd helped John manage the team lists, call parents, and check out equipment. I'd been his unofficial assistant, and yet this year I hadn't done a thing other than help with the parents' dinner a couple weeks ago.

The second half of the game had just started when I got a text message. I hoped it was Keisha, then instantly caught my breath when it was. I guess John hadn't cancelled her phone yet.

Keisha: I'm sorry.

The simple words made my throat tighten. I quickly replied.

Shannon: Are you okay?

Keisha: I'm really scared.

Knowing she was scared, scared me too.

Shannon: Where are you?

Keisha: Long Beach. Can u come get me?

I groaned low in my throat and glanced up to see John waving one of his players toward the goal. The kid got sticked in the chest, but not before he passed the ball. Landon caught it, swinging his stick back and forth to keep the ball cradled in the pocket while he dodged the opposing team on his way to the goal. I looked from Landon to John and back to the phone. I knew what John would want me to say to Keisha.

Shannon: I can't. I'm sorry.

Keisha: Please?

It ripped at my gut to hear her voice in my head begging me. She was sick, but she'd had the clarity to ask for help. How could I deny that?

Shannon: I'm at Landon's game. I can't leave.

It was a poor excuse, since it put the blame on timing rather than on my decision not to play along the way I had in the past. I didn't realize how poor a choice it was until she responded, however.

Keisha: What time can you be here?

I needed to tell her I *wouldn't* be there, but I couldn't bring myself to say it. She'd been gone for *five* days; she could be in the middle of any number of horrible situations. Could I really tell her to figure it out on her own? And yet she'd stolen from me and from Aunt Ruby, and though we hadn't found pawn receipts for John's things from the garage, they hadn't turned up either. She'd lied about so many things. But leaving her on the streets wasn't the answer. Maybe I could convince her to go back to rehab. I couldn't have any influence if I pushed her away.

Shannon: I don't know when I can come.

Keisha: Please come soon. I'm so scared. Here's the address.

And just like that, I was calculating how long it would take me to get to Long Beach. Landon's team made a goal, and all the parents around me jumped to their feet. I was a beat behind them but clapped as though I knew what was going on while looking over the field to try to figure out which player had scored.

"Did you see me, Mom?"

I blinked as my son appeared in front of me—almost eye level with me these days. He was grinning from ear to ear behind the facemask of his helmet, his eyes bright and his sweaty hair stuck to his forehead. "Did you see?"

"Of course I saw," I said with a big smile, squeezing his shoulder. "Your first goal of the season!"

His eyebrows pulled together. "I didn't make the goal," he said, sounding confused. "But I threw it to Coby."

"Right, that's what I meant. I mean, the goal is kind of half yours, right?"

He looked disappointed, but then John called him back into the game. I looked across the field at my husband. He was at least looking at me, making eye contact, but he didn't smile, or hold up three fingers—our signal for "I love you"—or come across the field to bask in the glory of our son.

After another second, the connection broke, and I sat back down while John called out commands to the players taking the field. Everything I'd done was filleted between us, raw and bleeding. I couldn't see how it would be put back together. I didn't know where to start. But I didn't agree with him cutting Keisha out of our lives so completely either. Had he considered where she would go if she had no one reliable to turn to? And wasn't the house half mine? He'd made the decision to change the locks and bar Keisha from our life, but didn't I get some say? I realized that maybe my behavior had taken away my vote, but I hadn't even had the chance to explain my side of things, not really.

Keisha needed me. I couldn't say no.

"I won't lie anymore," I said under my breath, letting the words penetrate every part of me. It didn't mean I was going to do things John's way, but I wouldn't lie to him anymore. Which meant the ugly between us was only going to get worse. But it also meant I would be helping Keisha the best I could. I couldn't turn my back on her when she was reaching out for me. I just couldn't.

Another goal was scored, but I didn't even bother getting to my feet this time. I was on my phone looking for a hotel I could check Keisha into. Maybe she would see how far I was willing to go to help her and that would drive her toward sobriety. She hadn't been using for very long, and she wasn't beyond saving. I cross-checked the hotels with locations for Narcotics Anonymous meetings within walking distance. She'd reached out to me for help, and I could not say no. Not when there was still hope left to hold on to.

Chapter 32

KEISHA LOOKED HORRIBLE, NOT MUCH different than the night John had picked her up in Compton two months ago. She was pale, fidgety, and seemed to be having a difficult time focusing her eyes on anything for very long. She jumped into the car when I pulled up and didn't say a word until I pulled away from the curb and asked her if she was okay.

"I am now," she said, turning to look at the house we'd just left—an ordinary looking home in an ordinary looking neighborhood. "Bunch of druggie freaks," she said under her breath before turning away from the house. She rubbed her upper arms with her hands as though she were cold.

I was glad she was safe, and yet disgusted at the same time. I turned up the heat in the car. I'd told John what I was doing before I left the house. He hadn't taken it well, and we both ended up saying more than we should have. I called him cold, and he called me stupid. I feared we were both right.

"I got you a hotel room," I said before turning onto the street with the Super 8 sign rising from the pavement. "I paid for two nights."

She looked at me in surprise. "I can't come home?"

"I'm sorry."

She started to cry, and part of me wished I could videotape this and show it to John. Would that help him realize how broken his little girl was?

"What about all my stuff?" she asked a minute later, wiping at her nose with the back of her hand.

"Maybe you can talk to your dad in a few days," I said. "Maybe he'll let you come back if you explain all of this to him." I wanted an explanation too, but I didn't need one the way John did. He was so blind to what was happening.

Keisha shook her head and said nothing. I parked the car and got her checked into a hotel room. The cheap carpet didn't match the bedspread, which didn't match the curtains over the window. It was depressing. All she had was her purse—no extra clothes, no makeup. Nothing.

"I work in Long Beach tomorrow until three o'clock," I said. "I'll try to bring you your things and find a meeting we can go to, okay?"

She sat on the edge of the bed and rubbed her arms without answering me.

I went to the heating unit fixed on the wall beneath the window and turned on the warm air, then came and sat down next to her on the bed. I put an arm around her shoulders, and she leaned into me like the little girl she used to be, that she still seemed to be sometimes. She smelled awful. Like body odor and tobacco and who knew what else.

"I'm really sorry, Shannon," she said softly. "I'm such a mess."

"You're going to be okay, Keisha," I whispered, aching with the need for her to feel my love for her. "You were meant for better things than this. We're going to make this work. I'm going to start looking into some rehab facilities, okay?"

"Rehab doesn't work for me," she said, wiping at her eyes.

"It *can* work," I assured her. "We just need to find the right one. And we can get you back in to see Dr. Livingston in the meantime. Maybe we can adjust your meds and find a better level for you."

She promised not to tell any of her friends where she was staying, and I chose to believe she meant it. It was as I was leaving that she checked her phone and we discovered that John had disconnected it. She cried all over again, and I promised to help her get a new phone tomorrow.

It was nearly midnight when I got home. The house was dark as I headed to the fridge to get a glass of milk that I hoped would help me sleep. I was tired, but I felt so much better knowing where Keisha was. When I was little and too wound-up at bedtime, my mom would heat up a glass of milk and add a little honey. She'd said it would help me sleep. I'd thought it was an old wives' tale until I learned that the tryptophan in both the milk and the honey really did have an effect on serotonin levels, inducing drowsiness. Combine that with the psychological component of mother's milk associations and you had a homeopathic sleep-aid. It wasn't Ambien, but it could help someone relax at the end of a hard day, and I had already taken too many sleeping pills this week.

While the milk was heating up, I noticed a business card on the counter and picked it up. Detective Samuel Pierce, Laguna Hills Police Department. My breath caught in my throat as I realized what this meant. John had contacted the police. I didn't think he'd do it.

I slid into bed a few minutes later but stayed close to my side of the mattress. John wasn't asleep; I'd listened to his soft snores for fifteen years, and he certainly wasn't sleeping now, but why *should* he be sleeping? He'd called the police on his own daughter—a daughter I'd just left sick and shaking in a hotel room with no means of communication. I kept my back to him, and he didn't initiate a conversation. I stared at the wall for a very long time.

In the morning—early, since I had to be to Long Beach by seven o'clock—I asked John about the detective's card. It was Saturday morning; John must have a job today or he'd have slept in.

John didn't even look up from his bowl of oatmeal. "She brought drugs into our house, and she stole from Ruby. That's illegal."

"She needs help. You should have seen her last night, John, she was fidgety and scared. I want to look into rehab."

"She just got out of rehab."

"It was the wrong one. Besides, it was only ninety days. We need something better. If you could have seen how sorry she was—"

"I talked to Ruby."

Heat washed over me, and my breath caught in my throat. John watched me as he continued. "She's agreed to press charges, and I'm pressing charges for Keisha having possessed drugs on our property. There will be an official warrant issued for Keisha's arrest this morning."

I fell back a step and stared at him. "I can't believe you're doing this."

His voice was softer when he spoke, but for whatever reason that made me angrier. "She can get help there, Shan. She'll be forced to be clean, and maybe she'll see what kind of life she's moving toward if she can't get her act together. Nothing else has worked."

He didn't understand. I turned away; I needed some alone time with my thoughts, but he called my name, causing me to stop and look back across the room.

"Are you willing to lose everything we have in order to enable her addiction?"

"Are you willing to lose everything we have to punish her for it?"

"I want her safe, and I think jail might be the last safe place she has. We've paid for rehab. We've loved her and helped her over and over again. She's lived in our home, we helped her find a job and get enrolled in school, and she's thrown it all back in our faces."

"That's not what she did," I said, crossing my arms, turning to face him directly. "It's not about us at all. It's about her being in a really dark place and needing our help. If we can break through this addiction, and convince her that—"

"I've done everything for her that I can feel good about doing, and she has made her choices over and over again. When there are no bad consequences for the bad choices she makes, she doesn't learn from them. You're protecting her from the chance she has to learn a better way of doing things. You're making this worse."

Rage shot down my spine as I glared at him. "I am *loving* her—a girl who has not had enough love in her life. How dare you be critical of me for doing what should be *your* job, John. You should be the one embracing her, but instead you're the first one to throw stones. She wasn't ready for all the responsibility we put on her when she came here. She's fragile and uncertain, and she *needs our help.*"

He grunted and shook his head, leaning back in his chair and crossing his arms over his chest. "And when does it stop, Shannon? She brought drugs into our home. She stole from your aunt. She stole from us. She lied to us over and over and over again. At what point do you draw the line?"

"I don't have to draw a line," I said, lifting my chin. "You've drawn enough for both of us. She's not here, is she? I followed your rule and made sure she didn't come back, but you should have seen her face, John, when I told her she wasn't coming home. It was heartbreaking. She is so lost and so sick, and now she has to figure it out on her own. You not letting her be here—the only safe haven she has—puts her at risk."

"Her being here puts *all* of us at risk," John shot back, anger in his tone again. He pointed down the hallway toward Landon's bedroom. "We have a son to raise, Shannon."

"And Keisha loves him," I said, balling my hands into fists. He was so obtuse. Why wouldn't he even try to see this from a perspective other than his own? "Landon wasn't hurt by having her here."

"Except that she stole from him too, and then you covered it up. What if he'd found her drugs? What then?"

"That didn't happen."

John let out a breath and shook his head, looking away from me, toward the window. The words we'd thrown back and forth settled into a wall between us. After a few seconds, he turned back to me. I held his eyes, poised and ready to pounce on whatever he said next.

"Let me be very clear," he said in a calm and even voice. "She will not come here again. She will not see Landon until and unless she is clean and sober for at least ninety days, and even then it won't be here. I hate the childhood Keisha had, and I wish more than anything that I'd done something more to get her out of that environment. I have blamed myself for so many things, but I won't put Landon in the crosshairs of my mistakes. Keisha is a grown woman now. She can work toward overcoming the hard things that have happened to her, or she can marinate in them. I will not help her be unhealthy, and I will not let my other child be anywhere near the same things that hurt her so very much when she was little. And if you're going to be as sick as she is, I will protect my son from you too."

My mouth fell open, and all I could do was stare at him. "I can't believe you just said that," I replied once I could speak again. Anger and hurt and sorrow and fear twisted around me like vines, but he stared at me, stoic, seemingly unmoved by the words he'd just said. When I spoke again, I kept my voice quiet but strong, wanting to wound him as badly as he'd wounded me. "How easy it is for you to turn on the people you love, John. How poorly I have judged your character."

I turned toward the garage as soon as the words hit their mark, and I closed the door behind me before resting my back against it. Was it only two months ago that John had dipped me into a kiss in the kitchen? Was it only six weeks ago that I'd watched him snuggle with his children on the couch and thought how ideal everything was? How could things have shifted so quickly? How could I have been so wrong about him? But even as I thought it, I knew I wasn't being fair. I didn't believe the accusations John had thrown at me, but I knew something was blocking my clarity, just as something was blocking his. I wished I knew how either of us could overcome it, but I feared it would take my abandoning Keisha to find out. I was not willing to do that. She was gone from my home, which meant I couldn't help her the way I wanted to, and John was right about needing to protect Landon from her choices, but I could take her to meetings. I could remind her she was loved. Would that be too much for John to handle? Would he see me as the enemy?

Tears came to my eyes. I loved John, and I loved our life together. Surely this was a hard road for us, but I couldn't help thinking that if Keisha could do better, if she could get clean and prove herself, then it would validate everything I had done. Love was always the answer. I needed to show John that while still taking full responsibility for having lied so often in the past that he no longer trusted my actions.

Chapter 33

JOHN AND LANDON WERE AT his parents' house when I came back from work on Saturday. Finding Detective Pierce's card had made me forget to pack Keisha's things before work, but I'd promised her I would bring them the next day. I'd picked her up a month-to-month cell phone in my name, though, so she could reach me when she needed to. Having John and Landon gone provided the perfect opportunity for me to pack her things, even if it broke my heart to clear the room of everything that belonged to her.

I put two big suitcases full of her things into my car so that I could take them to her tomorrow; then I put her sheets in the washer and moved the furniture around so it wouldn't look like her room anymore. It was what John wanted, but I secretly hoped he would feel something when he saw how completely she'd been removed from our home. What I hadn't expected was that her room would become John's room. Without saying a word about it, he got ready for bed once they got home and then fell asleep on her bed. I slept alone.

I worked a ten-hour shift at Fountain Valley the next day. I was falling behind in my management duties and was determined to be caught up by the end of the week. Afterward, I drove to Keisha's hotel and dropped off her things. She was shaky and irritable, but we got dinner at a café across the street. They had a Now Hiring sign in the window, and she promised me she'd apply tomorrow—she was too tired tonight. The whole time I was with her I was looking around for cops. John said there was a warrant for her arrest, and it was only a matter of time before they'd catch up with her. We parted with a hug at the door of her hotel. I paid for two more days and then headed home to my other family, wondering what would happen next.

Not much happened over the course of the next week. John continued sleeping in Keisha's old room, but he was polite when the two of us were together. Landon was more like his old self, but he was obviously struggling with making sense of what was happening, and while I was trying to be more involved and attentive, I could sense it wasn't enough. Sometimes I found myself wishing John and I would fight again. The strained politeness was horrible.

I saw Keisha every couple of days and moved her to a pay-by-the-week motel a couple blocks away from the Super 8 but that was still close to the daily NA meetings she was attending. I went with her when I could.

John's mother called to invite us to Easter dinner at their house on Sunday—how had I not noticed it approaching? I went shopping after work and bought all kinds of candy and goodies for the traditional hunt we would have in their backyard. I pulled out the Easter baskets, and John looked at Keisha's pink-and-brown basket a little longer than necessary. We didn't talk about it. I tried to talk her into coming to Easter dinner, but she wouldn't even consider it.

If any of John's family noticed the tension between us, they didn't say anything. I took Keisha her basket after work the next day. She gave me a big hug and thanked me for not forgetting her. I headed home in tears. I would never forget her. I would never give up.

I got home at six thirty, and John left for lacrosse practice at seven o'clock, giving me an unexpected kiss on his way out the door with Landon. He seemed to be offering just enough attention to remind me he was there when I felt ready, though it was hard to imagine I would ever feel ready to do anything other than what I was doing. Things were so muggy in my head I didn't know what to make of it. He hadn't told the police where Keisha was, which confused me, but mostly I felt desperate to figure something out before the warrants caught up with her or John gave her up.

At seven fifteen, the doorbell rang, and I looked up from my dinner—leftover chicken and broccoli casserole—and contemplated not answering it. I was so tired. After another bite, though, I pushed away from the table, hurrying to the door to make up for my not having answered it right away.

I pulled the door open with a polite smile, which slipped when Aunt Ruby smiled back at me, equally polite, though her smile didn't fall. She was dressed in peach, but the cheery color didn't improve my mood. I had no energy for this right now, and yet, it was Aunt Ruby. I looked at her feet, trying to think of what to say. She'd called me twice over the last few weeks, but I hadn't been able to bring myself to return the calls. I felt so bad for the situation that had put us on opposite teams, and yet looking at her on my doorstep had me questioning whether I could ever really see her as an enemy.

"Full disclosure," Aunt Ruby said to start. "John called and told me you were home. I didn't ask him to do it, but, well, you chose a good man, and he doesn't want this to continue to hang between us."

I looked up at her and said in all truthfulness, "I didn't know what to say."

Aunt Ruby nodded, her dangly earrings bobbing as she did so. "I don't know what to say either, except that I don't want this to ruin our relationship. You're the closest family I have, geographically and friendship-wise, and I don't want to lose that."

"I don't either," I said, wondering if maybe we could just talk about us and not say anything about Keisha. No such luck.

"Then you're going to need to forgive me for filing that report," she said, diving straight to the heart of things.

I hadn't thought about needing to forgive her because that seemed ridiculous, and yet if I were truly honest with myself, I *was* angry with her. I felt betrayed.

Aunt Ruby continued before I could defend myself; she was rather aggressive tonight. "*And* I need to forgive you for not telling me the truth. It should have been you, not John, who talked to me about it."

"I know," I said with a nod. "And I'm sorry about that, but—"

"You can't amend an apology," Aunt Ruby cut in. "As soon as you say 'but,' you're not really sorry." She paused, smiled again, and when she spoke her voice was softer. "Can we just talk about this? Lay it on the table so that we can put it away?"

"Yes," I said, wanting things to be okay between us even though I knew it would be hard to get to that place. I backed up and held the door open. "Will you come in?"

Aunt Ruby let out a sigh. "I thought you'd never ask." She swished past me and into the living room, where she sat on the couch while I took the love seat.

"I am sorry," I said once we were settled. "It wasn't that I wasn't going to tell you; I was just trying to figure out the right way."

"And I can understand that," Aunt Ruby said, smiling again. "But we're family, Shannon, and I love you. You could have told me any way it came out; I wouldn't have been angry."

"You pressed charges," I said before thinking it through all the way; it sounded snappy.

"John asked me to." She stopped herself and put up her hand. "But I'm not blaming him for it. I agree it was the right thing to do. Keisha's troubles run deeper than I thought. I hope this will help her get better."

Familiar anger zinged through me. "Going to jail isn't going to help her," I said, that snap still attached to my words. I took a breath and tried to even out my tone. "She'll be locked up with the very worst people out there, and she'll have a criminal record for the rest of her life. John's wrong to think this is the right solution."

"Are you sure about that, dear?" Aunt Ruby asked, cocking her head to the side. "She *did* steal from me. That's a crime I hope she never repeats. Getting away with it would only make it more likely that she'll do it again."

I was shaking my head before she finished and went on to give her the same argument I had given John, about how Keisha needed to get help for her depression and that what she needed from the people who loved her was understanding and support, not criticism, condemnation, and prejudice that, if she were arrested, would follow her forever. "I'm frustrated that no one seems to see the effort I'm putting into helping her. Maybe if I'd had some support, things would have turned out differently, but it feels like everyone's against her now, like she can just be written off."

"Shannon, honey, I'm sorry you feel that I'm working against you. That wasn't my intent. But I'm also just recently coming to terms with some hard truths in my life and realizing that pretending things are different doesn't change them. It's admirable that you want so much good for Keisha, but pretending she isn't responsible for her choices doesn't change the fact that she is. I don't hate her, and I don't love you less for what's happened and that you didn't tell me sooner, but I think John is right—you aren't seeing this correctly, and sparing Keisha from the consequences will help no one."

Aunt Ruby's allusion to Uncle Phillip poked holes in my defensiveness, and I looked up at her in surprise, trying to think of how I could ask where she was with all of that. It was a different topic entirely, but the correlation she'd made between Uncle Phillip and Keisha was uncomfortably reasonable. Pretending Uncle Phillip wasn't unfaithful hadn't changed the fact that he was, and the illusion Ruby had tried to create about her life being just right hadn't worked either. I wanted to bring up Keisha's mental health concerns again and my continued belief that the drugs were a form of self-medication and that if we could fix the disease behind her using, she could be better. But regardless of the cause, she was making horrible and devastating choices. And she wasn't getting better. No matter what I did.

Aunt Ruby must have seen the growing understanding in my eyes. She smiled again, but there was sadness there. "I've done so much soul searching these last weeks that my soul feels in need of new stitching around the edges, but the other night I had a thought that's made me very uncomfortable ever since." She paused, and I waited expectantly as she looked at her purse in her lap and straightened the strap between her fingers. "I wonder what would have happened if I'd confronted Phillip when I found out about the first affair." She looked up at me. "Instead I waited until after number two—Lisa—when I was beyond reconciliation in my heart. I'd held so much anger and hurt inside all through his first affair. And because I waited to confront him, waited until he'd gone even deeper down the path, I think it made our relationship impossible to reconcile. A woman might be able to forgive her husband one indiscretion, but two? I have to wonder what would have happened if, right after discovering those long distance phone bills, I'd served him his dinner, looked him right in the eye, and said, 'Are you being unfaithful to me?'"

She paused and took a deep breath. "Perhaps he'd have lied to me, I'd have believed it, and we'd have carried on like we did. But maybe he would have realized it hurt me and stopped. And there wouldn't have been all those women who followed.

"Or maybe he'd have made a choice between her and me. It would have been difficult for me if he chose her, but maybe I'd have found a different partner. If he'd stayed with me, then maybe we would have been better. Maybe I'd have ended up with a happy marriage, or at least a comfortable life as a divorcee." She shrugged and straightened the strap again.

"As it was, when I did blow up at him after affair number two, we were both too far down the path. I chose to suffer in silence and slowly grew to hate him because he was getting away with something horrible, and I was essentially allowing it so that I could keep the family together and both parents in the home for Tony. I was so afraid of Tony having to live in a broken home, being shuttled between parents, seeing his dad date other women . . . Despite everything I had to put up with, staying with Phillip was security. I was afraid of what our friends would say, what our neighbors would think, what my life would be like as a single mother. I didn't want to lose the security that Phillip provided."

She looked at me again and her gaze was intent. "Keisha isn't Phillip, and I know the situation is very different, but I hope you're not doing all this protecting because you're simply afraid of losing whatever security she gives to you. Fear is no way to live."

Any argument I may have had shriveled up and died in the glimmer of Aunt Ruby's enlightenment. I don't even remember the rest of the conversation, only that I promised to start reading the next book for book group. I didn't even try to get information about Gabriel from her. After a good-bye hug on the doorstep, she told me she loved me, and I said I loved her too.

I busied myself with household chores until the boys came home, then took over bedtime, working extra hard to tune into Landon, who seemed to bask in my attention. After he was in bed, I found John in the garage, regluing one of the rungs on a bar stool from the kitchen. He looked up in surprise when I leaned against the workbench.

"So, Aunt Ruby came over," I said, watching the guilt jump into his eyes. It was there only a moment, though, before conviction took its place. He knew I knew he'd told Aunt Ruby to come. And he didn't regret having called her.

"How did things go?"

"Do you think I'm helping Keisha because I'm afraid?"

"Afraid of what?" John asked, wiggling the rung a little before attaching the clamp to hold it in place.

"Afraid of losing her."

"Yes."

His answer was so fast it startled me. If that were true, then I wasn't helping because it helped *her*, I was helping because it helped *me*. I hated looking at it like that. *Hated it.*

John put a hand on my arm—it was the first time he'd touched me in more than a week—and when I looked up, he held my eyes for a few seconds. "You love Keisha," he said quietly. Tears sprang to my eyes. I did love her, so much. "From day one, you have wanted to include her and have a relationship with her and love her like a daughter. It's been a beautiful thing to watch. As her life has fallen apart, you've wanted to be that rock she can hang on to in the storms, and you *have been* that person. I have no doubt that the intentions of your heart are good and pure and based on love."

Tears overflowed, and I wiped at them quickly, as though John hadn't already noticed.

"But, Shan," he continued, and I braced myself, "your love can't fix her. My love can't fix her. Dani and Landon and Ruby's love can't fix her. You're afraid of losing her, and that's a valid fear. It terrifies me too, but she's using that fear against you, against all of us. She is so tightly connected to the drugs right now that she can't help but be manipulative, and she is squeezing every drop out of how much you care about her. She wants you to think that if you draw a line, you'll lose her because if you believe *that*, you won't draw a line, and she will be able to continue as she is right now."

"But . . ." I had to pause and take a breath, for courage as much as for oxygen. "Her depression," I said, begged really. "If she could just—"

"I know," he said, sounding compassionate but also tired. "If she could *just get well.* And if the economy hadn't crashed and made things hard for us you wouldn't have so much pressure on you, and if Landon weren't growing up so fast you wouldn't be worried about an empty nest. But there has to be a point where Keisha is responsible for Keisha and we aren't all dragged through the mud she keeps churning up. I want her to be well too, but *she* doesn't, and we can't force her to be different. If love were enough, she'd be well. If good intentions were enough, we could fix her. But that isn't reality. It's not giving up on her to say you won't suffer with her anymore."

"Oh, John," I said, dropping my chin to my chest and shaking my head as, for the first time, I allowed myself to consider letting go of Keisha. "It feels so wrong. What if I let her go and she never comes back? What if she only gets worse? What if she overdoses and dies alone somewhere?"

"It would be excruciating," he whispered after waiting for me to look up and meet his eyes that were misty with unshed tears. "I can't imagine it, but if we're not helping her get well, we're not really helping her at all. Somehow we have to come to a place of peace with the good we've done. But it's not okay that I'm not talking to her at all, or that you're putting her ahead of Landon and me. It's not right. Her choices are changing all our lives, and not for the better."

"I don't know how to do that," I whispered. I tried to imagine not talking to her every day. Those four days when I couldn't communicate with her after she left our house were horrendous. The idea of not knowing where she was or who she was with made me dizzy.

"I don't know how to do it either," John said. "Maybe we can find someone to help us figure out how to do it."

I rolled that around in my brain for a few seconds before looking up at him. "Counseling?"

John nodded, and I felt my eyebrows lift.

He seemed a little embarrassed, though I wasn't sure if it was due to my surprise or the idea of talking to someone. "I don't know how to sort through my feelings about all of this. I think some family therapy could be a good thing for all of us—Landon too." He lifted the bar stool off his bench and moved it to the side of the garage, out of the way. Then he faced me and crossed his arms over his chest in a protective-type stance. "The idea of getting some help gives me hope."

I nodded, the lump in my throat too thick for the words to get around. Hope would be nice.

Half an hour later we were getting ready for bed together—in our room—when I tested the waters between us with another topic. "Why haven't you told the police where she is?"

"I don't know where she is," John said before pulling his T-shirt over his head. He put it in the hamper, then sat on the edge of the bed, removed his socks, and left them in the middle of the floor.

"You know I'm paying for a hotel room. You could find out where she is through the credit card company."

He walked into the closet while I climbed into bed, pulled my knees up, and waited for an answer. When he came out, I took a breath before offering a possible solution. "Maybe you're not as ready to send her to jail as you say you are." I was still clutching at the idea of rehab. I'd be willing to work extra hours to pay for it, and it might be just what she needed. I'd looked into a few programs, though, and knew I couldn't invest in something that expensive without John's agreement.

"Or maybe I'm nervous about going around you for something so big." He crossed to the bathroom but paused with his hand on the doorframe, drumming his fingers before looking at me. "I don't want to choose between my daughter and my marriage."

My eyes fell closed, and my forehead fell onto my knees. It was all so ugly. I had to hold on to the hope John had talked about in the garage and the truth Aunt Ruby had spoken of this evening. I had to believe there were still good things to be had out there. I only wished it didn't feel like I had to put Keisha on the altar for it.

Chapter 34

THE NEXT MORNING I TOLD John that I still needed some time—one more chance to help Keisha. If nothing else, her being sober when she turned herself in would help her have a clear head through that process and maybe keep her from having to face withdrawal in jail. He was disappointed, and I feared he was going to give me an ultimatum, but instead he surprised me by asking me to commit to go to Landon's games on Saturday; it was a doubleheader in Orange, which meant it would take most of the day. I agreed, and we didn't talk about Keisha again.

I took Keisha to two NA meetings that week, and after walking back to her hotel room after the second one, I told her that we couldn't keep doing this forever. I had planned to tell her about the warrants, but when the moment came, I couldn't bring myself to do it. I worried she would think I was behind them. It was so hard to let go.

"I'm doing better," Keisha said. "It's been so great having time to myself, ya know, to think things through. And the meetings help so much, and you've just been wonderful." She smiled at me from her too-thin face, and I wanted so much to believe her. "You're helping me get better, Shan. You're the only one."

It was all so confusing. Maybe I *was* helping her—I wanted to believe I was—but then my conversation with John from Monday night came back and it felt like he was right. I didn't know what to do, so I focused on spending more time at home, which was feeling more comfortable, and pulling back with Keisha, which I hoped would help her stand on her own two feet. Each time I was with her, I talked about why she needed to be well, and we reviewed the steps she needed to take toward that. She claimed to be on step four of the twelve steps of Narcotics Anonymous—taking inventory of herself—but I knew she was still using.

I was almost home from having taken her some dinner Friday night when my cell phone rang, startling me. I pulled to the curb quickly, earning a honk from the car behind me. Moments before putting my phone to my ear, however, I saw that the call was from Tori, not Keisha or some law enforcement agency that would be giving me bad news. I lived in dread of that call.

"Hi, Tori," I said, taking a minute to put my Bluetooth in my ear before easing back into the street. I hoped I didn't sound too surprised. I hadn't talked to her since she'd brought me that pill to identify. That had been weeks ago.

"Hi," she said. "I hope it's okay that I'm calling."

"It's totally fine," I said, trying to sound even. "What's up?"

"It's Ilana," she said. "I'm sorry I keep pulling you into this, but I just don't know who else to talk to."

I'd never talked to Aunt Ruby about her prescription and cringed a little. Had Ilana taken Ruby's Percocet again? I hadn't spent two minutes thinking about Ilana's situation after the last conversation I'd had with Tori about it. "It's fine," I assured her. "What's happened?"

"Well, I tripped over this dolly at work on Monday—totally lame, right? I know; anyway, we have a nurse practitioner at the studio all the time, and he looked at it, told me to ice it, and then gave me a prescription, handwritten and all that."

"Okay?" I said, making sure she knew I was listening even though I had yet to see the relevance of this information.

"So, on Wednesday, I took Ilana to lunch. I've been texting with her a little, and she finally agreed to get together, so we went out to lunch, and in the course of conversation, I talked about the fall and the silly doctor giving me pain meds for my dumb injury. She got all intense, you know, and asked me what I'd been given. I told her I hadn't needed it, but she kept pushing. I finally said it was for Lortab and she, well, she asked me for some."

"Oh dear," I said. That wasn't good at all. I had reached my house and pulled into the driveway, but I stayed in the car. "Did you give her any?"

"Of course not. I hadn't even filled the prescription. I told her that and then added that I wouldn't have given them to her even if I had filled it—you're not supposed to share prescriptions. It was kind of awkward to say all that, but I wanted to make a point."

"No, it's good that you set a boundary." And wasn't I the *queen* of boundaries.

"I'm glad you think I handled it right," Tori said. "But then yesterday I went to throw the prescription note away—since I wasn't going to use it. I looked for it and couldn't find it. I mean, I don't want to jump to conclusions—in fact, I feel horrible that I *am* jumping to conclusions—but I haven't seen the prescription since that lunch with Ilana."

"Was she alone with your purse after you told her you wouldn't give her the meds?"

"Yeah, she was."

I let out a breath, fully flipped into pharmacist mode. I shifted the car into reverse. "Can you text me your full name and birth date? I'm going to head over to the pharmacy and look it up. If she filled it, or even tried to fill it, it will show up under your name."

"Really?" Tori said. "You'd do that?"

"Isn't that why you called me?"

"Oh, I don't know," she said, sounding embarrassed. "I just needed to talk to someone about it who could tell me if I was overreacting. I'm not so organized that I couldn't have lost the prescription or something."

"It will take me a few minutes to check it out, and then we'll know for sure. Just send me that info, and I'll let you know what I find."

"Okay, thanks so much."

Lucy was just starting to close up at the Fountain Valley store when I arrived and explained that I needed the computer. "Okay," she said easily, relinquishing it for me.

I logged into the Controlled Substance Database, then typed in Tori's full name and date of birth. I hit enter and held my breath, hoping the search would come up as unfilled.

It didn't. I let out an audible moan. The prescription had been filled at a pharmacy in Irvine Wednesday afternoon—a Walgreen's pharmacy, which was a big relief for me. It meant I had cause to do more checking; I was already pushing boundaries to have looked in the first place, but having the script filled by one of the pharmacies I sometimes filled in at was a good cushion for me in case anyone asked me about it later on.

"Everything okay?" Lucy asked.

I looked up at her. "Yeah, it's fine." Pharmacists were supposed to catch things like someone picking up a prescription made out in the wrong name, but it didn't always work that way—hence the epidemic of prescription fraud and black-market sales. I went back to the computer and tried to remember Ilana's last name so I could look up her history. For the life of me I couldn't remember her last name—I wasn't even sure I'd ever been told her last name. But I was pretty sure her husband was an ER doctor at Pacific Hospital in Long Beach—she'd mentioned it at one of our book club meetings, and I remembered it because I'd interned there in school. I called over there and talked to the unit clerk, asking about the different doctors there under the guise of trying to read a signature. When she said "Goldstein," I was sure that was him.

"Do you happen to know if he has a wife by the name of Ilana?"

"Yes, he does. . . . Uh, is everything okay?"

"Yep, just verifying some information, thanks."

It took me another half hour, and Facebook—which I could access on my phone—before I had what I needed to run Ilana through the database. Again I held my breath when I hit enter, hoping my suspicions would be wrong. A few seconds later, however, I stared at the evidence on the screen. She'd been seeing two different doctors, both of whom were prescribing her pain killers. That in and of itself wasn't all that alarming, but one was also giving her Xanax and Soma, and she wasn't using her insurance for most of her meds, which would prevent her from getting refills in advance. She'd received a few hundred pills in the last few months.

Though the CSD was a good program, it wasn't perfect, and Ilana's doctors—who should be the ones doing this background work—were obviously not checking the database before they gave her prescriptions. Many doctors just didn't have time, and Ilana was a doctor's wife and a polished and professional woman; she would seem low-risk to them. That she'd stolen a prescription in addition to all her other scripts took things to a new level. Ilana had a serious problem.

I went further into the system and looked at the signature log. I couldn't tell right away it wasn't Tori's signature, so I pulled up an old prescription Tori had signed for within the Walgreen's system. Upon comparison I could see that Ilana hadn't even attempted to sign Tori's name; she'd signed her own, probably saying she was picking it up for Tori.

To be doubly sure, I could confirm Ilana having signed for the prescription via closed-circuit video recordings, but I wasn't sure I wanted to take that step because it would alert other people to my concerns. I had an obligation because of my position, and yet I felt an obligation to Tori and Ilana too. I hoped I was choosing the right balance, but I felt sick to my stomach all the same. I knew pharmacists who had had their licenses put on probation because of things like this. I was walking a very thin line.

I thanked Lucy, who had put off closing down for an additional fifteen minutes in order for me to finish my investigating, then went to the parking lot and called Tori. I couldn't tell her anything about Ilana's history, or that I knew Ilana had signed for the prescription, only that her lost prescription had been filled.

"I can't believe this," Tori said, sounding angrier than I expected. "She stole my prescription. She is in deep, isn't she?"

"I can't get into details."

"It's obvious," Tori said. "Why else steal from me if she weren't desperate? So what do I do now—call the police?"

A tremor ran through me at the mention of the police. Keisha was part of my reaction, but my bending of professional boundaries would certainly be questioned if the police were brought in. "That might be taking it too far."

"Why? Isn't it illegal for her to have done that? I mean, she had to pose as me, right? I don't know how she even got it filled. Aren't there supposed to be all kinds of safeguards in place to keep people from doing that?"

"There are lots of safeguards, but nothing's perfect." I kept to myself the fact that, as a doctor's wife, she may have gotten more leeway from a pharmacist she might know socially or through her husband. "Calling the police is opening up a whole can of worms though."

"No, stealing my prescription is opening up a whole can of worms. You think I should do nothing?"

"I didn't say that," I said, but I had thought it. Was this really our business? But to not do anything wasn't right either. "We don't know for sure that she did this."

"Yes, we do," Tori said. "She took *my* prescription, and I'm taking that seriously. I've watched too many talented people in my industry flush away their lives for drugs and too many people turn a blind eye because they didn't want to kick up dust. I want to kick up so much dust about this that she never, *ever* dares do anything like this again."

The power and confidence behind Tori's words was shocking, and so different from my approach. I'd wanted to be soft and gentle and helpful; Tori was ready to have Ilana handcuffed.

"I mean, you see this stuff too, right? In your work, you've got to deal with junkies."

"Ilana's not a junkie," I said, and yet a voice in my head said, *But Keisha is.* Out loud, I continued. "Junkies use street drugs; Ilana is showing some serious drug-seeking patterns—it's different."

"Well, whatever the title, she needs to face the music for it."

"Tori, you just have to think this through. We don't know her very well, and her husband is a doctor. Prescription fraud is a felony; she'd face fines and jail time. It would follow her for the rest of her life."

"So you want me to do nothing?" Tori said again.

"No," I said, shaking my head even though she couldn't see me. "That's not what I'm saying." I paused and raised a hand to my forehead. "Can we just sleep on this? It's not going to change by tomorrow, and maybe if we can take a few hours to think it through, we can come up with the right approach."

Tori was quiet for a few seconds, but she finally agreed to call me tomorrow afternoon, and I returned home to John and Landon and two of his friends who were spending the night. I told John about Tori's phone call. He listened and then asked what I was going to do. I told him I wasn't sure, and though I could tell he had a lot he wanted to say, he didn't. Instead he gave me a kiss on the forehead and said he was going to bed.

It was only nine thirty, but I spent the rest of the night cleaning out the cupboards in the laundry room, thinking over everything that had happened. I was more objective about Keisha than I felt I'd been before in other evaluations, and yet I hadn't come to any conclusions by the time the cupboards were organized and the trash was taken out. I had told her something had to change, but I wasn't sure what I could do to make that change happen. I wondered how long John would wait before he told the police where to find her. I wondered if that wasn't the best option, because then I wouldn't have to feel guilty for making the call myself. But would I resent him for it? And didn't I want Keisha to be well before she had to face responsibility?

The next morning I made pancakes for breakfast—I couldn't remember the last time I'd done that—and Landon and his friends ate every last one of them. It was a good thing I'd promised John I would go to the games because his assistant coach had a family emergency just half an hour before we left and I spent the game helping on the sidelines and keeping the boys pumped up. It was invigorating not only to be a part of the game but to be working with John and seeing how much Landon enjoyed having me there. It helped me realize just how much I'd missed these last months, and yet I wasn't seeing Keisha today and couldn't stop thinking about her. She texted me between the first and second game—we'd taken the team to Arby's for lunch—and asked if I could bring her a hamburger.

I texted back that I was at Landon's game in Orange. She didn't respond, and it sat like a weight in my stomach to think that she was mad at me. Tori called a few minutes before the next game started. I let the call go to voice mail, then texted her that I'd call her when I was home. She responded that would be fine.

We won the second game, which meant John treated the team to ice cream. I ate my hot fudge sundae while trying to ignore the pit in my stomach. I hadn't talked to Keisha all day; I hadn't seen her. Had she been able to get something to eat when I couldn't bring her a hamburger? Did she feel abandoned? They were all thoughts I'd had before, and yet these ones had one different aspect—each time I thought them, a secondary thought came to mind that spending one day with my family should not be making me feel so much guilt.

"You okay?" John asked, sliding onto the bench next to me.

"I'm fine," I said, giving him a forced smile. He didn't call me out, which was good since I felt very fragile. I really hoped Keisha wasn't angry with me. I was all she had right now.

At home, I called Tori back.

"So, what do you think we should do?" Tori asked after we'd said hello to one another.

I took a breath and pushed everything else away so that I could focus on Ilana's situation. "I think we should talk to her."

Tori was quiet for a moment and when she spoke again, her bravado from last night was lacking. "Really? We barely know her."

"I know," I said, flipping into my professional mode. "But the most important thing is for her to get help, right? Isn't your ultimate goal for her to get better?"

"Well, of course it is," Tori said. "I'm just a little . . . uncomfortable with the idea of talking to her. What are we going to say?"

"I'm not sure," I admitted. I was in a precarious situation since I was the one who looked into the records and couldn't share what I'd learned. "But I think I can present it in a way that maybe she can admit what she's done instead of us accusing her."

"That's a good idea," Tori said, sounding relieved. "When should we do it? I don't think we should wait very long. Strike while the iron is hot and all that."

"Good point," I said, moving to the calendar on the fridge for a quick view of the week ahead. I was taken aback to see all the NA meetings filled in on the calendar—I'd written them in more than a month ago, believing Keisha would still be here and healing. Seeing the times written there gave me an idea, something that would take our confrontation with Ilana to the next level. The idea gave me butterflies. "Do you think you could see if she'll go to dinner with you Monday night? I kind of have a crazy idea, but I think it will make an impact."

"Impact is good," Tori said quickly. "I'm all for impact. What's the plan?"

Chapter 35

I stood outside the church Monday evening, tapping my toe while hoping I didn't appear as anxious as I felt. I hadn't seen Keisha since Friday, which was the longest I'd gone since I'd moved her into the hotel. I'd texted her a few times each day to check on her, and she usually responded that she was fine, but sometimes she didn't answer me at all. I'd get anxious and sweaty—it was hard to focus on anything but the text she hadn't sent. This morning I'd called her three times during my break. She finally answered and said she'd been asleep, she was fine, and could I take her to dinner tonight? I couldn't because of this meeting Tori and I had planned for Ilana. I felt horrible not being there when Keisha needed me, and yet I knew I was obsessing. Ruby and John's words were chipping away at my certainty that I was helping Keisha, but I still struggled to get past the "If she would just . . ."

Everything had come together in regard to what Tori and I had planned for Ilana, but now that I was here I was beginning to question whether or not this was such a good idea. If I couldn't help my own stepdaughter deal with her addiction, why did I think I could make a difference for a woman I barely knew?

And yet, the plan was in motion. Tori was taking Ilana to dinner, then they were meeting me here. Why had I thought a public place like this would be better than somewhere private? What if Ilana freaked out and made a scene? I wasn't good with scenes outside of work, where I dealt with them on a regular basis. I had that fabulous counter to keep me separate when those happened though. There would be no counter here.

"Hey, there," a voice said, forcing me to look up and focus. It was David, the guy Keisha had met at the first NA meeting she and I had gone to. "You're Keisha's mom, right? Is she here?" He looked past me and to the side, a hopeful look on his face.

"She's not here," I said, then took a breath and decided to practice the truth. "She relapsed."

His face fell, and he shook his head. "Dang, I'm sorry to hear that."

I nodded, out of words now that I'd been all brave about telling him. But he hadn't walked away, hadn't run away from the truth like I had for so long. I'd suspected David had had a crush on her, and it made me sad to look at the kind of person she could have been with right now if she'd chosen a different path.

"It's such a hard road," he said almost reverently. "But maybe next time it will stick."

"Maybe," I said, surprising myself as tears filled my eyes. Sheesh, what was wrong with me? I wiped at my eyes and was about to offer an apology when he spoke.

"This whole process is brutal—on everyone—but Keisha has to own her stuff, ya know? Don't let her drag you into it."

I nodded, a bit undone by his sincere concern, and blinked quickly to get rid of the tears. How could I love her and be there for her without being dragged into it? If I'd felt a little more stable, I'd have asked him that.

"So, if Keisha's not with you, why did you come?"

"Oh, I have a friend who's . . . struggling. I'm meeting her here."

He gave me a compassionate smile. "Good for you to be here with her. I'll save some seats for you guys, then. Two?"

"Three," I said. "Thank you."

He left me standing there, replaying his words before I looked up to see Tori and an anxious Ilana walking toward me. My stomach flipped. I'd already scoped out the building and found an alcove where we could talk before the meeting started.

"I don't understand," Ilana said, coming to a stop after looking up at the church. Oops, it was a Christian church; would that be offensive to her?

"Hi, Ilana," I said, hoping I could do this and hating how unnatural my voice sounded in my attempt to cover my anxiety. "I found a place we could talk."

"Talk?" she repeated.

I turned and opened the door without answering, and Tori walked behind Ilana, kind of pushing her inside. If she'd known us better, she might have resisted or challenged us, but she was just uncomfortable enough to not know what to do and therefore instinctively followed our lead.

They followed me down a side hall and around the corner, where a bench and two chairs were set up outside a locked door. I stayed standing while Tori ushered Ilana to a seat. Behind Ilana was a large wooden cross on the wall. I stared at it for a few moments before sitting across from them. Ilana's face showed that she was about to lose all her politeness.

"Ilana," I said, smiling slightly. "I'm sorry for the trick we played to get you here." She stiffened, and I pulled harder on all my resolve and my bedside manner while also praying for help. If this went badly . . . "But we're really worried about you."

That softened her a little, but confused her too, maybe even scared her. She pulled back and looked at Tori. "Worried about me? What are you talking about?"

Tori explained about finding the pill in Ruby's bathroom.

"Percocet," I added, drawing Ilana's surprised look from Tori to myself. "From a prescription bottle in Ruby's master bathroom."

"I don't know what you're talking about," Ilana said. She was definitely scared, and angry. She tried to stand, but Tori put a hand on her shoulder and pushed her back down. I don't know how hard she pushed, but it was hard enough to tell Ilana we meant business. She looked between the two of us and opened her mouth to speak, but I didn't give her the chance.

"There's a meeting going on in the next room, and I'd like you to attend it with us. Then we'll talk and we'll take you home."

"I don't have to stay," Ilana said, looking between Tori and me. "I can call my husband to come get me right now—you can't do this!"

"You *can* call your husband, Ilana," Tori said, a kind softness in her voice. "But we're trying to do you a favor. We could just have easily gone to your husband about this, or your doctor, or the police."

Ilana stood up, said she didn't have to stay, and turned toward the hall.

"It's illegal to possess someone else's prescription," I said. She stopped. "Either the paper script or the actual fulfilled product." I hoped my discomfort wasn't showing. I hadn't told her we thought she'd done it, I hadn't made an accusation, I'd just stated fact. She didn't turn to face us, but I could see her breathing had increased, and I could see the way her hand tightened on her purse strap. If she were scared enough, this could work, and if this worked, I wouldn't have to explain myself to the State Licensing Board. I stood and headed toward the meeting; Tory followed my lead, though she stopped behind Ilana, keeping her between us. I gave Ilana a look and then moved forward. She followed without us asking her to.

True to his word, David had saved seats for us, him on the aisle and the three of us along the row next to him. Ilana sat between Tori and me; we shared a look as we sat. Tori was as nervous as I was, but together we were apparently a force to be reckoned with.

A woman I recognized as the leader of past meetings was talking about a spring picnic for the group, then talked about a party she'd attended for work and how she'd drunk iced tea instead of wine. Everyone cheered for her and she raised her hands over her head like a conquering hero. It was hard to see her as anything different. She'd been where Keisha was and dug out of it. How I wanted that for Keisha too. My chest got tight with longing.

The woman turned the meeting over to anyone else who wanted to share. David was on his feet before she'd stepped off the platform.

"Hi, my name is David, and I'm an addict," he said when he reached the microphone.

"Hi, David," everyone in the audience said back—the reminder that everyone here understood where he'd come from. My chest got tighter as the tone of the meeting shifted.

"I'd like to talk a little bit tonight about the purpose addiction plays in our lives." A muttering washed through the crowd, but I kept my eyes trained on him. He looked down at his hands grasping each side of the podium. He couldn't be more than twenty-five years old, and although the geeky impression he'd made when I first met him was still apparent, standing at the podium gave him an air of authority and confidence that matured him in my eyes.

After a few moments of thought-collecting, David lifted his eyes and looked over the crowd. "Life is hard," he said with painful sincerity. "And each one of us encounters things in our own lives that we simply can't handle. It's not because we're stupid, or weak, or less than someone else; it's simply a fact that every person in the world deals with things that are too much. And when we encounter these things, we are offered a variety of ways to cope with them. Some people find that faith in a higher being can lift them just enough that they can keep moving forward. Some people have a special relationship with someone else that can carry them through. Some people find a bottle of one kind or another that takes the edge off enough for them to survive.

"For me, I found a pipe. The stuff I put into the end of that pipe softened the edges of the hard things I *couldn't* handle anymore. It was such a relief to get a break, ya know, to simply inhale deeply and feel as though I were suspended above the garbage instead of sinking into it. Maybe if that's all the drugs did for me—just gave me a break—I'd have been okay, but drugs are a tricky support system, and in time, the tentacles of the monster I thought I had on a leash began wrapping around me until the people in my life had to move away in order to save themselves."

His gaze flickered to me so quickly I could almost talk myself out of his notice. But the image he'd created was so real, so reflective of Keisha's monster too and the hold it had taken on the people who loved her. The hold it had on me.

"Maybe if those people had never left me, I'd have never found myself alone with the beast, and maybe I'd have never been able to truly feel the fear I should have felt in the beginning. I don't know if that's how it would have happened, though, because I chose my path and I can't go back and change it. But I *can* change how I handle stress now, and how I handle my obsessive compulsive disorder, and the abuse from my childhood, and the girl who broke my heart, and the college I didn't get into, and the loss of a grandmother I loved so much who died when I was too young to process my emotions." Another murmur washed through the crowd, and I felt tears come to my eyes. "I wanted to share today because last week I celebrated my twenty-four-month anniversary of being clean—two whole years."

The room broke out into applause, including Tori and me. Ilana was staring at David, but silent tears streamed down her face, taking away all my reasons not to give into my own emotion. David smiled under the attention, both shy and confident at the same time.

"Two years ago, I woke up on the floor of a crack house next to a woman I think I'd met the night before but whose name I couldn't remember. I couldn't feel my legs, and I couldn't take a full breath. I tried to call for help but couldn't make the words. I could hear a baby crying somewhere, though I never saw one. A few moments later my body started convulsing. I was aware of every movement but could do nothing to stop it.

"The woman took off, the baby stopped crying, and a few minutes later, after the shaking had gone away, two men picked me up, took me out of the house, and threw me into the backseat of a car. They dropped me off at a park—just left me there to die—but not before they took my wallet and the watch I'd stolen a few weeks earlier.

"Some kids found me on their way to school, and I ended up in the ER again. My mom came to see me for the first time in months, and instead of hugging me and crying over me and begging for me to let her help me, like she'd done the other times, she stood at the foot of my bed and asked me, 'Is this it, David? Is this the last time I see my boy alive? I think it would be easier to visit your grave than to see you like this over and over again. Maybe that's what I should be praying for.'"

The hush in the room was like a blanket, each of us wrapped tightly in the pain of those words. I glanced over my shoulder and saw many other people in tears. Every one of these people had parents, grandparents, maybe siblings and spouses and children. Friends, neighbors, church leaders, and—I glanced at Ilana, who looked completely overwhelmed— some of them had book club members, not sure what to do but doing the little bit they could in hopes that the monster David had described wouldn't win. I reached for Ilana's hand—something so out of character for me—but I needed to hold on to someone. When she let me take it, I wondered if she did too. I noticed Tori do the same thing with Ilana's other hand.

We turned our eyes back to the front when David continued. "I don't know why that moment was different than all the other times she begged me to get well, bribed me to get well, prayed for me to get well, screamed at me to get well, but something about her apathy that day made me realize how far I had fallen.

"I was in the hospital for three days, and even though I told her I was going to get clean and it was going to work this time, she wouldn't let me come home. We'd done that so many times, and I brought too much chaos with me. Mom contacted our pastor, and he found an older man from our congregation who agreed to let me stay with him. I went to a doctor and got help for my OCD and my anxiety disorder. I started talking to my family again and, perhaps most importantly, I started going to NA meetings regularly—every day. I met people like me—not bad, evil people with no willpower and no soul—but good, decent people who'd chosen the wrong way to cope with their struggles."

Tears finally filled his eyes as he took a deep breath and looked across the group. "This weekend, my parents are throwing me a party. I'm not supposed to know about it, but I do." Everyone laughed. "I'll get to celebrate my freedom from addiction with the people who never stopped loving me, even when they couldn't have me in their life. We'll eat cake and ice cream and drink homemade root beer, and it might just be the very best party I've ever been to." He took off his glasses and wiped at his eyes before putting his glasses back on again and sniffling slightly. "Thanks for letting me tell my story," he said, smiling and looking a little embarrassed, and yet confident and excited too.

David sat down, and I squeezed his arm and mouthed, "Thank you." He nodded shyly and looked away. Other people talked, but their words blended together, whereas David's had stood out. I knew he was telling his story for his own reasons, but I couldn't help but think that it was for me, too, that I was supposed to be here *this* night out of all other nights so that I could see his journey. His story gave me a different kind of hope than I'd had before, and in a way it let me off the hook. His mother *couldn't* fix him. It wasn't that she didn't work hard enough, or love enough, or hug, or kiss, or pay enough—she *could not* fix him. It wasn't her job. It wasn't my job either.

I'd become so wrapped up in my personal realizations that I almost forgot about Ilana's part until the meeting ended and everyone stood and began chatting and laughing with one another. David asked for a formal introduction to Ilana and Tori but then stepped out of our way when I finished, wishing us luck.

Ilana stood up and looked at the exit, her expression full of fear. She was shaking.

"Ilana," I said, quietly. "You're going to be okay."

She didn't answer me, and I understood that she didn't know what to believe anymore. Outside of the church, I explained as gently as I could that Ilana had a week to find help on her own, and then I would have no choice but to go through the professional channels of my position to enforce her accountability. It could have been a really awkward discussion and yet she was so humbled—or broken, I wasn't sure which—that she just nodded. Tori had her arm around her as they headed back to Tori's car.

I watched until they disappeared, then headed for my own car and drove back to my own home, with my own family—minus one. I wasn't sure who was helped the most with tonight's meeting, Ilana or me, but I hoped both of us would always remember this night as a turning point.

Chapter 36

I WORKED A TEN-HOUR SHIFT in Fountain Valley with the business card for Detective Pierce in my pocket the whole time. I filled prescriptions, processed the staff schedule for the next two weeks, inventoried, counseled clients, and ordered stock, but in the back of my mind was the question: What am I going to do about Keisha? Between Ruby, John, Tori, Ilana, and David, I felt as though my mind had finally cleared. What I was doing was not okay. I had to change this path, but knowing what I had to do didn't make it easier, just obvious.

I could call the detective and tell him where Keisha was, but that felt like such a betrayal. The other option was to try to talk Keisha into turning herself in. I didn't like that option either. The chances of Keisha agreeing to go to jail seemed thin, and yet it felt like the better reflection of our relationship. And I would get to see her one more time; it would give us the chance to do this together.

After work, I drove to the hotel. As I pulled up in front of her room, I could see a Do Not Disturb sign on the door but didn't think much of it. Once I reached the door, I raised a hand to knock just as I heard laughter from inside.

Male laughter.

I was shocked. Keisha had never had visitors when I'd come before, and yet it shouldn't have surprised me too much. Someone had to be giving her the drugs she needed. I knocked anyway. The laughter cut off abruptly, followed by the sound of movement and hushed voices, barely discernible behind the door. There was a peephole so I knew Keisha knew it was me when she asked who it was through the door.

"It's Shannon," I said. "Can we talk for a minute?"

"It's not a good time," she said, still not opening the door. "I'm really sick today."

But not so sick that she couldn't have company. I realized then that I hadn't texted her to tell her I was coming, which I had always done before.

"Did you get to your meeting today?" That was one of the things that had given me confidence these last few weeks—that she claimed to be attending her meetings regularly. But after last night, I wondered why it hadn't bothered me that the meetings obviously weren't working.

"Oh, yeah, I totally went," Keisha said from the other side of the door. "It was really good, but then I got sick and so I just need to rest."

It wasn't like she hadn't lied to me before; I should be used to it, right? But this lie hurt in a different way. I was keeping her off the street, but she wouldn't open the door for me? She would make up a stupid story she knew I would want to believe and tell it so casually?

"Please open the door, Keisha," I said, more forceful than usual. "If you're sick, maybe I can help."

"I'll be fine," she assured me, sounding the tiniest bit annoyed.

"Then let me in to make sure you're okay. That way I can go home and not worry." What a pathetic truth! If I knew she was okay, then I could be okay. "Keisha, please."

"Uh, okay, just a minute."

The was more movement, more whispering, and finally she pulled open the door, but only wide enough to let me slip past and into the room. She was wearing a tank top without a bra underneath it, and a pair of cutoffs hung on her bony hips. Her hair was brushed but she had what looked like yesterday's makeup on her eyes. She had the distant look of someone high, and her body moved back and forth slightly. I wondered if she noticed it. The room smelled like burnt diapers. The door to the bathroom was closed, likely hiding her visitor.

"See, I'm fine," she said, smiling, though her eyes didn't focus on me. "I really need to get some sleep, Shannon. I'm going to go out looking for jobs tonight. As soon as I'm feeling better I'm gonna hit it hard."

My anger began to dissolve into the familiar fear, but I couldn't let it rule this exchange. I had to be stronger than that. "Keisha, what's going on?"

"Nothing. Gosh." She rolled her eyes. "I'm sick." She pretended to cough. "And I don't want you to get it, so you should probably go. But I'm fine, I swear. And guess what, I'm four days clean today, I haven't used since Friday." She smiled wide at me, like a little girl awaiting praise. "Aren't you proud of me?"

I looked at the closed door to the bathroom, then at the bed and finally into her eyes. I could tell her that I wasn't paying for the room anymore, that I didn't believe she was going to meetings or applying for work or any of those things. I could force a confrontation and . . . then what? Confront the man in the bathroom too? I felt the tears rising. I tried to blink them back, but if she noticed them she didn't comment.

"I better go," I said, turning back to the door, which she was still holding open.

"'Kay," she said. She followed me across the threshold, hurrying to close the door behind us, though she didn't shut it all the way. "Oh, uh, could I borrow a little more money? I'm out of food and stuff. I swear I'll pay you back when I get a job. It'll give me a good excuse to keep seeing you when I'm back on my feet, ya know?"

"I don't have any cash," I said.

"There's an ATM in the lobby," she assured me, pointing toward the front desk of the hotel. "You could get some cash from that, right? Not much or anything; I'm fine just eating granola bars, you know. The hotel provides coffee—thank goodness, right?" She smiled that we're-best-friends smile, and I found myself nodding.

I went to the lobby and paid the three-dollar transaction fee to withdraw twenty dollars. When I knocked on Keisha's door a minute later, she opened it, pretending to cough again. I held out the money and watched the disappointment on her face. She'd thought I'd give her more—I usually did.

"It's all I've got," I said, still watching her face.

"Okay," she said with a shoulder shrug, taking the money as though she was doing me a favor. "Thanks." She stepped back and started to shut the door. "Um, why don't you text me before you come over next time— you know, just so I can get ready and stuff."

"Sure," I said, still watching her. She closed the door until it was only open about six inches, then coughed again. Was this what John saw when he looked at me? The same fool Keisha was taking me for? In the next breath, however, I played along. "I hope you feel better."

"I'm sure it's not serious," she said. The door narrowed to four inches. "It's just tough getting clean, you know? But I'm doing it, Shannon. I'm fighting the fight!" She grinned widely at me. "I'll talk to you tomorrow, okay?"

"Sure," I said automatically as the door closed some more.

"Love you, Shan." The door snapped closed. The chain slid into the lock, and a few seconds later I heard muffled voices again, more laughter; Keisha's this time. I couldn't help but wonder if she wasn't laughing at me.

"Love you too," I whispered as I turned back to my car. Once in the driver's seat, I pulled Detective Pierce's card from my pocket and stared at it for a few seconds before getting my phone out of my purse and doing the hardest thing I'd ever done in my life.

Chapter 37

SATURDAY WAS MY DAY OFF, and I welcomed the break. I went to Landon's games—another doubleheader—and then cleaned the house, paid bills, and dug in the flower beds, but thoughts of Keisha hung over my head every second of the day. I had been waiting for her to call for four days, but I'd heard nothing. John had talked to Detective Pierce, who had handled her arrest, but John hadn't talked to Keisha either. It was killing me to not know how she was doing. Would they give her anything to help her with the withdrawals? Was she through the worst of it, or was she still feeling as though she were going to die?

I thought of every cop show I'd ever seen and felt sick to my stomach, imagining Keisha as one of those people in handcuffs, getting fingerprinted and then thrown into a cell. I couldn't understand why she didn't call me. She needed me more than ever now, right?

At six o'clock, I cleaned up and went to book group. I had promised Aunt Ruby I'd go and wanted to make sure she knew I was ready to rebuild things between us. I was late though—again—so I planted a smile on my face and made my apologies while I took my seat. Ruby gave me an extra squeezy hug, but I knew we wouldn't talk about everything with the group here so we both headed into the living room and took our seats. Ilana wasn't there, and I felt my shoulders drop. Had we scared her away? Had we made everything worse? Tori caught my eye from where she sat on the far side of the room and smiled, but I was wishing I'd stayed home. I didn't even know these women.

I'm so lonely.

The admission took me off guard enough that I said it again: *I'm so lonely.* The truth settled around me like feathers, and my chest tightened with emotion. Here I was, surrounded by these women and doing nothing to get to know them better. I'd been coming to this book group for nearly eight months, and the only reason I knew Tori even a little bit was because she'd come to me for help. Yet these women were friends with each other; they were laughing and talking and leaving me alone—like I wanted them to. But was that what I *really* wanted? How could I change it? I was who I was. Where could I start? I didn't even know, and that depressed me more than anything. Did I know what healthy friendships were? Did I know how to be a part of one, or could I only feel connected to people in crisis?

The doorbell rang, and Ruby got up to answer the door. If Daisy was still on bed rest, then it had to be Ilana at the door. I looked at Tori again and wished I had time to talk to her. She gave me another smile and lifted her shoulders. She didn't know any more than I did.

I relaxed a little bit as I listened to Ilana and Ruby talking in the foyer; then Ruby came back in, and Ilana followed behind her, pausing in the doorway to scan the room. She made eye contact with me, though not long enough for me to gauge her mood.

The conversations had started dying down when Ruby had left to answer the door, and everyone seemed to be facing Ilana, as though we could start now that she was here. She lifted the book and said, "Great selection, Ruby."

I tried not to make it obvious that I was watching her, but I was, and when I glanced at Tori, I thought Tori was too. I shifted in my seat, feeling uncomfortable and yet aware of every movement Ilana made. Would she pretend Monday night hadn't happened?

"Now that we're all here, we can get started," Aunt Ruby said, picking up the book Gabriel had given her from the coffee table. She fluttered the pages, then pulled out a paper from inside the back cover. "I looked up some information about the author," she said, then cleared her throat and started reading. I tried to pay attention, I really did, but I couldn't keep myself from checking my phone in case Keisha had called and I'd missed it since I'd set the phone to vibrate. Was she not calling because she didn't want to or because they wouldn't let her?

"I just loved this story," Aunt Ruby said. I met her eye and smiled, distracted from my own thoughts for the moment. "One of my favorite parts is how he had all these friends all throughout the journey, different people he'd known from 'before' and was visiting again after so many changes."

I had no idea what she was talking about since I knew nothing about the book. I didn't even know if the book was fiction or not, but she kept talking about the "story," which made me think it was. Though it sounded as though there was a lot of philosophy in it too. Fictional philosophy? Now that was a genre I didn't see getting its own shelf at the bookstore anytime soon.

She read a few sections from the book, then talked about electric shock therapy and said again how much she liked the book. You'd think it was the Bible for the conversion she'd had to the different passages. I couldn't help but smile, though, because I was pretty sure her love of the book might have something to do with the person who had given it to her. Maybe I could talk to her about *her* life someday soon, though thinking that reminded me of the night she and I had hashed things out about Keisha. I checked my phone again.

"As you can tell, I loved the book. Anyone else like to jump in?" Aunt Ruby said. I was careful not to make eye contact with anyone, hoping I wouldn't have to admit that I hadn't read it.

"I'd like to share some thoughts I had about the book," Ilana said, surprising me. She was going to talk about the *book*?

She said she hadn't really loved it at first, but a few days ago—she looked quickly at Tori and me—she'd picked the book up again.

"Truth is, I've been living in denial for some time," she said, and I felt a tremor go down my spine. Was she going to confess everything? Here, at book group? "And I've been angry. Blaming everyone and everything for my miserable life and the pain I was in, although I won't deny I really was in a lot of pain. But that wasn't an excuse. I looked around for excuses and a way to fix everything, to make myself feel better and not be so aware of my problems."

I nearly dropped my jaw as the words she said washed through me— they could have been my words. I had been looking around for excuses and a way to fix everything too. I had wanted to make myself feel better through helping Keisha get well, rather than focus on the hard things I was facing in my life. They might not be of the same caliber as Ilana's, but they were hard all the same. Ilana had wanted escape; what had I wanted? To be the hero? To be the one person who would make a difference with Keisha after everyone else tried and failed? Gosh, that sounded pathetic.

Ilana kept talking, mentioning a hysterectomy she'd had before she hurt her elbow and about the difficulty of accepting a different future than the one she and her husband had worked toward. It wasn't until Paige handed me a tissue that I realized I was crying. Ilana explained how she'd taken the pain meds because her arm hurt, and then because her heart hurt, and then for any reason she could think of. How did that relate to me?

Something about tonight, or yesterday, or this whole last week must have opened my heart a little more than I was used to, because it was all suddenly so clear. After my parents had moved away, I had started working so much that I hadn't left much room for other relationships. I was also feeling left behind by my son, who was growing up and not needing me so much. And despite all the good things in my marriage, I could see that I was angry with John for not bringing in his share of the income. I was horrified to think it, and yet I knew it was true. We were best friends, but I was mad at him, and lately, we had less time together and more stress than ever.

Having Keisha to take care of filled all those broken places for me. I had someone new in my life—to replace my parents—and someone to take care of—to replace Landon—and someone to hang out with and encourage and feel close to—to replace John. She was my friend and my child and my chance to prove myself powerful. She really was my drug, wasn't she? She helped me cope with things I didn't know how to fix. She masked my feelings of insecurity and insignificance just enough that I could pretend they weren't there.

I could barely keep up with the tears streaming down my face as I made that connection. My heart ached with the acceptance of it.

"But the truth is, I do have a problem. I'm an addict."

I looked up at Ilana. She'd said it out loud, but I repeated a similar declaration in my mind. *But the truth is, I do have a problem. I'm codependent to my stepdaughter's addiction. I have made it possible for her to be sick because it makes me feel better.*

Ilana talked more about the book, and I took a deep breath, finally getting ahold of my emotions. The women must have thought I was insane. None of the rest of them seemed to be as emotional as I was, though there were some shiny eyes around the room.

". . . I won't be at next month's meeting."

Ruby audibly gasped and put a hand to her chest. "You aren't quitting, are you? Please say you aren't."

"We want you to stay," Athena said with a nod.

"We really do," Paige agreed.

"I'll come back," she assured us. "But not until I've done the work I need to do to fix this mess. On Monday, I'm checking into an inpatient rehab center, and I'll be there for as long as it takes. It may be a month. It may be longer. I hope to be back for July's meeting if I miss June."

The group finished up on a hopeful note. Ilana was getting help, and she'd called us her friends. I wasn't sure how to make the transition to also feeling like these women were my friends, but I wanted to start. Somehow. Ruby would help me, I was sure.

I checked my phone again when I got into the car. I needed to come to terms with the fact that Keisha might never call. I had to find a way to be okay with that.

It was after nine o'clock when I walked into the kitchen, still in this bubble of discovery that was exhausting and yet freeing and confusing and hard. I smiled at John, who looked up from the paper he was reading, but from the expression on his face I knew something was wrong. My heart seized up.

"What?" I asked, terrified of the answer. "What's happened? Is it Keisha?"

"No," John said. "But I called Dani to see if she'd heard from her."

"Had she?"

John nodded.

My back straightened. Keisha hadn't talked to her mother in months. "She called . . . Dani?" I repeated. *But not me?*

He nodded. "And she had a lot to say. She said Keisha said it was awful living here, that you were so demanding and that I hated having her here. After I kicked her out, you were buying her drugs and then got a hotel room for her and this guy, Tagg, so that they could deal in order to pay you back for the money she owed for school—even though school was all your idea. She told Dani that all she'd wanted was to go home, but that we convinced her that Dani didn't love her and didn't want her."

I blinked at him, taking a few seconds to catch my breath. "Keisha didn't say that," I said, shaking my head. "Dani's making it up."

John shook his head, a sympathetic look on his face.

"But why would Keisha say something like that?" I said, feeling my chest tighten. I still didn't believe it. Couldn't.

"Because she's an addict, Shannon," John said sadly. "And she'll say anything she can to whoever might help her get a fix or, in this case, bail her out. I would guess that she called Dani because she felt like she'd used us up, that we wouldn't buy into the games anymore. When she runs through Dani's patience—of which there isn't much—she'll find another tactic to use on someone else. I've already told my parents not to take her calls if she tries to contact them. We should tell Ruby and your parents the same thing."

I felt my chin quivering as the depth of Keisha's betrayal washed over me. John came over to me, wrapping his big arms around my shoulders as I crumbled even further. She turned on me? After everything I'd done? My whole body started shaking in reaction to the acceptance of things I'd fought so hard not to believe, an acceptance that had started when I'd listened to David's story and continued as I'd listened to Ilana's story tonight.

"I'm sorry, Shan," John said into my hair as I completely fell apart. "I really am."

Chapter 38

John went to see Keisha on Wednesday afternoon, but I wasn't ready. He said Keisha had begged him to bail her out, which he refused, then she asked him to hire her a good lawyer, which he also refused. He came home and spent the evening researching family therapists, ready to make his head and heart right about this and find a way to be her dad without giving in or shutting her out. We set our first appointment for the next week.

I took the week to come to terms with all that had happened, and on Friday night, John and I attended an Al-Anon meeting, a twelve-step program for families of addicts. I found it completely uncomfortable and painful, and yet the stories I heard were so similar to ours. Good people who wanted to help but had to accept that they could not change the choices of their loved ones.

On Saturday morning I felt as though I couldn't wait any longer. I was still hurt by the lies Keisha had told Dani about my enabling her, but it had helped me realize just how sick she was, how desperate she was, and how manipulative she'd become. I didn't love her less, but I was no longer so desperate to prove my love to her.

I went to the Orange County jail alone, still battling my many emotions and feelings and wishes and hopes. I sat down on my side of the glass and took a deep breath. I'd seen scenes like this a hundred times on TV but never imagined I'd be in this sterile, echoing room, waiting to talk to my child through a pane of glass.

After a few minutes, the door on the other side of the glass opened, and I straightened as Keisha was led in. She was dressed in orange—so cliché—but wasn't handcuffed. She looked thin and pale, but she was clean and her hair was pulled back from her face. She looked so much better than she had the last time I'd seen her, and though it hurt my heart to see her incarcerated, I was relieved to know she was safe.

We picked up the phones on our respective sides of the glass at the same moment.

"Hi," I said in an eager voice, smiling at her, hungry to take in every inch of her. This was my girl. "How are you doing?"

"Terrible," she said, tears filling her eyes. "It's horrible here, Shannon, and I'm so sick. They won't give me anything to take away the shakes—look." She held up her shaking hand for me to see, then put it on her forehead. "I'm in a room with three other women—one is a gang member, another one deals drugs, and the third one is a prostitute who hit another hooker with her car." She leaned forward and put her hand on the glass. "I don't belong with these people." Her voice cracked and tears spilled from her eyes. "Can you please get me out of here? I swear I won't use. I'll even go to rehab again. I'll go to therapy, I'll take my meds. I'll do *anything*."

I felt emotion rising in my face, and I tried to blink the tears away. It broke my heart to see her so desperate and to imagine what it must feel like to live the way she'd just described. "It's not up to me," I said. That was something I'd learned at the Al-Anon meeting—the importance of reminding the addict of their responsibility rather than taking it on as our own. "But I'm so sorry all this happened, Keisha."

"But you could post bail," Keisha said, wiping at her tears. "You could get me out right now."

"I don't have $10,000, Keish."

"They can put it on your house or something."

"I can't do that either," I explained, shaking my head.

She started to sob. "Why? Why won't you help me?"

It was surreal to consider putting my home up as insurance that Keisha would do what she needed to do, and I was proud of myself for not feeling the least bit tempted to take such a risk. I no longer believed that jail was the worst thing that could happen to her; I no longer believed that, because the cause of her drug use—depression and childhood trauma—was beyond her control, her choices were beyond her control as well.

"I've done everything I can do, Keish," I said softly. "And some things I should never have done. I think that maybe this is the best place for you."

Her eyes narrowed, and her face hardened so fast it startled me. "The best place for me? Are you nuts? This is hell, and you think I should stay?"

"You *have* to stay," I said carefully, hoping she'd calm down and really listen. "It's not really—"

"You *want* me to stay, don't you? You don't care how awful it is in here because at least I'm not your problem anymore." She went from anger to tears again. "No one cares about me," she said, her chin trembling as she covered her eyes with her hand. "No one has ever loved me."

"I love you," I said. "You know I do, and your mom and dad, Landon—"

"Then get me out of here."

"I can't," I said, shaking my head again, wanting her to understand. "Like I said—"

"If you really cared, you'd get me out. You'd find a way. If it were Landon in here, you'd do whatever it took to get him out of here. But I guess he's your *real* son, isn't he? I'm just something you got stuck with because you married my dad."

I opened my mouth to dispute what she was saying, but then some of the things John had said echoed back to me. *She'll do or say anything she thinks will get you to help her.*

"That's not fair," I said instead. "I've done everything I can think of to help you, Keisha. I was there when no one else was."

"But now you'll abandon me just like everyone else has."

"I'm not abandoning you, but there isn't anything left for me to do."

She sniffed and wiped at her eyes again as her face hardened one more time. "You know, it wouldn't have gotten so bad if you'd have kept me to that contract."

Something shifted inside me, and more of John's words seemed to quickly block the burn of what she'd just said. *She's sick, Shan. She's being run by her need for the drugs. All we can do is love her.*

There was truth in her words though. If I had held her to that initial contract, maybe things *would* have been different. If she hadn't gotten away with her lies and half-truths, maybe she wouldn't have said so many. And yet, at the end of the day, I hadn't done this. Though misguided in my efforts to help, I couldn't carry the burden of her addiction. In the space of two minutes she had begged for my help, asked me to risk my home for her release, accused me of not loving her, and told me it was my fault she was an addict.

"Keisha, have you ever heard the term *codependent?*"

She furrowed her eyebrows, probably because I wasn't playing along the way she'd expected me to. I supplied an answer before she tried to distract me again. "It's a term used to describe someone who becomes as dependent on an addict as that addict is on their drug of choice. I haven't been able to sleep unless I know you're safe. I haven't been able to be happy unless I think you're okay. I risked my marriage, my job, my relationship with Aunt Ruby, and my role as a mother to make sure you were okay. You were addicted to drugs, and I was addicted to your validations. I needed you so badly that I didn't help you the right way, but I'm learning from that now, and I will not help you be sick anymore."

Tears filled her eyes once more. She put her hand on the glass. "I do need you, Shannon. You're the only person who understands me, who really wants to help."

"A minute ago you said I'd abandoned you."

She shook her head. "I'm just so sick, and my thoughts are out of control. I'm so depressed; I'm so, so, low right now. They won't even give me my meds, did you know that? And there are drugs in here—if I wanted them, I could get them, but I don't because I want you to be proud of me. But I've got to get out of here, Shannon, so I can get better. You've *got* to get me out. You're the only one I have left."

Tears filled my eyes, but not because I was scared for her and desperate to help. This time the tears were a kind of mourning for what I thought I'd been working toward. I'd been so wrong. Keisha was an addict, a thief, and a liar. She was also kind, and good-hearted, and loving, and . . . my daughter. "I love you, Keisha," I said, letting the tears fall. "And I want all good things for you."

"Then get me out!" she nearly yelled, clenching the phone with both hands. "Get me out of here, Shannon!"

She wasn't hearing me. "I love you, Keish, and I'll be in court next week to see what the judge decides to do." He could sentence her to prison for up to five years, or he could refer her to a year-long treatment program. Maybe this would be the time she'd embrace the help being offered. I believed she could claw her way out from her addiction—thousands of recovered addicts attested to that possibility—but it would be up to her. I stood.

"You're leaving me here!" Keisha said, her eyes wide and her voice rising to the extent that a guard started moving toward her. "Shannon, don't—"

I hung up the phone as the guard came up behind her. I couldn't look at her; it hurt too much to see her disappointment and anger. The glass didn't drown out what she said—or rather, what she screamed—as I turned and left the room, my heart breaking with each step as a sob filled my chest. I so wanted a different solution than *this*.

On my way out of the jail, door after door shut behind me, sealing Keisha in and cutting me off from her. The moment I stepped into the sunshine, I thought about the fact that we both needed to get well and that our wellness would be dependent on the choices we made from here on out.

I got into my car, turned on the engine, grasped the steering wheel, and cried until my eyes were swollen and my chest ached. I had made so many discoveries about myself and my motives, but I knew I wasn't done. I knew I would revisit all those things over and over again, I would want to save her in the future, I would want to be that hero again.

I pulled out my phone and Googled the nearest Al-Anon meeting. There was one in Laguna Beach that started in an hour. I would be there with a prayer in my heart that it would help grant me the serenity to accept the things I could not change, change the things I could, and find the wisdom to know the difference.

Chapter 39

AFTER DINNER WITH LANDON SATURDAY night, John and I sat on the couch like a normal couple and watched a Netflix video while Landon played video games with his friends down the hall. I popped popcorn for everyone and called my son "Baby Boy" when I brought it into the room. He rolled his eyes at me, but I knew he secretly liked it.

Later that night, John took Landon's friends home while I lay on the second bed in Landon's room and listened to him update me on his life. He requested Pop-Tarts again, but this time, instead of refusing, I said, "I'll see." Maybe I could use them as bribery for chores or something.

John came home, said good night to Landon, and then told me what work he had lined up for next week while we cleaned the kitchen together.

"Sounds like a full week," I said when he'd finished listing his out appointments—four bids, a final measure, and an install.

"It feels good to be busy again," he said while rinsing his hands. He turned off the water and picked up a dish towel. He leaned against the counter. "How about you? What's on your agenda?"

"I'm meeting some of the book club members for lunch on Monday," I said with a nervous smile. I still could hardly believe I was going to do it. "I even turned down a shift at the Long Beach store so I could make it work."

"Really?" John said, smiling in that funny way of his that made me think he was half teasing me. But I knew he liked the idea. I'd confessed to him how lonely I felt and how I was beginning to think Keisha had been part of me trying to resolve it. Or run from it.

"It was even my idea, though Ruby helped me choose the place. Apparently she and Gabe had lunch there last week."

"Good for you," John said, truly impressed. "And good for Ruby."

"And I'm going to run on Monday too," I said, hoping that would help prove to him I was healing. "I'm hoping I can do four miles even though I haven't run for months."

His smile widened, and he stepped toward me, wrapping his arms loosely around my waist so he could still look at me. "I'm proud of you, Shan," he said, soft and intimate.

I basked in his words. I *wanted* him to be proud of me. I wanted him to trust me. I wanted him to feel about me the way I felt about him: grateful, safe, better.

"Thanks," I said.

"You coming to bed?" he asked.

"In a few minutes," I said. "I've got one more thing to do." I wondered if he would question me or think I was being too vague—he had reason to be suspect when I wasn't completely upfront—but he didn't bat an eye.

"Do whatever you need to do," he said, letting me go and giving me a quick kiss good night. "You know where to find me."

He went to bed while I headed for the desk in the study, sat down, and pulled out a piece of off-white stationery. When had I last written a letter by hand?

I liked the feel of the pen in my hand and hoped it would help me break through my remaining resistance and help me be more involved in the words I put on the page. So many new starts in my life right now—or restarts, depending on how I looked at it.

I brushed invisible dust off the paper, adjusted the pen in my grip, and started writing.

Dear Ilana,

I've thought about you a lot this last week and sent some prayers your way—I'm hoping they reached you intact. I know you can't write back for a couple of weeks—Tori explained the rules when she gave me the address—and maybe you won't want to write back at all, but, just in case you, like me, could use a friend, I thought I'd tell you about the impact your situation has had on my life—how you've inspired me.

For you to really understand, though, I should start by telling you about my stepdaughter, Keisha . . .

Butterscotch Brownies

½ cup butter
2 cups brown sugar, light or dark
1 tablespoon vanilla
¼ cup milk
2 eggs
2 cups flour
2 teaspoons baking powder
1½ teaspoons salt

Preheat oven to 350 F.

Melt butter in 2-quart saucepan. Remove from heat and add brown sugar. Mix well. Add vanilla, milk, and eggs. Mix well. Add flour, baking powder, and salt. Mix until just combined.

Spread batter into a greased 9 x 13 pan. Bake approximately 30 minutes. Remove from oven when brownies are lightly browned and edges are just beginning to pull away from the sides of the pan. Do not overbake or brownies will be hard once they cool.

For variety, add 1 cup chopped nuts, toffee chips, butterscotch chips, or chocolate chips.

RUBY'S SECRET
COMING OCTOBER 2013

Heather B. Moore

A NEWPORT LADIES BOOK CLUB NOVEL

Ruby's Secret

Preview

Chapter 1

I tapped a long coral-pink nail against the book-club list on my counter as I listened to my daughter-in-law, Kara, reprimand me.

"Ruby, you've got to stop doing everything for everyone." Kara's voice was a bit shrill today. "You should join the senior center—I hear they have wonderful activities. You'll love getting to know women your own age."

My own age? I scoffed. Although my birth certificate claimed I was sixty-two, I felt I could be forty—if it weren't for my aching knees—or thirty . . . well, maybe not thirty. That was the year I discovered my husband's first affair. I'd never wish to be thirty again—at least not thirty and married to Phillip.

I actually gasped at my horrible thought and said out loud, "God rest my husband's soul," as if that would erase the poison running through my mind.

"Amen," Kara said, then she plowed on, and I continued to tap. I loved my daughter-in-law, but she could also be quite irritating. Not that I wasn't grateful she lived in Illinois with my only son, Tony, but she wasn't exactly what I'd imagined having a daughter would be. Shouldn't we be like bosom buddies and support each other in everything?

Finally, just to stop the stream of words, I said, "I'll think about it, sweetie. Now I should really let you go. Love you."

Any thought of the senior center immediately fled as I hung up. I refocused on the book-club list. Seven names graced the book-club list now—seven women who were quickly becoming nonirritating daughters to me. The Newport Ladies Book Club had turned out to be a success after all. A few fliers and several phone calls later, we started out strongly and had now already met four times.

I read through each name slowly so I could forget my tortuous thoughts. There was a reason I had a locked box . . . and it did its job well by keeping certain things locked away—literally.

Every couple of weeks, I did something special for one of the women on the book-club list. I knew Kara would really chide me about it, so it was something I kept to myself. Like pretty much everything in my life— kept to myself. I glanced at the calendar to mentally map out who was doing what today. Tuesday . . . February first. My heart stilled.

Today was the second anniversary of Phillip's death. No wonder I felt off. It hadn't even taken much to practically argue with my daughter-in-law. I took a deep, cleansing breath, determined to not let myself get rattled.

I mulled over the names on my list with a new fervor. Paige, Daisy, Athena, Ilana, Olivia, Victoria, and my niece, Shannon. It had taken some convincing to get Shannon to join, but maybe she felt bad that she was my only relative in California and didn't want to turn me down.Each of the women at book club was so different, yet we'd bonded over our love for books and fabulous characters and twisty plots, not to mention delicious refreshments. Food was always the great equalizer. I bypassed Athena's name on the list since I'd taken her to the spa recently—hoping to give her a bit of relief from the cares of her ailing father. I was plainly having a hard time deciding which lady to focus on this week. Usually, my intuition was keener, intuition I learned to trust at thirty for reasons I refused to think about now.

Finally, I settled on Ilana, with no specific, clear reason, except I just felt I should call her. So Ilana it would be. I called her before I wasted another second. After all, this was the time I'd set aside to make the phone call. The rest of my day was scheduled down to the minute, as usual.

When Ilana answered, she sounded quite harried, so I got right to the point. "I know you're probably working right now, but I wondered if you would like to meet for lunch today or tomorrow." I felt I'd have more of a chance if I gave her more choices.

Ilana sighed, small but unmistakable. I gripped the phone a bit tighter, waiting for her answer.

"I usually only have a short time for lunch—"

"That's all right," I said. "I can meet you anywhere—some place quick will work for me too."

A pause, then she said in a more cheery tone, "Maybe in a couple of days. Let me call you if I think something will work out."

Trying not to feel completely deflated, because I didn't want to doubt my intuition, I said, "All right, dear, that would be wonderful."

Her good-bye was equally pleasant, but I knew better. She wouldn't be calling me.

Disappointment pulsed through me as I ended the call. A lunch would have been wonderful with just Ilana. She was the one lady I felt I knew the least in the group. She'd been married for three or four years, didn't have children, but seemed completely wrapped up in her career. Although, when the other ladies at book club discussed their kids, I saw the wistful look in her eyes. I thought if she needed someone to confide in, I could be that person.

I circled her name on the list and wrote, "Call back on Thursday." I didn't want to be a pest, but I hoped she'd know the door of friendship was wide open.

What are you doing? I mouthed to myself. I was being obsessive, I knew, yet I couldn't help it. Ilana wasn't a stain in the carpet that needed scrubbing over and over. She was a grown woman, who knew her schedule and who didn't want to hang out with a senior citizen—well, *barely* a senior citizen.

Maybe my daughter-in-law was right. Her words rang through my mind—*You'll love getting to know women your own age.* Just because Kara's voice wouldn't leave my head and today of all days I needed a distraction, I grabbed the phone book and looked up the Oasis Senior Center. Maybe I'd pay a visit, glance over the activities, and then I could tell Kara I'd done at least that.

A phone call wouldn't tell me about the atmosphere of the place—first impressions were so important. I read the address listed in the phone book and realized it was closer to me than I thought and in the same vicinity as Athena's father's rest home. "Rest home" left a bad taste in my mouth, and without thinking about it, I moved to the refrigerator and poured myself a glass of lemon-fresh filtered water.

Washing and drying the glass so it wouldn't be alone in the dishwasher gathering bacteria, I set it back in the cupboard, rim down. Not everyone kept their cupboard shelves clean enough to store glasses in the proper fashion, but I didn't mind adding the cupboard shelves to my weekly cleaning routine.

Since I was at the cupboard, I decided to organize the glasses into straighter lines. When satisfied, I moved to the next item on my day's agenda—watering the huge haciendas along the front walkway. They did best if watered before the heat of the day set in.

Stepping outside, I noticed the cloudy sky looked oppressive and grayer than usual. The California sun would be missing today, and I worried that my hair would wilt before I had a chance to visit the senior center. I turned on the hose to low pressure and watered the base of the flowers, watching the soil darken and swell. It was a small pleasure I'd indulged in a few weeks after Phillip's funeral. We'd been traveling so much for the last ten years that I'd never been able to tend any sort of garden or flower bed, not even a row of flowers, always having to rely on the landscapers.

Besides, Phillip didn't care for haciendas, so it was with a bit of guilty delight that I brought home three dozen from the nursery right after his death and learned everything I could about them.

The wind pushed through my cropped hair and raindrops started to fall—I'd definitely have to redo the styling now. But perhaps I'd delay it for a while; I hated running errands in the rain. I hadn't expected the day to be overcast, and my favorite thing to do on rainy days was read something deliciously amusing. And today of all days, I needed an escape.

I had no idea what the book-club ladies would think of my devouring regency romances. Perhaps I'd suggest a specific one—a notable one—at the next meeting to gauge their reaction. Jane Austen always seemed to be well respected, but there was so much more out there than just Jane . . .

I would be the first to admit there was not much value to reading them— unless I counted sheer contentment, the ultimate relaxation in delving into a world of the past where people were concerned with frivolous nonsense, notions, and ideas that had no consequence in today's world . . . unless one wanted to study human nature. Why someone did what they did. Why a *man* did what he did.

Perhaps there was more value than I thought besides a historical study.

The rain no longer fell in innocent drops but made great splashes on the pavement. It seemed the sky would water the flowers for me today. Turning off the hose, I went into the house. Passing by the kitchen, I paused and looked at the calendar again. February first . . . It had been a horrible day. Even with the passage of two years, it was still fresh in my mind.

But I didn't want it on my mind. I'd given most of my life to that man, and now I wanted to put everything in our relationship behind me. So . . . I decided to forget my schedule and do something different.

I left the kitchen and headed upstairs. I had several bookcases stationed throughout my home, but I kept the nearest and dearest in my bedroom— no longer the master bedroom—that room I had converted into a guest suite. When my son had questioned me about it, how could I tell him I no longer wanted to sleep in a room I'd shared with my husband?

I converted Tony's old bedroom into my sanctuary, with a queen-sized bed, two elegant bookcases containing my favorite books, and long, flowing, gauzy curtains. I had the next book-club book, *The Help*, on the coffee table downstairs, but that could wait. I needed something light . . . something that could take me completely away from Newport and memories of my husband's last day alive. Running my fingers along the spines, I stopped at my Georgette Heyer collection. I bought all of her books in a single, crazy afternoon browsing on Amazon, but I'd only read about half so far.

The next in line was *Bath Tangle*.

Ah . . . Bath . . . the place of healing and relaxation. The perfect respite in winter to get away from cold London.

I smiled to myself, already feeling the magic of the era seep into my skin as I turned the first page. If I closed my eyes, I could very well imagine that I was in drizzly England, if even for a short time.

* * *

A barking dog woke me, or was it hunting hounds sprinting through the forest of a grand estate? I shook off half thoughts of ballrooms connected to endless hallways and sat up. Falling asleep hadn't been on my agenda, and the barking dog could only mean one thing.

Lance was home.

Not Lance in the *knight sense*—or any sort of hero—he's the farthest thing from it. Of course, he might argue with you—one of his better talents—that he's just the man for me. Who else but a financial planner was in a better position to take care of a lonely widow with a healthy inheritance left by her late husband?

The only thing even Lancelot-like about Lance was his purebred hunting dog. It was supposedly trained to catch the finest pheasants at some prestigious farm, but I'd never known it to be gone from the neighborhood. However, its training had at least taught it to bark only when it saw Lance coming home.

I parted one gauzy curtain and watched the thinning head of hair make its way to the door of the next house. Sunlight peeked through the clouds, making Lance's gray hair look golden in the late afternoon. One thing about financial planners on the West Coast—they started early and closed up early. Predictably, when Lance opened his front door, his ivory Labrador bounded out, putting its narrow paws into Lance's waiting hands, and Lance promptly leaned down for the mutual nuzzle.

I drew back with a shudder, remembering the single attempt Lance had made at kissing me. It reminded me of that nuzzle, although it was probably much shorter than what he gave his dog, since I'd promptly screeched, nearly causing Lance to lose his balance. The timing wasn't good, since it had been only a couple of months after Phillip's death, but even if it had been a couple of years, I would have still been surprised at the move. Especially since a second marriage, or any sort of relationship with a man, was the farthest thing from my mind.

Besides, Lance and Phillip had been friends, at least they'd chatted about the economy and stock market on occasion.

Turning away from the window and realizing Lance was the only person I really saw apart from the book club ladies, I decided that perhaps Kara was right. Perhaps I did need to meet a few more people—ones my age and ones who didn't live next door to me.